SON OF THE SUN

Books by Moyra Caldecott

FICTION
Guardians of the Tall Stones series:
The Tall Stones
The Temple of the Sun
Shadow on the Stones
The Silver Vortex

The Egyptian Sequence:
Daughter of Amun
Son of the Sun
Daughter of Ra
The Ghost of Akhenaten

Weapons of the Wolfhound
The Eye of Callanish
The Lily and the Bull
The Tower and the Emerald
Etheldreda
Child of the Dark Star
The Winged Man
The Waters of Sul
The Green Lady and the King of Shadows
Adventures by Leaf Light and Other Stories

POETRY
The Breathless Pause

MYTHS AND LEGENDS
Crystal Legends
Three Celtic Tales
Women in Celtic Myth
Myths of the Sacred Tree
Mythical Journeys, Legendary Quests

AUTOBIOGRAPHY
Multi-dimensional Life

SON OF THE SUN

Moyra Caldecott

Published by
Bladud Books

First published in Great Britain in 1986 by Allison & Busby

Also known as *Akhenaten: Son of the Sun*

This hardback edition published in 2018 by Bladud Books, an imprint of Mushroom Publishing, Bath, BA1 4EB, United Kingdom

www.bladudbooks.com

ISBN 978-1-84319-351-7

Contents

I tell you this three millennia
after these events took place.
Mark them well.
They did not end with my death,
and they will not end with yours.

1

THE THRESHOLD

TODAY THE CHOICE IS MINE: I live or die. When I enter the House of Many Thresholds, the ancient pyramid, the tomb which is no tomb, my duty as oracle is to travel, clad only in my soul-double, to the regions of the gods and there to intercede for my people, pleading for the rising waters, the inundation of the Nile, which yearly deposits the rich black silt on our farmlands, that we may eat and thrive. This year, the year before and the year before that, the waters have not risen at the appointed time: the fields have baked and cracked in the heat, the seed shrivelled, the people died of famine. No ordinary prayers will serve this day. The oracle himself is to be sent beyond the earth, held by a slender silver thread to life, to speak with the gods directly. When it is done I am to return to my body with their answer and live out my life of waiting, my life of service, my life that is no life.

Today, the choice is mine, and I have decided that I will not return. I will kill myself.

That music I hear? A flute playing notes as lonely as my heart.

Am I afraid? Yes, I am afraid. I am Oracle. I speak with the gods; but I have no name that is my own. How will the spirits call me to the weighing in the Hall of Osiris? What name will my heart bear on the scales as it lies beside Maat's feather of Truth and Justice? Like an enemy or a criminal, a name has been denied me: but worse for me, since it has been denied since birth.

It is known that a man is of nine substances. He has his shadow, his double, his soul, his spirit and his body. He has his heart, his intelligence and his power. He has his name. Into life he comes blinded by splendour: into death he goes knowing what he knows. But wherever he goes his name is with him. In the silence, in the waiting and the listening, the cry of the one without a name is lost. Because I have no name I will live no more when I am dead. I will become nothing and will fall back into the void.

I see a star, brighter than any other star, still hanging from Nut's nipple even as Ra rises. It is Sopdt, the star that I was born under, the star that should herald the rising waters. I call it "deliverer", "fire-quencher", "bringer of life", but it does not answer. For three years it has been a dry star, pitiless: no inundation has come at its beck, no Osirian green has touched the barley into life, nor drawn the corn shoots from the earth.

They gave me no name in a world where everything is named, but perhaps I, who am nameless, will be named in my death: "Deliverer", "Fire-quencher", "Bringer of life". I will pull the cloth of waters across the world as I die, and leave it as rich as they left me poor, as hopeful as they left me hopeless.

Reflecting in the pool at my feet the star shimmers briefly among the sleeping lilies and then disappears, swallowed by the sun.

Now, it is only as I remember it.

In the west the full moon plunges. The day in which I have chosen to die is with me.

From the dark house the priests, my gaolers, come, padding softly on the flagstones of the courtyard. I hear their voices chiding me, feel their hands pulling me back into the darkness even as the sky bursts into light. Inside, the lamps are still lit because inside it is always night. I should not have been in the high-walled court. I have missed the first incantations, and there is no time to repeat them now. I will have to go on my dangerous journey without the full invocation. No matter. Our words are but the creatures of Time.

I am stripped of my night-clothes, my head shaved, then squeezed into the hard, painted wooden head-dress that tells the world that though I am lesser than the lowliest man because I have no name of my own, I am mightier than the mightiest because I speak for the gods.

4

I? Speak for the gods!

Why do I not scream and rage, now, while they are pushing and pulling me into their ceremonial robes? They understand nothing of the spirit realms. Some of those they call gods are no more than servants of the Most High, and others are but named aspects and attributes of the One Beyond all Others. The priests teach—but they have not learned. And I? I fear my gaolers. I fear the physical pain they can inflict when I do not obey. But most of all I fear the demons of darkness that they conjure to torment me.

Once again I keep silent. But this time I know that there will be an end to my suffering, to the lie I live. I will not come back from this journey. I will be out of their reach forever, beyond their filthy spells and their stinging whips.

They never talk to me except to give me orders. How can one talk to a person without a name? But they talk among themselves, and I hear the king himself is to be there to watch the procession and the sealing. Shall I call out to him? Shall I tell him how they treat me, how they lie? The voices I speak with are false, tricks of Ma-nan, the so-called priest of Amun. I will tell the king. I will shout out with my own voice that has never been heard outside this house. I will tell him everything. I will destroy my captors. I will pull down their edifice of power. Beggars will spit on them, dogs urinate.

Ma-nan narrows his eyes and looks at me. I have never been sure whether he can read thoughts or whether he is just shrewd at interpreting the signals of the face. He looks at me hard and then mutters something I don't catch to the thin one, the one who is always bowing to him. The creature, Pi-en (even he has a name!), slobbers off and comes back running with some thin sticks of that resin I hate.

"No!" This time I scream and struggle, but Ma-nan holds me down, his arms like a vice, my bones almost cracking under his grip. The resin is already lit and the smoke waved in front of my nose. I try not to breathe, but my lungs rebel and finally, after enduring almost unendurable pain, burst open, and I suck in the foul stuff, Set's cursed breath, the dark god's poisonous effluvium.

Ah, but now the pain is gone and I float, float on soft cushions of air. . . Sleep is near. . . Do I drift to my golden bed, or do the men lift me? I am as docile as a doll as they arrange my arms across my breast and slip the symbols of my high office into my hands. . . smooth my brow and close my mouth for me. Then a third eye is drawn upon my forehead with kohl, with powdered malachite and lapis lazuli—the eye that will see what no ordinary eye can see. Then the black plumes are set in place at the four corners and we are ready for the tall Nubians who come so swiftly to Ma-nan's call.

I must have dozed off, because now I am in the open air. My body feels numb, and I cannot move my head to see what is on either side of me. I can see the shoulders of the men carrying me, the tall black plumes fluttering in the air, the high, high arched sky, totally blue, totally blank. I try to remember the star Sopdt, but even that memory is fading. . . I taste bitterness with my tongue, but I can say nothing. Ma-nan has played this cruel trick on me before. Inside my head I scream. But no one can hear.

The carrying-bed tilts as the Nubians walk down a ramp. Without moving my head I can see the crowds now, thousands and thousands of people crushing forward, ragged, dusty, starving, anxious. . . pressing forward to glimpse the great oracle who will speak with Hapi, the great river god himself, and Osiris who was dead yet gave life, who was buried yet lived again. He will bring the green and golden grain back to the land and save the people from famine. They see me encased in gold, painted with powerful magic symbols. They do not see the one who lives in that house of darkness, a prisoner of loneliness. If they were to look more closely, they would see the tears leaking out of the corners of my eyes.

Level ground is reached, and I can no longer see the people, the parents clutching the hands of children, the youths sidling up to young girls. The tears stop flowing, but I can still feel their uncomfortable dampness at my temples. The bitterness knots in my heart. I can feel the tightness of it squeezing the life out. Let them do what they like; after today they will have no more power over me. I know from experience that the effect of the resinous fumes will last only a certain time. Ma-nan has become very skilled in judging just how much he needs to use to keep me docile for the required length of time. But he knows that he must not use so much that when the time comes for me to "perform" I will be unable to.

Today is a very special performance. Instead of going to the temple as I usually do, I am to be taken to a pyramid, the House of Many Thresholds, and sealed in. There, there will be no priests to harass me as I separate that part of my soul we call the "ka" from my body. In death the ka is naturally released from the body, and may travel freely through the many realms of matter and spirit, earth and sky. In life, usually only initiates of a very high order can separate the various substances of their being while they still remain attached to the body. But I have been trained for this—if for nothing else.

"What if the gods refuse my plea, refuse to give the waters to the Two Lands?" I had asked Ma-nan. "Must I bring this message to the people?"

I see by Ma-nan's face that, as usual, the words I bring will be rephrased by him, cunningly, ambiguously, and without hesitation.

The Nubians stop moving.

This will be because we are about to board the barge that will take us by river to the House of Many Thresholds. There will be singing. The rowers will sing rhythmically and the water will slap the sides of the boat.

There seems to be a longer delay than usual, and my muscles ache with the unsuccessful effort to lift my head to see what is happening.

Suddenly, a man stands beside me, looking down into my face. Beside him is a pale, thin young man whose crisp pleated kilt and golden menat collar seem too large for him. The older man is broad-shouldered and strong, and on his head the double crown fits snugly. The king himself! And, probably, the prince who will succeed him.

Now I should speak out and tell them what I know and how I am being treated, but though my voice, fumbling at first but growing stronger every moment, sounds clear to me I can tell that he is not hearing a single word. I begin to shout and cry and plead, but he hears nothing, sees nothing except the beautiful young painted body with its mask-like face, lying completely still on the bed of gold.

"Look into my eyes," I scream. "My eyes will tell you!" He stares into my eyes sombrely, and it seems, for a moment, that he is deeply troubled.

The young prince takes a step forward and leans over me, looking into my eyes. He starts, and turns to his father to say something, but at once Ma-nan steps forward, bowing, and speaks to the king. The king and the prince withdraw and I can no longer see them. The bed that is to be my bier is picked up again, and carried aboard. The river journey has begun. This time, I think fiercely, for the last time!

I listen to the drumbeats of the time-marker, the rhythmic song of the rowers. I listen to the swish and slap of the water, to the captain calling to the steersman. But mostly I listen to my own breath and my own heartbeat, and wonder if, when I come to it, I will have the courage to give them up.

As long as I can remember I have been in the dark house. It has a name: "the House of the Oracle"; but I never call it that. I have been told nothing about my parentage, nor why I have been chosen for this office. I am treated with remote respect by the few servants who work in the house, all deaf-mutes. My meals are brought to me by them on rich and elegant dishes. There is a tutor who teaches me the holy texts, but he will never answer my questions. There is a girl flute-player, but I have never seen her. I don't even know for sure that she is a girl; I just find myself thinking of her as one. Her music is always so haunting and sad I believe that she is not only beautiful, but blind, and I long to run away with her, far from this place, and teach her to see with my visions. Yes, I have visions of my own. Real visions, nothing to do with Ma-nan and his sorcery.

Ma-nan, who is in charge and has been always, treats me with cold severity, and it is he who inflicts pain if I refuse to do what he demands of me. His underling, the thin one, seems as frightened of me as he is of Ma-nan, and avoids me as much as possible. When I am taken to the Temple of Amun I see other priests, but they are always encased in rigid ceremonial robes and their faces are as expressionless as masks. Beneath the robes and the paint I wonder who the real men are.

Everything that is said and done in the temple is ritualised. The very way the lector priest reads from the holy texts in his high whining voice hides, rather than reveals, any meaning the texts were once supposed to have. How can they expect me to believe the god is really there when they themselves do not address him as though he were?

After the chanting it is my turn to perform. I am placed before the god in the high place of the sanctuary and am expected to stare into his eyes with the one eye painted on my forehead. I have to stare and stare, unblinking, until my own eyes sting and water in the smoky atmosphere. I am never told the "why" of anything, only that I have to stare until Ma-nan gives me a signal by moving the taper he holds up to the god. Then I have to speak out the words Ma-nan has taught me

8

to say. If I try not to say them, knowing that they are his words, and not the words of the god I am supposed to be speaking for, he will rouse his familiars; and I will be surrounded by ghastly figures, man-bodied, animal-headed, like the gods, yet not like the gods, demon figures who surround me and torment me.

No one else sees them. Only I.

Then, if I have rebelled, I will be punished when I am taken back to the dark house.

I shudder as I remember the punishments. I hear my heart beat faster. I know I cannot go on like this. I *will* not go on like this! This river that bears me now alive, will bear me tomorrow, dead.

We arrive at the jetty. The bier is lifted again. Again the plumes flutter against the sky, as the Nubians lift me and carry me along the causeway to the pyramid, the place where all the worlds meet, the only place I know of where man can leave his body, travel in the other worlds and return to his body, without experiencing body-death.

I shiver as we pass through the low door and into the long gallery of stone. Warmth and sunlight are gone and I will never see them again. For a moment I weaken and think: *A little longer. . . perhaps I could endure this life a little longer, just so that I can occasionally feel the sun's warmth and see its light. . .*

The darkness oppresses me.

I smell the sticky black blood of the torches, and see the soot-grimed rock ceiling getting lower and lower as we go deeper and deeper in, further and further from the sunlight.

I'm afraid. I don't want to be sealed in. I don't want to be left alone in that impenetrable dark. I begin to scream; but my lips do not move. No sound comes from my throat. The footsteps of the Nubians are enormously loud on the stone floor. I can hear them panting with the effort of climbing up the narrow ramp. I feel I will suffocate long before I reach the chamber at the centre. Huge and grotesque shadows flicker over the walls and the ceiling.

I am going to die with no one knowing my story. No one knowing what I have suffered, am suffering. No one has ever loved me, known me, cared. My loneliness is huge. Having no name, my story cannot even be scratched on the walls, cannot even be written in blood. In my death I will cease to exist. I will never have existed. . .

9

We have reached the chamber, and I am lowered carefully on to the slab of cold black granite.

I hear them leave. I hear the hollow clang of the rock door as it is shut. Every muscle in my body is straining to lift me off the bier, to call out, to plead for them not to leave me. The Nubians will listen. I suspect they don't like Ma-nan any more than I do. But Ma-nan's resin has worked well and my body is still paralysed, though my consciousness is agonisingly active. I smell the different kind of resin smell, the kind that is used for sealing. They are sealing the cracks around the chamber door. No one may break these for three days and three nights.

Ma-nan thinks that when he opens the door again, he will find me as he did last time, on the floor, my fingernails broken and my fingers bleeding from trying to dig away the resin and open the door. But this time he will find me lying on my bier as he left me, my face composed and calm: and he will no longer have me in his power. This time when I leave my body I will not return, but travel on until I am transformed and become one with the mighty splendours of the Secret God who is beyond all gods.

But to achieve this I must keep calm. I cannot die of starvation in three days, and there are no weapons with me to kill myself. No, I will do what I have been sent to do. I will leave my body and travel to that realm where I have been before in soul-form, the abode of the free spirits who have chosen to help our world. There I will plead for the water for the fields, for life for the people of Egypt. When this is granted, and only then, will I plead for myself. If they will not take me I will defy even them. I will not return to my body, no matter what.

But first the preparation and the journey.

I try to conquer my fear. I can feel the paralysing effect of Ma-nan's drug wearing off, and I can move my limbs again. The temptation is to jump up as I did last time, and tear at the door. The darkness is absolute. The cold is the cold of the tomb. My heart is pounding. My thoughts race about in my head like rats in a trap. What if I can't control myself, and at the end of the three days I am gibbering and whimpering at the door of life, whining to be let back in?

I waste precious time, weeping.

Now I have the full use of my limbs back. To give that up, voluntarily. . . I have had few pleasures in this life, but one of them is to sit by the pool in the tiny walled garden of the dark house and watch the water-lilies open. Can I give this up? Can I?

I take a deep, deep breath and bring myself under control. I must not think of the water-lilies, the one star of dawning, the moon, nor of the faces of the people I sometimes glimpse when I am taken to the temple. I must think of the pain, the loneliness, the darkness, the constant harassment from Ma-nan; the demons waiting to get me if I say or do something against his will. . .

What if Ma-nan has planted his familiars in this chamber? I look around fearfully. But it is as though I am blind, the darkness is so complete. My skin does not prickle as it does when Ma-nan's demons are near. I feel increasingly calm and relaxed, as though there are good spirits present. . . or at least. . .

I begin to do my breathing as it should be done in preparation for the separation. I flex all my muscles, rejoicing that they now obey my commands, and gradually relinquish the use of them, one by one. Every time my old fear threatens to rise to my throat and choke me I say the words I was given in one of my visions, words not even Ma-nan knows. I think, with brief satisfaction that Ma-nan does not know how to leave his body as I do, that in this he cannot interfere—though he will no doubt insist on giving me the words to say to the people when I come out. But in here now—I am alone, and what I experience is my secret, and the secret of those I reach towards. If only I can keep my fear under control.

It gradually becomes easier.

I know my ka is slipping from my body when I begin to see again. The darkness no longer exists for me, and I can see my body as though it is a stranger's, lying on the dark stone. I see inscriptions and paintings on the walls in minute detail, yet I know that the walls of the chamber are not painted or inscribed. To anyone existing only in the body the dark stone is smooth and unmarked. To the ka it is filled with signs and symbols needed for the journey. This is the threshold between the known and the unknown, and there is a map here of the universe beyond the stars, of the realms where the gods sail throughout eternity—and I do not mean the eternity of endless time, but the eternity that only the gods know, the eternity that has never known time. The words inscribed are not of worldly matters, but are written in the old language, almost forgotten, hinting at mysteries too deep for the human mind to grasp. I feel strange—as though as I look at them they are keys that are turning lock after lock in my invisible self, and as each one turns, a little more of me is released from the world I know.

I hover, enjoying the freedom from the restrictions of the body.

I look dispassionately at the youth lying so still. He is thin. I can see his ribs and his prominent shoulder bones. The kohl has run down his temples where his tears have soaked it off his eyelids. His lips are set in a sad line as though he rarely smiles.

I speak the words of praise I have been taught to Hapi, god of the Nile, spirit of the inundation who lives in a great cave under the river and in whose power it is to draw on the primeval waters beneath the world.

"Thou who canst not be sculpted in stone, nor seen in the images that are set in the crowns of the South and the North. Thou who accepteth no works nor offerings and cannot be brought forth from Thy secret abode, for the place wherein Thou dwellest cannot be known. Thou who canst not be found in inscribed Shrines, for there is no habitation which is large enough to contain Thee. . . nor imagining that can fashion an image of Thee. . . Whose blood flows with the green waters of the great primeval ocean from which we all come. . . hear my prayer. . ."

I visualize the river swelling as it does at times of flood, flowing with its rich green and brown over the fields; the festivals of greeting in all the towns and villages; the fleets of little boats decorated with coloured streamers by day, and torches by night, passing from village to village over areas that a few short hours previously had been dry, cracked earth and withered shoots.

And then I invoke Osiris, the great spirit of fertility, who will bring from Hapi's waters and from the rich black silt they have deposited, the bright green growth that will feed the people of the Two Lands.

"Homage be to Thee, O King of kings, Lord of lords, Ruler of princes, who from the womb of Nut hast ruled the world and the underworld. Thy members are like bright and shining copper, Thy head is blue like lapis lazuli, and the greenness of turquoise is on both sides of thee, O Thou god of millions of years, whose form and

whose beauty of face are all-pervading in the underworld. Thou art Nepra and Thou givest all green herbs and all flowers. Thou art the Lord of Food, presenting all lands with thy abundance. Grant Thou unto me a path whereon I may pass in peace."

Slowly I climb the ladder of the sacred words. Slowly I say the spells that have come to me from ancient times. The scene around the youth is no longer there. Without passing out of the chamber I am no longer in it. I am in a boat. I look over the side and the water is crystal clear, and beneath it I can see the continents and the oceans of the world laid out as though on a map. I see my country is small; is one of many.

I drift to the masthead and see that there are no horizons. We are sailing towards a huge darkness, and behind us I see that we have come from a darkness equally vast. I pray for spirit-sight and that I may not be afraid of the dark.

My prayer must have been granted, because out of the darkness looms a huge and beautiful figure. I can see the stars through her body, and feel her breath on my cheek like the whisper of a great and potent secret. It is Nut, who is the spirit of the sky, created before the earth. . .

I bow as low as it is possible to bow, and my heart breathes the prayer my lips are now too awed to speak. I ask to see Osiris, he who has power to give life on the other side of death. She reaches out her closed hand to me, and as I stare at it enquiringly, she opens it slowly in front of me. Resting on her palm is a golden falcon. He spreads his wings and flutters on her palm, light sliding from his feathers like drops of water. He is a being of light beyond anything I have ever seen. I understand he is to be my guide and my protector. Silently I follow him as he wings away from her towards the darkness. One by one we reach the guardians of the way, monstrous figures, fierce beyond belief, who reach for us—but when the falcon cries the name of Him we go to seek, fall back and let us pass.

"How can such hideous demons serve the Lord of Life?" I ask.

"Look back," the falcon says, and as I look the guardian that had seemed so dangerous and harsh, is now as beautiful as fire on the hearth. I remember Set, whose other name is Violence, the slayer of Osiris, the enemy of Horus, standing at the prow of the Boat of Millions of Years and in his role as Protector, destroying the enemies of Ra.

13

We reach the Great Waters out of which the first hill rises. Osiris, green god, rooted in the earth, his branches reaching to the sun, is before us.

How can I speak to such a one? Who am I, to address a spirit so lofty? My throat is dry: my words sticking in it like bones. And then I remember the suffering of the people without food and water; the pot-bellies of children with skeletal bodies; the withered vegetation; the cracked red earth. I forget myself, and pray for them, for the mysterious waters that will bring the rich black earth to my land.

He hears my words, and lifts his hands to receive them, and then he lets them go again so that they drift upwards like smoke. . . higher. . . higher. . . until they disappear into a light-source impossible to look at, so dazzling, so great, that our own sun if placed before it would appear to be a dark hole; our own gods, like moths around that sun.

I tremble, and find myself back in the chamber with the youth who has no name. I remember that I have forgotten to ask for his death.

I can feel his suffering drawing me to him again. Soon I will be back with him, and he will have to face the life he hates.

I am no longer in the world of spirit, but I pray to Isis who has suffered more than any mortal, who has known loneliness and loss. I will pray to her though now I know the gods we pray to, the gods we worship, are no more than mediators between us and the unknowable—bridges that span for us the mighty chasms between reality and reality.

Suddenly, the youth and I are not alone in the chamber. A figure stands to one side of me. He is very beautiful. Not young. Not old. Where have I seen him before? Was it on a granite wall carved by a sculptor with the seeing eye, or is it that he has the eyes of the falcon who was my guide on the journey to Osiris?

"I am Khurahtaten," he says quietly, proudly. The name is unknown to me. His golden eyes watch me.

I look at him, not knowing what to make of him.

"Many things will become clear to you soon," he says gently. "Let my name stand on your doorstep, sit at your table, walk with you in the evening. . . All things will become clear. . ."

"Why do you come to me? What have I to do with you?" I ask.

"I seek help."

"How can I help you?" I say. "It is I who need help."

"Nevertheless it is you who must help me."

"But how? I have a body that is kept prisoner by the priest Ma-nan."

"It is a body that houses the soul of a true adept in the mysteries. With recognition of who he really is will come freedom from whom he thinks he is."

"But now he is lonely and afraid. He does not know who he is. He has no name."

The being looks thoughtfully down on the young body.

"I will help him with my strength. He will grow strong," he says.

I feel the urge to return to my body, to cling to what I know. It is as though I have glimpsed for a moment what we truly are, and am as frightened as someone who had thought he was a child, and finds suddenly that he is expected to be a responsible adult. There is a moment when I have partly returned to the motionless figure of the boy, and partly not. I feel the searing of his pain, his fear returning; yet I am still separate and he screams at me to keep away.

"I won't let you return!" he cries. "Leave me! Leave me! I want to die! I want to die! I must die."

His body shudders and jerks as I unite once more with him.

I HAVE FAILED. . . FAILED. . . NOW THERE will be no escape.

The blackness is oppressive. How can there be such darkness? I, as nameless oracle, struggle to my feet and rush forward, feeling for the wall. I tug the hated wooden head-dress from my head and start to beat my bare skull against the wall, again and again, with all my might. The pain is terrible but I seem unable to kill myself. I remember nothing of what happened while my ka was on its journey. . . I can think of nothing but my fear of returning to life.

Blood fills my eyes where tears filled them before.

I join the darkness, and fall unconscious to the floor.

2

THE JOURNEY

MY RETURN TO THE CITY OF Men-nefer passes like a dream, I am only partially aware of the sun's bronzed disc low against the horizon, the river sounds—a boatman calling to the boy who climbs the mast, the cry of birds. . .

Sometimes I am aware of nothing.

Then images swim into view and through a mist I see the crowd being held back, while the young prince moves forward to gaze at me. There is something in his face. . . I cannot tell what it is. . . but it is as though he desperately wants an answer from me and does not know how to word the question. I see horror and pity in his face when he notices the blood that has seeped out from under the formal head-dress and dried on my temple. I look over his shoulder half-expecting to see his father, the king. . . but I meet Ma-nan's eye and close my own with a sigh. What if the king is there or not? What if the prince pities me? There is no escape. No way out.

In the night the prince is in my dreams. We are reaching out towards each other through a jostling crowd of people who are driving us further and further apart. Behind him I see his father, Amenhotep Neb-maat-Ra, and his mother, Queen Tiye, calling to him. . . behind them is a young woman weeping. . .

* * * *

17

WHEN I WAKE I AM AWARE of nothing but the throbbing of my aching head. I am told that by the king's command I am to be taken at last from this dark house, this place of sorrow. I know not where I am to go, but Ma-nan is agitated and shouts at the thin one. The servants scuttle about seizing things and hurrying them into boxes. For the first time in all the years I have been here routine is broken.

I lie on my bed swathed in bandages, unable to die. Is the move to be a punishment because I tried to kill myself? Is some worse prison awaiting me? Ma-nan, of course, tells me nothing. Through the thundering of the pain in my head I hear snatches of words not meant for my ears, and gather that it will be a long journey. I ask no questions, knowing that if I did, they would not be answered. Worse, my voice would he ignored as though it had not entered their ears, and I would feel again as I have often felt, as though I have no existence except as a tool for them.

When all the house is empty and the echoes double each footstep, each word, Ma-nan comes to me and stands over me, looking down. I cannot read his expression. Is it triumph or bitterness? Only Ma-nan knows how to combine these two. Snatches of my ka's journey have been coming to me, but my head is too painful to sort them out into real and not-real, memory and imagination. Did I do well for the people and Ma-nan in the House of Many Thresholds? I am not sure. I am sure only that I failed to take my own life, and now I am worse off than before because my head is in agony as well as my feet.

I shut my eyes and Ma-nan's face disappears, but I can still sense him beside me. Why doesn't he speak or go away? At last I hear him clap his hands, and then feet without sandals pad across the floor. The Nubians. Surely not another performance already? But it can't be, because a cloak is put over me and I am placed on an ordinary stretcher, the kind for carrying sick people. The rich trappings of my office as oracle are nowhere in sight, packed up no doubt with the kitchen utensils and the excretion bucket—where they belong.

I am taken through the early morning streets back to the harbour, only a few citizens out to see me pass. Very different from yesterday, when the crowds were staring, pleading with me to bring them salvation. When a prince tried to speak to me...

The streets are narrow, mud-brick houses crowded together. The administrative capital of the Two Lands, placed strategically at the junction of the broad, rich delta lands and the narrow strip of green hedged in by desert that comprises the rest of the country, is an old city, sprawling and ungainly. The huge Temple of Ptah dominates it, the streets close to the temple less oppressive, the houses of the noblemen who provide most of the priests to serve the god, more spacious and elegant than those we have been passing. Palm trees in their gardens rise above the walls and flowering vines flow over the brick almost to street level. We pass the south gate of the Temple of Ptah and my heart skips a beat as I meet the eyes of the two gigantic alabaster sphinxes that guard it, unsleeping day and night. I have passed between them many times—never happily. In this temple too I have spoken lies. I have been taken from the Temple of Amun, the Hidden One, to the Temple of Ptah, the Creator—in both I have been manipulated like a puppet by Ma-nan. Can I hear the chanting still? Ptah who created all I see around me, mighty and powerful energy beyond imagining, reduced to the small figure of a man carved of stone with a skull cap, holding to his chest the sceptre, the wand, the rod of power—the means to create, to bestow life. Ptah speaking with my voice. Ptah taking the piping voice of a child to mouth his Wisdom Words. Sometimes he has spoken to me alone and I have told no one. He has reassured me that everything has a reason and a purpose, even my own shadow-life. He has told me that I must not despair, that my time will come.

In these temple precincts there is also the smaller temple of Ptah's consort, Sekhmet. I have been used for her too. She I fear as much as I love Ptah. Visits to her I dread. Great scarlet woman, fearsome lioness, drinker of blood, the Destroyer that shakes the earth and tumbles cities down. When I am in the chamber behind her shrine and am told to speak with her voice, I tremble. Many a night I dream of running through the desert with Sekhmet padding after me, her sinewy limbs rippling in the starlight, her eyes seeing in the dark, seeing through rock, seeking me out wherever I try to hide. Sekhmet the Destroyer, angry. Angry with me!

But today we do not enter. We skirt the high walls that keep the secrets of the god and goddess safe from the uninitiated and head for the river that laps one of its sides. We board a sailing-boat of the kind that plies up and down the river for long distances, not the narrow barge I usually travel in. I find my heart contains a tiny shoot, a bud. . . possibly it is hope for a better life. . . possibly excitement that whatever happens it, at least, will be a change.

The day goes by and I lie under an awning, protected from the worst heat of the sun; the banks slide past. I doze and wake and doze again.

Where the green of the cultivated lands ends, behind the forest of palms, rises the desert and there on the escarpment of reddish rock and sand we glimpse something of the ancient necropolis of Men-nefer, the tall step pyramid of King Djoser rising higher than any of its fellows, towering above the smooth walls of his mortuary temple, like the first mound that rose from the waters of chaos and on which the shining spirit-bird of the greatest god landed to lay its golden egg. I have heard tell of this place in the ancient texts but, as far as I know, I have never seen it before. Yet, as I look at it, I know it is familiar. As I look at it, I know what I will find if I turn my gaze to the north and the south of it. I know what will be on the other side of it, though from here I cannot see further than the gleaming walls of stone. I have seen this place in a dream and in the dream I stand in the moonlight with a roll of papyrus in my hands and, as I try to read the hieroglyphs, it disintegrates into fine dust and is blown by the mocking breath of Set to every horizon. Is that sound a dog howling or my own voice howling in despair for a great wisdom lost and an opportunity missed? The sorrow in my heart tells me it is my own voice. I have been here before and I have not been here. Is it a memory from a long-gone life—or are the gods trying to tell me something?

We pass the landing quay, the entrance to the causeway that leads from the river to the field of many pyramids. Here the great funeral barges would have come in the old days, here the royal burial processions would have started. Nowadays kings are buried in the far south, at Waset, in tombs cut into the western mountains. The great days of pyramid building are over. Even here some are crumbling, their fine casing stone loosening and slipping, quarried for the sumptuous buildings of the living city to the north, their secrets violated by the tomb robbers. Only Djoser's stands as perfect as it was at the time of its building, the greatest of them all, constructed by a visionary, the god Imhotep himself, surrounded by ancient glories and the tombs of priests and high officials.

I am drawn to the place and long to stop, but the oarsmen pull even harder against the current and we sweep on to the south.

There are other people aboard, but they are kept well away from me. In the long, dark, moonless night I think that perhaps, when I am stronger and the pain has eased off, I can creep to the side of the boat and leap off. They will not notice that I have gone until the morning. I can hear Ma-nan's ugly snore beside me. But not now. Now, I have not the strength. I drift off to sleep again. Strange dreams. Someone seems to be trying to reach me. I turn my back on him. I know he wants me to do something for him, but I am too tired. . . too tired. . .

"Go away," I say, "go away. Leave me to sleep. Leave me alone." I wake and am in a huge night. . . people all around me sleeping, but I alone.

Days pass and I gradually grow stronger. Ma-nan changes my bandages from time to time, and gives me food and drink. He never talks to me. It is as though I am deaf and dumb like the servants. Perhaps I am dumb, I think. I haven't used my voice for a long time.

A north wind begins to blow, cooling the air. A Horus wind that presages the inundation.

I sit up, feeling considerably better. I had thought I had noticed a change in the motion of the boat and now I see what it is: the river is running strongly against us, very strongly. I take a deep breath, hardly daring to hope, and look closely at the banks. I was right. The floods have come, the river is on the move to cover the fields with its beautiful, deep, rich, life-giving black silt. I look at Ma-nan, half expecting him to show some spark of gratitude for what I have done. I, done? Even as I think it, I know he will show me no gratitude. Quite rightly. It is not I who have brought the water. . .

O Osiris!
They come, the waters of life which are in the sky.
They come, the waters of life which are in the earth.
The sky is aflame for you, the earth trembles for you.
The god comes into being, the god has power in his body.
The month is born, the fields live.

Each night that comes I think that I should jump overboard, and either die in the turbulent water or escape. But each night that comes, I put it off to the next. Is it possible that I am beginning to enjoy life and want it to continue? I am still kept away from the others and treated with cold contempt by Ma-nan, but now I don't care because every day my eyes are dazzled by beauty. Ducks, with a green translucence in their wings, fly over me. Flowering water-reeds shimmer above the surface where the banks used to be. Flotillas of little boats bob beside us, their occupants waving joyfully. At evening I am awed by the splendour of a procession of shining beings accompanying the mighty golden disc of the Sun as he enters his unseen realms, his hidden kingdom. I never cease to catch my breath with surprise at the sudden flare of fiery light that suffuses the whole sky, long after the disk has disappeared. Slowly, slowly fading, easing us into darkness. At dawn my heart beats with love, as first light stains everything pale green like a new shoot, and I see my star still there when all the others have faded from the sky. The nights are lighter now, as the moon steadily grows from silver feather to polished wing. The only pain I feel now is fear of losing all this beauty, this day-by-day growing intensity of love for the earth and sky and water—the gift of life I have received. When I sleep, I see the one who had wanted to reach me that first night, and I welcome him. We stand on the deck at night with the stars like enormous lamps above us, and he talks to me, telling me that his name is Khurahtaten, an incarnation of the great spirit, known to us as Horus, sent once before to guide me and now returned to guide me again. He tells me he has a task for me, something that I started when I last lived on earth but failed to complete. He wants me to work with him. At first I argue that I cannot, and then I say "maybe". And now I know I shall.

At first he came only at night when I was asleep. But now he comes in the day. . . at any time. I might be staring at a hawk circling, and I hear his voice inside my head. I might be admiring the infinite shades of blue and pink in a distant mountain range, and he is beside me. I ask questions, and am answered, but I am worried that our time together will be brief and that at any moment Ma-nan may notice the strange trances I slip into, and find a way to stop them. Khurahtaten asks me if I am prepared to take a step from which there is no turning back. Eagerly I cry *Yes!* And then I know that where Ma-nan used to paint the Seeing Eye on my forehead I now need no paint. I am no king, but on my forehead I feel the golden ureaus, the cobra poised to strike at darkness, like the sun. There is no mild recognition, but fission and terror as meaning leaps to meaning, like lightning in iron mountains. Words split in revelation. The crust of my former understanding shatters, and inside, like a geode, an unimaginable crystal landscape is revealed. The myths of my people take wing, and leave behind the shabby trafficking of priest-magic and empty incantation as the golden eagle leaves behind the sparrow. I know my task is to find the living truth behind the holy words and the holy rituals, to bring understanding to a people who have so misunderstood the ancient revelations that they believe the body has to be preserved in Time for the spirit to live in Eternity, and that magical formulae alone can open what is truly closed.

My instructor, day by day, night by night, goes deeper into the truth for which my soul thirsts. His knowledge comes into my mind and becomes my knowledge. I grow in wisdom and strength moment by moment.

Now I do not care that I am kept isolated in one part of the boat, and that no one is allowed near to talk to me. I welcome it, and dread the breaking of my silence. People sometimes come to where the cord is drawn across the deck to keep me separate, and stare at me.

I squat on the deck for hours, unmoving, staring at the blue water rushing past the boat, or stand, still as stone, my eyes fixed on some distant rock-formation from the moment it appears until the moment it disappears. The clarity of the air makes it possible to see great distances, and figures of stone a morning's walk away seem only arrow-far, every cleft and cranny clear.

I presume Ma-nan has strengthened the effectiveness of the cord with some spell, because no one attempts to push it aside and come to me, though it looks easy enough to do. And I too make no attempt to escape my confinement.

From time to time we change the oarsmen. More rarely we stop, pulling in at some small quay to take on bread and beer. Often I have no idea of the name of the village that serves us and I do not care to ask, but one day I notice more than the usual flurry of excitement that characterizes these pauses in routine. I hear the name "Abedju" and realize we have reached one of the holiest sites in the Two Lands. It is here the head of Osiris is said to lie and it is here everyone from king to commoner wants to be buried or at least have some monument raised to associate himself with the great King of the Underworld. The place is a forest of stelae and cenotaphs. The temple itself on its sacred mound lies some way back from the river and it is clear there is no intention that we should visit it though some people leave the boat and do not return. I lean over the side and gaze into the heat-haze that almost obscures the town and certainly the hills beyond it. I wonder at the long centuries that have seen this as a place of pilgrimage and miracle. I picture the continual seasonal re-enactment of the death and resurrection of the Great God—the battle he loses against his brother, Set, his dismemberment—the long search of his sister-wife, Isis. . . I wonder at the magnificent Book of Coming Forth by Day that is buried with so many kings—the book that gives such clear instructions for their progress through the Underworld where they endure trial after trial until they stand at last before the throne of the Living One, the resurrected Osiris. I look at the water of the inundation lapping high upon the banks, covering the low-lying fields, and know that when it recedes Osiris will bring the green world to life again.

> "Hail to you who are pleased with justice; you are Lord of Abedju,
>   and your flesh has enriched the sacred land. . .
>   . . . All hearts are at peace for what you have done, for to you belong
>   eternity and everlasting. . ."

We leave Osiris and travel up-river again. The next stop is at Tantere. Here Hathor, the daughter of Ra and wife of Horus, gave birth to her son, the god of music. Here music and dancing enliven her temple, the Lady of Turquoise, the Beautiful One, the Mother of the earth. I have always loved Hathor, fantasizing that she is indeed my mother, that I have suckled at her breast, that she comes for me and visits me in the night to comfort me when I am lonely and afraid. I long to visit her cult-centre and put flowers on her altar—but Ma-nan refuses to let me set foot off the boat. I have never known a mother of flesh and blood, and I weep secretly for Hathor who is also kept from me.

One day I am standing urinating over the side, when I see that we are approaching a great city. I hear the others on the boat excitedly shouting and pointing, and gather by the collecting together of possessions, the squabbling over position on the decks, that this is our destination. I have a twinge of disappointment. My journey is over and

I am still prisoner. No, I think, *never again*. I look across at Ma-nan giving curt instructions to his servants, and find that I no longer fear him. I will stay Oracle, for Oracle has power. I will bide my time and take this power when I am ready, and neither Ma-nan nor anyone else will know the moment of its approach or be able to understand it when it comes.

With apparent docility I wait, peering at the great city, Waset. Men-nefer was huge and sprawling, but, nothing like this. It always gave the impression of clutter, as though it had grown up haphazard and too many people had crowded into it. Here there is shape and order. Hugging the earth are the mud-brick houses of the people. Above them rise huge stone edifices, obelisks with glittering pyramidal points reaching to the sun; mighty temple-gates under the protection of the winged sun disc colourful with the fluttering pennants of the pharaoh and his priests; noble houses, palaces with green and leafy gardens beside the waters of the Nile. . . Set back on the west side of the river lie the silent hills of pale stone which hide the entrance to the Underworld, the tombs of the kings. And between the river and the mountains is the huge mortuary temple of the present pharaoh with its tall painted columns, its magnificent cedar doors inlaid with golden silhouettes of the gods, and, flanking the entrance pylons, two gigantic seated effigies of the king himself set to keep him in the minds of his people as long as time lasts. I cannot help being impressed. If I had not seen the king (shorter than myself, though I am scarce full-grown) from his statues I would have believed him to be a giant among men.

I try to re-establish contact with my friend and counsellor, Khurahtaten, but he has left me alone to find my own way and form my own impressions in this new place. He warned me that he did not want to be gaoler of my mind as Ma-nan was of my body. But I find something of the old fear creeping into my heart as I see the huge walls of the temples, and the darkness from inside lurking behind them. The sun blazes down on them but does not penetrate.

3

THE MEETING

THE INUNDATION HAS COME AND GONE several times since the day I
pleaded with the spirits in the House of Many Thresholds. My body is
changing and growing and day by day I seem to be a different person.
Sometimes I am consumed with restless indignation at my plight, at
others I am indifferent to what happens to me. I live in the crowded
precincts of the Temple of Amun and come in contact with many more
people than I ever have before. Some of them are women and young
girls and I dream of touching them but never dare to do so. Ma-nan
still has an extraordinary hold on me. Whether it is by his orders or
because there is something about me that repels others, I am somehow
still alone. I have noticed on more than one occasion when I have tried
to befriend someone that they withdraw from me with something like
fear in their eyes. I am nameless. I am an oracle. My body is a vehicle
inhabited by the gods from time to time. They are made uneasy by my
presence and do not want to get too close to me. Sometimes I wonder
if I was not better off alone in that house in Men-nefer than I am now,
lonely in a crowd.

Ma-nan finds it necessary to control me with charms and hypnotic
spells and more and more frequent use of the smoke. My only comfort
is Khurahtaten. He and I speak many secret words together, and l learn
it is almost time for me to show my strength and find my living partner for the task. My spirit companion tells me that charms and spells

27

and smoke will have no effect on me when my time comes, and I must abide till then in patience, storing knowledge against the time it will be needed. When I ask him who my partner will be, he tells me to be patient. He will find me, and I will find him, when the time is right.

Meanwhile day follows day and at least there is a great deal of activity in the community in which I find myself, even if I take no part in it. The temple itself is sacrosanct and no one enters unless he or she has a specific role to play in the elaborate rituals of the day. Even the sweeping of the floors with brooms of soft green reeds is done by an initiate priest. But in the cluster of buildings kept separate from the city by vast mud-brick walls there is a microcosm of the world outside. Here there are rivalries and jealousies as people jostle to improve their status in the temple hierarchy. Here there are loves and hates, courtships and disappointments, intrigues, frustrations and triumphs. Farmers bring in a proportion of the produce of their labours to be offered to the god and consequently consumed by the huge temple staff. Scribes record what is brought in and what goes out, contrasting strongly in their crisp white linen kilts and their clean and perfumed bodies, with the rough and dusty workmen of the fields. Cattle are brought in and driven, lowing, to the cattle pens, stirring up the dust with their hooves. Geese cackle and honk on the sacred lake. Gardeners shout to each other as they tend the gardens, while novices squabble and adepts debate. My favourite sight and sound is a group of young girls, chantresses of the temple, walking together with their flimsy robes floating out behind them, lotus blossom in their hair, laughing and chattering as they leave the temple for their dormitory quarters, pretending to ignore the admiring whistles of the builders who are almost constantly working in the area, but giving covert glances over their shoulders to see whether the whistler is handsome or not. Sometimes I meet the eyes of one of them as they pass me and fancy I see a spark of interest there, a curiosity that is not as unfriendly as usual. Nothing more ever happens—but I begin to dream and my dreams keep me awake at night.

The higher orders of priesthood have their dwelling houses outside the temple precincts, but usually close by. Most of them have other houses as well on the outskirts of town or in the country—huge mansions rivalling the palaces of the king, with storehouses and columned halls, with lily ponds and shady walkways of sycamore and palm. They retain quarters in the precincts as well, but when the day's work is done I see them striding out between the guards at the gate, glad to get away from the hubbub surrounding the god's house.

I long to go out into the town, but am not allowed. It is continually impressed on me that I must stay ready, and absolutely pure, for the moment when the god or his representative, the High Priest, wants to use me. Whenever I make an attempt to stray beyond the areas that have been allotted to me, I find someone there to turn me back.

THE PREPARATIONS THIS YEAR FOR THE Opet Festival, Amun-Ra's journey from his great sanctuary at Ipet-Esut to Ipet-Resut in the south where his consort, the goddess Mut, has her sanctuary, have been as elaborate as usual. The young Prince Amenhotep, in whom Ra-Horus glories, and who will succeed his father to the double crown, is to be present; his father being, at this time, confined to bed with an illness that has been troubling him more and more lately. I have been instructed as usual in the words I am to speak as Oracle, Ma-nan manipulating my mind with the power of his dark and piercing gaze, his smoke, his incantations. I wait, in the darkness of the chamber behind the sanctuary of Mut, dazed, scarcely thinking, the words Ma-nan having fed me lying dormant, to spring forth when he gives the signal.

Idly, my mind's eye follows the progress of the procession of Amun-Ra. There will be thousands upon thousands of people to see the journey; more than usual because of the illness of the king, and their curiosity to see Prince Amenhotep, who was not born to wear the double crown, but became heir only on the death of his elder brother, first-born and beloved of the king. They expect the prince to ask for the oracle's pronouncement on his father's health, and for confirmation of his own right to succeed him.

At the quay the god, safe in his curtained shrine, will be placed on a gilded barge, beautiful with fluttering feathers and ribbons, and towed from Ipet-Esut to the southern sanctuary, the crowds following on the towpath, children running and jumping, adults shouting and cheering, traders selling ribbons and fans, and small effigies and amulets. Everyone is happy at last to be near the great god—or at least because this is a holiday and the musicians are playing lively tunes.

Once disembarked, the chief prophets of Amun-Ra, now a

tremendous power in the state, walk ahead of the procession. The bearers of the jewelled model of the sacred boat in which Amun-Ra sails towards his beloved are all relatives of the king. One is the prince himself, older than I, but smaller, thinner and round-shouldered. His coronet, his pectoral collar, the stiff and jewelled apron that overlays his kilt, all seem too heavy for him, dwarfing him in some way, making him look outlandish and ungainly. Beside him walks his uncle Ay, the brother of his mother, the Great Royal Wife, Queen Tiye. Ay has been many things to the old king, from household confidant and steward to Master of the King's Chariots. He has carried the ceremonial fan and sat at the king's table when feasting was in favour. Having chosen his queen from one of the minor noble families instead of from the royal line, King Amenhotep Neb-maat-Ra has always been at pains to honour his wife's brothers almost above anyone else. Other priests from Ipet-Esut walk behind, while Ma-nan and Na-aghte, responsible for the Amun Oracle on loan to the Temple of Mut for the day, wait with the priests of Mut in the great courtyard of the southern temple for the procession to arrive. They stand almost as still as the statues of the pharaoh-as-god that guard the entrance.

The darkness is very silent in this chamber. I can almost feel it, touch it, as though it were solid. I am seated on a gilded chair raised on a platform, carved with devices from the earliest days, the magical formulae of my trade. My fingers read them as a blind man would, tracing their shapes, bored with the time of waiting. I wish I could see the crowds, the sunlight glinting on the silver and precious jewels of the bark and the divine effigy. I am looking forward to seeing the prince again. I still sometimes puzzle about that dream I shared with him. I have heard that he is something of a weakling, nothing like his father. The rumour is that his father was bitterly disappointed in the death of his eldest son, and barely tolerates his younger. It is to his mother, Tiye, that Amenhotep must look for encouragement; it is said that there are times when she half smothers him with her love.

I have seen the king twice, once when I was on my way to the House of Many Thresholds, and a year ago at this same ceremony. He had looked into my eyes as I declaimed the words Ma-nan had put into my mouth, and his expression had been very strange. For the second time I had tried to fight the spell I was under and say the words that I believed needed to be said, rather than the words that had been prescribed. For the second time I had failed.

The configurations on the chair are beginning to give me strength. Khurahtaten has taught me many things about the ancient texts that the priests these days seem to have forgotten. The saying of names is not enough, the drawing of signs, the carving of figures—you have to know the inner meaning of the names, the signs, the figures. As my sightless fingers work I feel the circle that is the wholeness of all things, the spot inside the space within it that is the dimensionless moment from which all things grew. . . *Who sees, when they see me, that I am many? Who sees, when they see me, that I am One?*

I find the shape of a falcon's eye and remember that Horus gave his eye to his father, that blind Osiris might see. It was given with love, and with it the seeing is clear and true. There is a left eye and a right eye. The eye of the moon: the eye of the sun. The one to illumine the secrets of the heart: the other to illumine the secrets of the mind. Slowly, slowly I work around the chair as far as my fingers will reach, my mind gradually clearing of Ma-nan's spells as I do so, my own mind taking over.

I hear the distant cry of the crowd and know that I have not much time left. The sign I touch is Maat's feather, that which is weighed against the heart in the Halls of the Two Truths, after the first death, the death of the body. I remember inscriptions on the walls of tombs thought to mislead and placate the forty-two assessors:

O thou being, broad of stride, who comest forth from Yunu,
I have done no evil!
O thou embracer of flames, who comest forth from Kher-aha,
I have not robbed!
O thou nose, who comest forth from Khemnu,
I have not been covetous!

On the walls of my tomb, if I have one, there will be no such inscriptions. I know no words can turn aside the last judgement, no green heart-scarab of stone prevent the real heart speaking for itself. It cannot lie, once it is free of its physical sheath, no matter how loud one cries: "*O my heart of my mother! O my heart of my mother! O my heart of my transformations! Do not stand up against me as a witness! Do not create opposition to me in the council! Do not cause the pan to sink in the presence of the keeper of the balance!"* The secret motives that have lain hidden in the heart will out!

I hear chanting now, and know that the procession must have passed under the protective winged sun above the entrance gate and have entered the great courtyard. Most of the people would have been left outside the walls of the holy precinct: only a few privileged ones are allowed through to participate further in the ceremony.

The sounds are muffled and very distant. I think I hear a drumming, but it is my own heartbeat. I have decided that this day will be the day I make my stand, partner or no partner.

After what seems a very long time, the pitch of distant sound rises again, and I know the next stage has begun. The uninitiated people will be left outside, and the small group of initiates, including the prince, will enter the antechamber. Prince Amenhotep's training as a priest was at Yunu in the Mysteries of the Sacred Nine, though no doubt he has been instructed in the rituals of Amun and Mut. Once in the antechamber they will all be sprinkled with holy water, while the incantations for cleansing are made. Then they will come into the first hall. Their progress through this will be slow, for they will stop every few steps by some particular inscription, while the priests of Mut intone sacred words and the priests of Amun utter the responses. Once they reach the sanctuary, the chamber immediately in front of the one I am in, the ritual will take even longer.

What are they thinking, I wonder, these priests mouthing these words, making these ancient gestures? Do they think the gods are children taken in by make believe, enjoying the same bedtime story over and over again?

My hands begin to sweat.

I try to pace out the ritual in my mind so that I will know exactly when my time is come.

Now they will be placing the effigy in its costly boat beside his consort Mut, on the plinth kept ever ready for it. . .

Now they will be bowing. . .

Now they will be praying. . .

Now the offerings will be brought and laid before the god and goddess. I wonder what rich gift the young prince has brought.

More praying.

32

Now the two high priests will be preparing to lead the prince, in his role as representative of the pharaoh, through the door to me.

I hear Ma-nan breaking the seal that had been placed over the lock when I was led there early in the morning. I compose myself. I sit as straight and still as a statue, the paint so thick on my face it feels and looks like a mask. I hold so tightly to the sign of the ankh, the symbol of eternal life carved on the chair, with the one hand, and to the sign of the seeing eye of Horus with the other, that my knuckles hurt.

As the light from the tapers shines into them, my eyes are momentarily blinded. I cannot see the figures that enter and take up their positions in the small dark room, but I know the prince will be in front of me, priests of Mut and Amun on either side, a step or two behind the prince. I know Ma-nan will be looking at me, anxious to see whether the spell he has put on me has stayed—confident it has, but checking nevertheless. I keep my face still, my eyes staring straight ahead, trying to fool him.

Gradually my eyes adjust, and I can dimly make out the figures, the small flames grotesquely accentuating noses and the hollows of the eyes. I can feel the young prince's fear at the same time as I can feel mine. We both suddenly know that this is a significant moment in our lives and are afraid of it.

Ma-nan has instructed me under spell to promise the prince the life of his father, in exchange for unbelievable amounts of bounty. But he has worded the lists of gifts for the god so carefully, and made it so complicated, that if the king dies it could be claimed that it was because the prince had omitted something from the bargain, not because as Oracle I had failed.

Prince Amenhotep speaks the asking prayer, and I notice that his voice is faltering. His face is so sensitive it is almost luminous, his eyes deep-seeing, his lips full.

I stay silent for the required amount of time, taking my cue for speaking from the signal Ma-nan always gives me, the raising of his hand.

I pause slightly longer than usual after the signal, gathering my strength. It is not easy to push aside Ma-nan's powerful spell and I know the effort to do so could destroy my sanity. My companion and counsellor, Khurahtaten, has given me advice for the chosen moment and I try to follow it, knowing that if my mind wanders a second from the task in hand I could be destroyed.

I visualize a tremendous source of light beyond and outside everything I have ever known, yet infusing everything I have ever known, just as my soul saw it in the House of Many Thresholds, our own sun dark compared to it.

I visualize the secret source of the river and in its turbulent spring I plunge and wash myself, the water as clear as the clearest crystal, colder than the coldest stone at dawn. I visualize myself rising from the spring washed clean of everything that has gone before... And then, and only then, I begin to speak.

At first, what I say is no more than the expected words anyone would use honouring the prince and his forbears, but then I startle them all by breaking tradition and standing up. I begin to speak my own words, telling the prince that his father's time for death has not yet come, but that from now on he will not be as strong as he has been, and the prince must prepare himself for the day when he is pharaoh.

"When this day comes," I say in a voice that seems louder than any I have ever known. "When this day comes you will have a task that is mightier than the expulsion of the Hyksos, mightier than the conquest of Nubia."

Open-mouthed he looks at me. I cannot afford to make a long and subtle speech, for Ma-nan is already recovering from the shock, and is reaching into the small pouch I know he keeps hidden in his kilt.

"Turn the people round, beloved of god," I cry, "set them to search their own hearts for the meaning behind the ancient texts, set them to listening for the voice that speaks in the silence. Behind the many names of the gods is the one beyond all names. No man can give it to you. No man can take it away from you."

I feel the icy prickling on my skin that tells me Ma-nan's demons are near. I am determined to look neither to the left nor the right, where they are lurking in the shadows, but stare, as before, only into the eyes of the prince. Above his head it seems to me I see the light in all its splendour. I cry out in awe of it, holding up my arms. Around me I hear the rustling of wings and feel the air stir with their beating. Is it Mut's vulture, or is it the Horus hawk? With eyes blazing, Ma-nan leaps forward waving the resin smoke that I dread in front of my nose. The instant it enters my nostrils I stagger, my body twitching convulsively, my tongue cleaving to the roof of my mouth.

Prince Amenhotep moves forward, reaching up to me, in astonishment and alarm; but two of the priests take him, one by each arm and, whispering urgently but soothingly, lead him out of the room. He looks back over his shoulder, but I see that his eyes are rolling strangely. It is more than likely the resin fumes have affected him too.

Ma-nan gives me a look of fearful malevolence, and backs out of the door after them, clanging it shut behind him. I try to get off the chair to open it before the bolt is drawn, but I cannot move. I am slumped half-on the chair, half-off, and around me in the dark I hear the howling of his familiars and see their ghastly eyes.

"No," I scream. "No! No!" But they are already clawing at me, and my skin is coming away from my bones like the grey rotting skin of a corpse.

The dark beasts almost make me forget that I am man and have within my flesh that which is not flesh, that which cannot be touched by man or demon.

"Take my flesh," I cry, trying to stop whimpering with pain. "I don't need it. All that was ever mine I still have, and all that ever will be, you cannot touch."

Why do I see Djehuti here, the ibis-head, and Khnum with his potter's wheel consorting with demons? Anubis with jackal-head; the wolf-head Wepwawet, and many others whose presence should give comfort. These are gods from the regions of the other world who should record with wisdom, guide and guard. Why do they consort with Apep the serpent of non-existence? Why with Ammut the Devourer, Set and Sekhmet? Round they go, their howling chilling me to the heart. . . demons all. . . all demons! Who shall I pray to if the gods are demons! Who shall be my help when there is no help?

I know Khurahtaten is trying to reach me; like a trapped golden hawk he flutters against the ceiling of the chamber, bruising his wings, his beak like the flashing of a blade moving for my benefit, pecking at an eye here, ripping an ear there. Snarling, my tormentors turn on him and leave me alone. Feathers fall from his wings as jaws snap and teeth tear. His screeching is beyond any sound the ear can hear. There is no human word that can give expression to what I witness.

Shuddering, I pull my grey skin from the floor and wrap it round me like a cloak. It warms me, comforts me. It is familiar.

His claws sweep close and then are gone, the flesh of demons dripping from them.

I am alone in the dark chamber, sobbing.

What is the meaning? I plead for meaning. I as man cannot live without meaning. Without it my limbs have no strength, my heart no power. I fall back into the first chaos and know nothing.

Khurahtaten in his human guise stands before me, strong and whole.

"You have seen the meaning of things corrupted. You have seen the image and the cipher take the place of those truths they were chosen, in the ancient time, to represent. Priests now play the "gods" like counters in a game of senet: kings move them like the knuckles of their own hands. You have been tormented by the shadows of shadows, the withered shell of a good that has lost its goodness; of a protector that no longer protects; of a teacher who does not understand what he teaches; of a recorder who records what he has not witnessed. . ."

"Help me to bring back meaning to the gods," I cry.

"I will help you, if you help yourself. I must not play you like a counter in the game of senet. I must not move you like the knuckles of my hand."

"I will help myself, if you help me."

"This bargain is well struck. See—the light is a seal on it."

I look around and the dark room is light. I have confidence. I can see. But Khurahtaten, my counsellor and friend, my defender and mentor, is no longer there.

I look at the heavy wooden door. I know the huge bolt will be in place on the other side. Ma-nan will want me dead.

I sit back in the oracle's chair. I compose myself; calming my breath; straightening my back; my arms lying on the two arms of the chair. My ka, half in my body and half out, folds its luminous wings around me like a healing cloak, its head resting on my head, its eyes looking through the door, through the carved walls of the shrine in the sanctuary to the silver statue of Amun-Ra resting in its jewelled boat. Amun the Unseen, ceasing to be as soon as seen. Amun the creator of multiplicity out of potential: become the destroyer out of greed. My gaze is so intense that the metal seems to melt and run, until there is nothing left in the shrine but a shapeless pool of molten silver and a few deformed gems, their crystal shapes mutilated by the jeweller.

My next task is to release the inspiration that in the beginning brought Amun into existence.

My fleshly brows are frowning, but the soul-bird who rests his head upon my head, is smiling. The joy of recognition darts from his heart to the heart of the god, and, from horizon to horizon, the images of Amun give forth the song they were meant to sing. In temple after temple, horrified, the priests shut their ears, slam shut the doors, trembling as the pillars of the holy halls shake and rumble, the statues of mighty kings tumble down.

Here at Waset in the southern sanctuary I hear footsteps running, and see the priests gathering in the hall, approaching the shrine with cries of astonishment as light blazes out of it.

The shaking of the building dislodges the bar across the door of my prison. Ma-nan, Na-aghte, Ay and the other priests gasp as I stand before them, the wings of my soul spread above me with feathers of light. My eyes, my own two, and the one Horus has lent me on my forehead, seeing into the roots of their souls, the shrine doors opening, and from them the Unseen gliding away like a breath of wind, the shrine left empty.

"HE RETURNS WHERE HE BELONGS, IN THE ONE."

Are these my words? They come from my mouth like thunder. Yet I have not spoken.

I begin to shiver, remembering suddenly that I have no name.

The eyes of my body gaze across the chamber, and see the young prince once again. He has heard what Not-I have said. He has heard.

The wings of my soul are folded in my heart once more.

I walk with careful dignity across the room to the far side that leads out from the sanctuary to the great hall. If I do not look back perhaps they will not stop me. I intend to leave the prison of the temple and go out freely into the great world.

"Stop!"

I hear the shout, but do not stop moving.

The prince is close now. He looks pale and bewildered but he is Pharaoh's heir, and no one dare touch him.

"I put myself under your protection, my lord," I say quickly to him.

He looks from me to the angry faces of the priests approaching. Behind them the shrine is closed, no longer emitting light. Shadows are gathering close again.

Will he?

He looks back at me, frowning, confused.

"Please, my lord," I whisper urgently. "It is in your gift."

He seems to make up his mind suddenly and straightens up, looking into Ma-nan's fierce eyes with something of his father's commanding strength at last.

"He is to come with me," he says. "He is under my protection."

"He is Oracle, my lord, and cannot be taken from the temple," Ma-nan says smoothly.

"I am son of Amun-Ra and to be Pharaoh of the Two Lands. I say he is to accompany me."

Ma-nan tries to control him with the magic of his gazing, but I take the prince by the arm and turn him quickly away.

"My lord," I whisper urgently, "there is danger here. We must go."

He turns with me, and we walk out together.

We both know we are breaking every kind of temple rule and that we are taking a great risk, but he, as well as I, seems convinced that now it is the only course to take. We try not to hurry. We try to give the impression that we are walking out in perfect command of ourselves and with a perfect right to do so, yet I can feel by the tautness in the muscles of his arm under my hand that he is as nervous as I am.

The priests follow a little way behind. They seem nonplussed. There is no precedent for this. No rules laid down.

We do not look back until we are safely through the final courtyard and almost ready to pass under the great pylon. Then I cannot resist turning my head to look at my old enemy.

He is standing very stiff and straight, his eyes blazing at me, and, as clearly as though he were saying the words aloud, I hear his thoughts: "You are dead, Nameless One. And in your death there will be no journey to the kingdom of Osiris. You will be dead beyond all death, and I will see your soul pinned for ever to your rotting bones. There will be no going out and coming in. No travelling through time and walking in other bodies on this earth. You without a name, will never have a name. . ."

I shudder. The curse is the most fearsome I have ever heard, and I believe he has the power to implement it.

4

THE FRIENDSHIP

THE LONG NIGHT OF MY HALF-LIFE is over. I stand as a free man stands beside my prince. The sun shines on our friendship, and he has forged a name for me in its fire and pinned it on my forehead, that anyone with eyes to see might see it. Djehuti-kheper-Ra. Now, when my name is called, I answer. Now, when people ask who I am I say my name is Djehuti-kheper-Ra, and they go away satisfied, thinking that they have been given an answer. It has always been believed that without a name the spirit returns at death to the great void and is as if it had never been. The worst punishment a criminal can suffer is that he be declared nameless: the greatest honour a man can receive is to be endowed with a new name. From the words a mother cries out at a child's birth the first name is chosen. Later, in maturity, another may be added, expressing what he has become or what he has achieved. In death all the names are called as he or she starts the journey through the Duat. I had thought that because I was nameless, I was no one, but now I see an earth-name is only a mask like other masks, a branch to grasp in the roaring of the cataract; no more. The only name I need, or have ever really needed, is the secret one I had at my creation as spirit endless aeons ago, and that no one knows, or will ever know. It has held me in the Light of the Creator and identified me to the Great He-She. It is longer than time itself, and contains within it all that is and was and ever will be. No man has breath enough to say it: but the One

41

speaks it in the heart and knows every nuance of it. When it is called I will know it is mine, and go forward. "Great One" I will say, "here I am," and I will speak it for the first time myself, and in it will be all my thoughts and deeds, all my fears and hurts and joys. . .

AS THE MONTHS PASS THERE ARE fewer and fewer secrets between Prince Amenhotep and myself. We walk beside the lake at his father's palace at Per-hay and open our hearts to each other. I tell him of the hardships of my life as oracle, and he tells me of the hardships of his life as prince. Sometimes I think that there is not much to choose between them. He has always been a dreamer, a thinker, but has never been allowed time to dream or to think. As a young boy, scarcely adolescent, he was sent to the eastern frontier to learn soldiering. Although the pharaohs of his dynasty, Thutmosis III and Amenhotep II, had secured territory far into Djhai, the peace there is always uneasy and there are always places where corrupt officials exploit the people, where men who do not know how to love can ease the itching of their disease by violence and bloodshed, where Pharaoh's soldiers and the boy Amenhotep with them, can learn to kill.

He tells me that his learning of this most degrading of all sports had started in the marshlands of the delta, long before he reached the eastern frontier. The tall papyrus sedges were alive with duck and waterfowl of every kind, geese and herons, storks and cranes, waders on spindly legs, divers and plungers, which the soldiers had great enjoyment in killing. He himself soon became an expert fowler, though the only thing he enjoyed about it was the time he had to himself, hiding and waiting, the sun glinting through the brown-gold puffball clusters of flowers shimmering in the breezes above his head, the columns of sturdy green stems enclosing him like the tall columns of a temple. He could imagine Isis living hidden in these marshes. Amenhotep as a young boy had shivered with excitement when he had heard the tale of how she had sought her husband, Osiris, tricked and killed and cast into the sea in a sealed coffin by his own brother, Set: how she had found him within the trunk of the tree that had grown round the coffin at Kepel, and how she had brought him back to Khemet and hidden him in the papyrus marshes of the delta. The prince's eyes had grown round with amazement when he was told that she had brought him back to life from death by the power of her magic and her love and had conceived a son by him: no ordinary son but an incarnation of the mighty spirit Horus, one of the companions of the Most High. Once again Set had found his brother and torn him apart, scattering pieces of his body across the length and breadth of the Two Lands. Once again Isis had hidden in these same marshes, protecting her son, teaching him her wisdom, that one day he would be able to challenge the dark and re-establish the light.

But the young Prince Amenhotep couldn't hide dreaming for ever, and from time to time he had to return to his companions with a kill. He described to me how his marksmanship eventually drew praise even from the young captain he knew to be closest to his father's ear, Horemheb. This pleased him particularly because he had felt Horemheb's disapproval blowing on him like a hot wind ever since they had set off.

Each night in the marshes they had eaten well, and each morning they had wakened to a cacophony of bird calls, a honking and a squawking, a trilling, rilling and a chirping so loud that some of the men had laid about them with sling-shots and curses. For his part, he had listened with delight, astonished that there could be so many sounds emitted by the feathered kingdom. If he had massed his father's musicians from every palace they would have been drowned by this excitable chorus of birds.

The lotuses were in flower, and he had secretly composed a song for his cousin Nefertiti, to be sung on his return. He had no means of writing it down, and he dared not let the others know that he composed songs and poetry. Pharaoh's son or no, they already teased him about his short breath, his thin arms, his womanish habit of dreaming rather than boasting of his past exploits like the rest of them. He suspected that his father had passed the word that he was to be treated no differently from the other new recruits. He repeated the words of the poem in his head as he walked, using it to buffer himself against weariness and the weight of the pack he carried. Suspecting that he had a secret way of escaping the taunts of the others when he limped or lagged behind, the group responsible for most of the cruel tricks played on the young recruit in the name of fun engineered trap after trap for him. On one occasion they very nearly brought about his death. He had been, "accidentally" eased into the water, and found himself out

43

of his depth, being pulled down by the entangling water weeds. He struggled silently, trying not to show his fear; his chest hurting, his limbs powerless. The men were laughing at him as usual, pretending to offer him a rescue pole, and then deliberately moving it beyond reach just as he was about to grasp it. Suddenly Horemheb appeared beside them and his heart leapt to think that now at last they would haul him out. Perhaps they would be punished for their disrespectful treatment of a royal prince. But to his horror, as his head went under the muddy water once again, he saw Horemheb fold his arms and stand beside them, watching him dispassionately. Anger mingled with his fear now. It is possible they did not realize that he was drowning and that he could not hold out much longer; it was also possible that this was a deliberate attempt to murder him. Rage and the will to live combined to give him unusual strength. He heaved himself out from under once more, and, his face distorted with anger, strove and floundered until, without their help, he broke free of the rope-like weeds and managed to grasp a bunch of reeds that gave him support and leverage. Spitting green slime and sodden feathers from his mouth he finally dragged himself on to the bank. His tormentors had melted away like marsh mist at sunrise. Only Horemheb towered above him, still with his arms folded, looking down.

"Get yourself back into line immediately," he said coldly. "We are about to move off." Then he strode away without a backward glance.

Amenhotep tells me how he had lain on the bank sobbing; how he had looked at the sky and wanted to put a curse on his tormentors, and on Horemheb, that would blast them and their descendants until the end of time; how words had formed in his head so fearful that Set himself would have been proud of them.

But something had stopped him. Quiet, strong words had unravelled in his mind like a long golden thread: "More powerful than the curse, the love that unfolds the lotus." He had listened to them with surprise. They were from his own song. He squeezed the mud and water out of his soldier's kilt and knew that he could send the vicious circle of his anger and their cruelty spinning through time, and neither he nor they would ever be free of it, or he could break the circle now, and there would be an end of it.

When he rejoined the others he appeared so calm and composed they looked at him with astonishment. He took his place in the line as though nothing had happened. One by one, over the next few days, his tormentors came up to him, each claiming that it had not been his idea to leave him in the water, but that he had just gone along with the others. He remembers smiling. Where was this mysterious person whose idea it had been then, if not a single one of them was responsible? Was it possible they were not lying, that someone else had been present, invisible, sly, deadly, feeding thoughts of darkness to them as surely as he had been fed thoughts of light from another source in the lotus song? Yet they were still responsible.

Being fed thoughts is one thing; accepting them and acting on them is another.

It seemed that even Captain Horemheb treated him with slightly more respect than before. Had the whole thing been, perhaps, a kind of test devised by his father to "make a man of him"? He had earned points in the moment he ceased calling for the help of others, and decided to help himself.

BEYOND THE RICH FARMING LANDS OF the delta and the marshlands and lagoons they had had to skirt lay the desert, and to the north of the desert lay the ocean, the Great Green. He had heard of it, of course, but until that moment, reaching the top of a dry and rocky hill, out of breath and running with sweat, he had never seen it.

He was stunned. A water-desert as far as eye could see, a fit companion for the sand plains that stretched ahead of them. Day after day they walked beside it, thirsty, beginning to hate its tantalising wetness. Sand chafed his feet and scratched his eyes. The sun almost blinded him as it shone off the water. He was not sorry when the route took them out of sight of it for a while. How could such vastness be? Sky and desert and ocean. . . sky and desert and ocean. . .

He began to lose identity, believing himself less than an ant climbing the great pyramid. From time to time they came upon huge statues, stelae and monuments extolling the deeds of kings and their armies who had passed this way, in every case encouraged in their violence and their arrogance by the god Amun. He remembers one erected by his ancestor, Men-kheper-Ra, Thutmosis III:

"I have come that I may cause Thee to tread down the princes of Djahi.
I spread them out beneath Thy feet throughout their countries.
I cause them to behold Thy majesty as the Lord of Radiance,
Thou shinest in their faces as mine image."

Some had been overturned as the fortunes of war changed, and the sand was already burying them, but the Two Lands were in the ascendant at the moment, and the monuments of Thutmosis I and III, and of his own father and grandfather were still standing proud, hardly weathered by the blasting of the sand-winds. Amenhotep wondered if it was because people felt so small that they built so hugely; so insignificant that they carved in stone such absurd and grandiose eulogies of themselves.

THE YOUNG PRINCE AMENHOTEP STAYED IN the eastern province until he had learned everything his father thought necessary for him to learn, and many things his father would not have approved of his learning. Amenhotep would never make a warrior king like his great ancestors, but he learned enough to talk knowledgeably about troop movements, tactics and provisions. He learned to march, to shoot, to ride. He learned to defend himself in close combat, and inflict death on others if need be. In the early days he hardly saw his father, but once Amenhotep Neb-maat-Ra decided to visit his eastern dependencies, the prince was expected to attend banquets, standing behind the king's chair, observing the delicate art of diplomacy. He learned to say one thing and mean another, to hear what was not said, to couch a threat in a compliment and a compliment in a threat.

WHEN HIS FATHER RETURNED HOME THE prince was left under the special tutelage of Horemheb. The man was hard, and determined to make the king proud of his son. At first, each day seemed longer than the last as they drilled and marched, rode and practised, the few breaks filled with the soldiers' boring anecdotes of how much they had drunk the night before, how many women they had laid since they left home. The nights passed in oblivion brought on by desperate weariness. He despaired of ever having a real life. His limbs ached, his blisters festered, his eyes were red and sore. But in the sixth month after his father had left, when they were faced with a sudden raid from over the border, time suddenly speeded up. He found himself to his surprise remarkably agile and fit, as he rode his chariot into action, even killing without thought when Horemheb gave the word.

The prince having proved himself, the captain was not so vigilant, and Amenhotep found, as time went by, that he could get away from the others more often, and pursue a study that fascinated him: the religious practices of the countries in which they were stationed.

There were gods to whom the people sacrificed bulls, gods to whom the people sacrificed rams, gods with the tails of fish, gods that lived in trees, gods of the sky, gods of the earth; Astarte riding on her lion. Baal worshipped with fire. Everywhere he looked there were gods of different shapes and sizes and names; but when he looked closer it seemed to him they were not so different from his own gods, each an element of the mystery of life given features and a name, but not whole as a person is whole. It seemed to him that in a sense a god was an inferior being to a man, for each god had only one aspect, or at most two or three, while a man has many. Huge god may be and man may be small, but in a man's heart lay unfathomable things, distance beyond distance, and time at the movement of a thought. He stood before statues in temples as he had stood before statues in the temples of his own country, and he heard the words of the priests and suddenly he knew; knew why the temples were so oppressive, so dark, so alien.

The true temple for the true god is in the heart. His being is dimensionless, invisible light. It takes up no space, extends through no time. . . Amenhotep remembered how, since he was a very small child in Waset, he had witnessed the carrying of the god Amun from his sanctuary, his holy of holies, down the great processional way to the river and thence, to sojourn, for the full cycle of a moon, in the great southern sanctuary. He had seen the joy of the people, the dancing, the singing, the solemn faces of the priests, the beautiful robes, the glittering jewels he and his family wore as they walked behind the god. He knew that when he was older he would be required to train as a priest. But even then he saw Amun's eyes, stone staring out of metal. He knew he should not think like this, this was blasphemy, heresy. He knew that the Amun he saw was only a mundane shell into which the divine could step from time to time if it so wished, and the real Amun was unseen, the father of the gods, the Great One, the Mighty. But everywhere he went, each country claimed this for their god or their goddess. He saw many Great Ones worshipped, many Mighty.

He walked by a great river far from his homeland, and his thoughts thrashed about like a trapped animal. At last, wearily, he sat on a rock at the water's edge and watched the image of the sun dancing in the water in front of him, its reflection distorting its true shape, ripples causing it to break up and appear as many different images. He looked up to the magnificent arc of the heavens. He tried to look directly at the sun itself. Instantly the pain made him shut his eyes. An afterimage of the fire danced on the inside of his lids. He remembered the words that are written in the book for all those who leave this earth and travel in the Duat—the guide that leads the being through all the transformations necessary for life beyond life: "*He is not the Sun of this or that moment, but of yesterday, today, and of all eternity, the 'One proceeding from the One'. We call him Ra, Ra-Harahkti, Kepher, Aten and Atum in his different aspects, and in all the naming we forget he is none of these but mysteriously, powerfully, ultimately the One proceeding from the One.*"

When he tells me of this vision I am tremendously excited. Now there is no doubt in my heart that he is partner with me in the great task that Khurahtaten has set us.

"Djehuti-kheper-Ra!" My prince calls my new earth-name and I go to him. We walk beside the lake in the cool air before dawn, the last stars like flecks of light in lapis lazuli. I remember how Khurahtaten has told me that lapis lazuli was brought from the east where the sun rises and used for the eyes of the gods, not because it has magic properties in itself, but because it reminded our forefathers of the deep blue sky of evening and of the dawn: the times when the invisible sometimes becomes visible.

I see that my prince is troubled. He has taken me from my prison and I love him for it. His trouble is my trouble. He is pacing beside the lake, and I can see that he has not noticed the mother-of-pearl sheen on the water turning to molten gold as the sun suddenly bursts over the eastern desert. He has not noticed the tall obelisks tipped with gold, igniting with the sun's light like a line of running fire. A kingfisher hovers, and then dives so cleanly that scarcely a ripple shows where his beak has entered the water. He rises again, with a struggling blue and silver fish.

"What is it, my lord?" I ask quietly, not wanting to break the fragile mood of the dawn, but knowing that he needs to be asked. He looks up at me thoughtfully.

"There are so many things I want to know—so many things I need to know," he said, "but life goes by too fast and now. . ." He paused, frowning.

"And now?" I prompt.

"And now it seems I am to be king before I am ready." I look surprised.

"Is the king's condition worse?" I ask.

Amenhotep shakes his head.

"No, not worse," he says, "but last night he called me to his room and spoke to me in a way—" he hesitates—"in a way I had never thought to hear him speak."

I wait patiently, knowing that I will he told.

"His fever had broken, and he seemed quite calm and relaxed. It was better than the time before," Amenhotep says. He has told me of his father's strange fantasies when his fever was high, when even the touch of his queen, Tiye, whom he loved beyond all others, offended him, and the intoning of prayers and spells by the priests drove him crazy with rage. He had spoken then as though he didn't know whether he were alive or dead, confusing his feverish dreams with his journey through the Duat after death; calling his pleasure lake at Per-hay the "Great Lake of Peace", and claiming that the barge named *Aten Gleams* was in fact a spirit-barge ferrying him to the kingdom of Osiris. Was it Horus himself, Lord of the Sun and of the Two Lands, or a hawk, circling over him with outspread golden wings? Were the stars he saw the jewels of Nut—the spirit-lamps in the throne room of Osiris where he would face the Great judgement—or the flickering candles lit by Tiye in his room at Per-hay? Sometimes, the creature lurking in the corner looked like Ammut, the hideous Devourer of those souls that had failed to satisfy Maat and the forty-two assessors, and at other times like one of his own physicians.

When the king first became ill he had become obsessed by Sekhmet, the goddess with the body of a woman and the head of a lioness, the Lady of Destruction, consort of Ptah the Creator. She had come to him in dream after dream and he had begun to believe that he had offended her in some way and his only chance of returning to good health would be to placate her. He had called upon his workmen to make statues of her in her benign aspect, seated on a throne, a lotus wand in her one hand and the ankh, the symbol of eternal life, in the other. They were carved of fine-grained black granite and imported basalt. One after another they were polished and erected, each one accompanied by prayer and sacrifice. Surely the river of blood he caused to flow at her feet from the slaughtered animals would turn her anger from him? In the night when he could not sleep he prayed to her, sometimes visiting the place where so many images of her stood. It was in her power to purge the earth and its inhabitants of their sins and their diseases however painful and cruel the process was, and when she was finished, it was in her power to set the scene for healing and renewal.

Something gnawed at the king's heart and no one, not even Tiye, could reassure him. The statues of Sekhmet grew in number, the craftsmen who created them working night and day, trying to satisfy his desperate impatience.

Now he was tired, and longed for rest. The burden of being god-who-walked-on-earth was sometimes too much, and this was one of those times. He was weary of being the fulcrum on which the invisible and the visible turned, the shoulders that bore the teeming millions of the earth. When he was young and strong, dressed in his full regalia with his crown upon his head, everyone bowing, everyone listening to every word he said, and jumping to carry out his commands, it had seemed an easy and a pleasant thing to be a divine king. As he grew older and less arrogant he had realized that he, the man who grew tired and angry and disillusioned, was very far from being a god... but the pretence had to be kept up.

Prince Amenhotep pauses. He is obviously deeply moved by his father's confidences, but he has reached a point in the telling of them where he thinks perhaps he should be silent. Again I wait.

He hinted that he had done things at one time that he was now ashamed of. I tell him that he must not reveal to me what his father had said, if he thinks it wrong.

"There was a moment when I thought he was going to tell me something about you," my friend says, and looks at me for a moment doubtfully. My heart skips a beat, but I say nothing. "He has never approved of my bringing you here," he continues. "I've never understood it. It is almost as though. . . almost as though he fears you in some way." Amenhotep looks at me very closely. "Should he?"

I shake my head. "I can think of no reason why he should."

"Nor can I," he says, suddenly with conviction.

"What did he say?"

"Oh, it wasn't anything. . . his mind seemed to wander for a moment, and then he was quite clear again, and talked about how, after his illness, he feared he would not be vigorous enough again to shoulder the full burden of the two crowns. He said he felt it was time to share the government with me."

"A co-regency?"

"Yes."

I pace beside him in silence. I know he is not ready to be king. But regent? How would this affect the task Khurahtaten had set us both, the task of opening the mouth of dead ritual, that the living truth might be heard again in our land?

We hear a call and turn at the lake edge, both finding it difficult to leave our thoughts. From the flowering terraces in front of the palace we see the figure of a young girl running towards us, fine pleated muslin billowing out like a sail behind her, the curves of her figure as beautiful as Hathor's, the lady of the southern sycamores.

My pulse quickens. Nefertiti, whose name means "the beautiful one comes". Nefertiti, beloved of Prince Amenhotep, daughter of his uncle Ay.

We begin to walk to meet her. Her cheeks are flushed with the exertion of running, her eyes alight with the news she carries. She flings her arms about him and dances him around, laughing with delight.

"You'll never believe the good news I bring!" she cries. Her dark eyes are the night sky at full moon, her hair a raven's wing. He holds her and kisses her. I notice her breasts—yes, her breasts.

I ache. And turn away.

"The marriage is arranged at last! After the next full moon we'll never be parted again," she sings.

I don't hear his reply. I step closer to the lake, stoop down and pick up some pebbles, and start to skim them across the water. A heron standing sombrely on a rock surveying the scene, flies up with a loud and indignant cry, and wings away low over the water.

But they insist on sharing their joy with me. They put their arms around me and make me dance with them along the shore, singing a ridiculous, happy song. Tears are running down both their cheeks. They have been in love as long as they can remember, but there had been talk that Amenhotep would have to take another as his Great Royal Wife. But the king must have relented, perhaps persuaded by Queen Tiye, whose brother was Nefertiti's father, and who indulged her son Amenhotep whenever she could.

The prince is not handsome. His body is somewhat out of proportion; hips too wide for a man, shoulders too narrow, chin long, lips thick; but Nefertiti loves him and in her love he becomes beautiful.

I am handsome. I am tall and well proportioned, my features regular. But because Nefertiti does not notice me, I am ugly.

As soon as he is declared co-regent at his father's jubilee festival, the prince takes the name Nefer-kheperu-Ra Wa-en-Ra Amenhotep: Amenhotep IV. He begins to plan a new temple at Ipet-Esut to Ra-Ha-rahkti—the combination of Horus and the Sun—which he hopes will rival the might and splendour of the great Temple of Amun close beside it. The dedication in this temple is the first public hint he gives that there is to be a change in the way the gods are viewed.

He uses the name Aten frequently, as the one closest to what he wants to express, pleasing his mother and father who have always had an affection for this ancient sun-god, but who do not realize that his concept of it is slightly different from their own. He is watched closely by the priests of Amun, jealous of their privileged position as custodians of the Two Lands' current most powerful god.

In spite of what I have told the prince about my experiences as Oracle, he does not at first think it is necessary to forbid the use of oracles in the temple of the Two Lands.

"Many have proved reliable," he says. "Not all priests are as corrupt as Ma-nan."

That is true, I think. The skills of an oracle are important, and these, combined with an honest and reliable priesthood, can make communication between the different levels of the spirit-world and the physical world so much easier. I know from my own experience that I do speak words that are sometimes not my own, nor those of Ma-nan. These occasions are precious and rare, and it was after one or two of these that my reputation as medium for the gods grew so great. Ma-nan was in an awkward position. My very aptitude for true mediumship gave me credibility—yet he could not rely on the gods speaking when he wanted them to or saying what he wanted them to say. It was then he started to control me with the smoke so that I would appear to be in a trance, yet be incapable of being a spokesman for anyone but himself.

One day, not long after the prince has built his temple at Ipet-Esut and made it clear that his support when he is king will be almost exclusively for the Sun-god, an oracle in the Temple of Amun, amidst spectacular lightning flashes and crashing of thunder, declares that the Two Lands will be all but destroyed if Prince Amenhotep becomes king and that an heir for Neb-maat-Ra must be sought among one of the lesser princes. The heir is not specifically named, but the prophecies of what will happen if my friend becomes king are frightening. Under guise of trance-possession, the oracle speaks harsh calumnies against the prince.

My friend is called before the king at once and is closeted there with only Tiye as witness for a long time. When he comes back to me he is white with anger but will not tell me all that has passed between his father and himself. I gather, however, that the king himself has expressed doubt that he is capable of ruling effectively, but that Tiye had spoken so eloquently for him, he had, in the end, apologized to his son.

Whether it was Tiye or the king who stages the next scene with the oracle I don't know, but the boy is taken suddenly ill and on his death-bed confesses dramatically before many witnesses that it had been the god Set who had spoken through him, and not Amun, that day. Set, the fearsome storm god, the cunning predator, who had tried to destroy the prince because he knew he would be the perfect pharaoh and guard his people well from Set's dark and dangerous schemes.

Prince Amenhotep tells me that when he is king the temple oracles are to be abolished. I see by his face that with this latest example of corruption the priesthood of Amun have roused a formidable enemy.

* * * *

Soon after building his temple he and Nefertiti build themselves a separate palace. They use mud-brick and painted plaster, and tile the floor with lively, colourful ceramic tiles. It becomes a cheerful place to be, the evenings noisy with young people enjoying themselves. Amenhotep himself is not particularly interested in the revelry, but Nefertiti enjoys every moment of it. He tends to carry on long, rambling discussions about the new theories of art and religion he is trying to introduce, with anyone who will listen, while she is enjoying the dancing and the music, passing among her guests like a butterfly with brilliant wings.

It seems to them a new age is about to begin, and they are set to change the world. I share in all their plans and all their hopes, but sometimes wonder if their enthusiasm is not blinding them to difficulties and dangers.

The temple to Ra-Harahkti at Ipet-Esut is not to have darkly roofed halls, though there will be colonnades for shade. The worship of Aten will be in the open air, and the altar for offerings is to be placed so that at no time during the day will the sun's rays leave it. There is no dark and secret inner sanctuary where the god will be kept behind closed doors, no gloomy places for shadows to gather.

"His sanctuary is everywhere," Amenhotep declares, waving his arms to indicate the desert cliffs, the green and fruitful strip of land beside the river, and the wide and arching skies above. This brings uneasy mutterings from those who are used to the sun-god in his other forms; vividly portrayed on stone and papyrus, and available in handy amulet form.

But as the shining sandstone columns rise, the pylons receive their fluttering pennants, the obelisks their caps of gold, young Amenhotep seems unaware of the undercurrent of dissension. He surrounds himself only with his friends, people who find excitement in the new ideas and have hope for the new age. Throughout the land new temples to Aten are built, old ones refurbished.

Nefertiti is pregnant, and gives birth to a daughter. They call her Merytaten and carry her at once to the new temple, though it is scarcely finished, to lift her in their arms above the altar and dedicate her to the deity they believe was before all others, the mysterious one, the great He-She, symbolized by the light of the sun.

In his delight he orders the building of a new chapel entirely devoted to Nefertiti. The queen is to be seen in her relationship to the sun alone,

54

in her own right—not as his consort. In this he has broken totally with tradition and convention. In the cartouche bearing her name the sign indicating the sun is to be turned round to face Nefertiti herself, as though she and the sun are equal divinities.

If there is murmuring among the priests and the craftsmen who carved the reliefs at this extraordinary departure from the norm, Amenhotep does not hear. I wonder about it—but say nothing.

BEFORE DAWN ON THE DAY THE carved wall-blocks are to be put in place in her private chapel, Nefertiti calls on me to accompany her. The rest of the temple is almost finished, but her own chapel is no more than a shell constructed of rough filling-blocks.

We take torch-bearers to light the way, but no one else. I give the password to the guards and we pass through gateway after gateway until we stand at last in the sacred space her husband has dedicated to her. Life will come to it when the carved facing-blocks are in place, when the rituals are performed, when the god takes up residence.

She paces the walls with long strides, touching the blocks from time to time. She has told me to bring holy water, and she takes the jar from me and begins to sprinkle it, anointing the stones, laying the dust. Her face is transfigured. I cannot hear all that she is murmuring, but the words of the prayer she utters are not the traditional ones. She has brought her own passion to this place and broken with centuries of rigid custom. I thrill to hear words from the heart spoken in such a way, in such a place.

As first light comes she stands in the centre of the space prepared for her chapel and lifts her arms to the sky. Quietly I send the torch bearers away and we are alone.

But it is not only I who hear her hymn to the rising sun. I fancy I feel the presence all around of other great beings; other voices seem to join with hers in praise of the disc—the mighty cipher for the divine source of all light. At this moment there is no question that she is the channel through which this light will reach the earth. Her husband has deliberately stepped back and given her this sacred responsibility. There is no precedent for this in the records, but I have the feeling we are entering a time when new records will be written and old ones discarded.

She stands so long entranced that she is still there when I hear the sound of workmen approaching. The foreman's voice is loud above the chanting of the men as they heave the great blocks along on rollers.

What shall I do? I do not want to interrupt her.

I slip away and wave my arms at the approaching throng. The foreman barks a command and the men come to a halt. The sound dies down like a wave retreating from the shore as each group of men in turn react to the command.

We wait. The men do not know why, but obey without question. The foreman approaches me, the question in his mind almost visible, I am too near the royal priestess and do not want to speak aloud. I try to indicate in dumb-play that there must be absolute silence and stillness.

At that moment I hear a sound from the waiting men that reminds me of wind through corn, a hush that becomes a roar, rises to a crescendo and then dies down again to a sigh. I look at them in surprise. Every eye is on something behind me. I turn around.

She stands there framed in the entrance, and not a man, however distant, but can feel her power.

I hesitate before I walk towards her—awed. Sometimes she is like a kitten. Sometimes she is like a lion. At this moment she is a divinity.

They can put the carved pictures up, the inscriptions, the images that will keep her memory alive for thousands of years—but bare and rough as it is, this chapel is now a living, holy place.

AFTER TWO OTHER DAUGHTERS HAVE BEEN born, Maketaten and Ankhesenpaaten, and have been blessed in the new Temple of Aten at Ipet-Esut, I am told that a new city is to be established on virgin ground, half-way between Waset and Men-nefer: a threshold sacred only to the Aten, free of the clinging spells and the dark ghosts that haunt the environs of Amun's temple.

At Ipet-Esut the two temples are separate, and the worship of Amun and his family, Mut and Khons, go on unhindered as before; only the young friends of the co-regent and his wife shun their precincts entirely. The old king still worships in the traditional way the traditional gods, and pays as much tribute to Amun as before, but he sometimes honours us with his presence. I am often disturbed by the way he looks at me. What is he thinking? His queen, Tiye, seems to dislike me and does everything in her power to discourage my close friendship with her son.

I have not seen Ma-nan for years, for the prince had banished him under strong guard to Nubia soon after he had given me my freedom, but I am very much aware that Na-aghta of the Temple of Amun is my enemy. He does not attack me openly, because I am the favourite of the co-regent. His position is not as secure as it used to be, and he takes care to ingratiate himself with the old king, while leaving the co-regent and his protégé well alone. I see by his eyes when I meet him that he has not forgotten the incident in Mut's temple, and is biding his time for revenge. I often ponder what went wrong with the worship of Amun, and at what point human corruption destroyed the ancient archetype.

What makes men, when they have so much, demand more? I have seen peasants with scarcely enough food to keep themselves and their children alive made to fear that they will be punished by the god because they have not brought a generous enough offering to the temple. I have seen so much cynical misuse of power, so much greed for material possessions and so much ruthless exploitation of others all in the gods' name that I fear the gods will grow impatient with us and destroy us as we destroy the pest that threatens to undo all our good work in the garden.

The elaborate rituals of the temple have become meaningless.

The temple, the sacred place, was set aside originally to be a space where the human and the divine could meet and communicate in privacy and quiet, uninterrupted by the noisy hubbub of everyday life. It was a place chosen because of its association with some extraordinary numinous event, built to represent and symbolize that event. The temple was a place where a great spirit could cross the threshold between the realms and speak with us, listen to our petitions and advise us on what we should do through the mediumship of the chosen ones, the initiates, the pharaoh and his priesthood. Just as the building had to be kept clean and perfumed and beautiful in anticipation of the arrival of the honoured guest, the god, so those who were to talk with him and pass on his messages had to be pure and dedicated and honourable.

But now I see that the cleaning and purifying of both building and man is done as an empty act. No one expects the god to arrive. The priests themselves play god, using his name to demand anything they wish for themselves, ignoring the general good of the people and the land, and indeed anything at all that might conceivably be the wish of the god himself.

Sometimes, at night, I feel that malevolent spells are reaching me. My childhood fears return and I sense Ma-nan's familiars around me. But now I have Aten's strength, and prayers that are more powerful than any spell keep me safe.

It seems to me there is a purity about the worship of the Aten. The concept of the god has existed since the beginning as part of Ra, but perhaps because it has never before been singled out for the particular attention of a district or a pharaoh it has so far escaped the usual corruption that follows the accession of power.

The love of the young Amenhotep for his god and for his wife, Nefertiti, knows no bounds. Nefertiti is his partner in everything and is depicted as such publicly. In statues and reliefs and paintings she is at his side, proudly taking her place as his equal in the Divine Light of the Aten rays. Her figure is life-size in proportion to his. Rarely is she shown smaller as other Great Royal Wives have been. More than once she is depicted alone worshipping the sun's rays, taking the life-giving gift of the sun into her own body on behalf of the people. The priests of Amun who do not like this upstart temple crowding them out at Ipet-Esut, stealing the royal attention from them, try to encourage an undercurrent of dissatisfaction and alarm—complaining that a queen should not be accorded the same relationship to the god as is traditionally and immemorially accorded to a king. But though the older generation is nervous about the innovations, the younger generation loves them. Nefertiti, the Beautiful One, is idolised and wherever the royal couple go, it is she who draws the attention of the crowd.

MEANWHILE KHURAHTATEN COMES TO ME LESS and less as I feel my own strength. Sometimes I long to ask him questions, but I soon learn that if the questions are important to me I will be given the answers—either in dream, or in conversation with someone I casually meet, or in some ancient papyrus I happen to be studying at the time. All I have to do is look around me with eyes to see. Everything and everyone is my mentor.

I AM GIVEN A POSITION OF honour in the new temple, and take up residence there. One day Nefertiti and Merytaten come to the temple to see me. Merytaten runs to me at once holding out her arms. I lift her in mine and swing her round. She laughs her lovely, bubbling, child's laugh and my heart sings. Young as she is, she is very like her mother.

Nefertiti looks at us both fondly.

"She insisted on coming to you today," she says.

Merytaten's arms are around my neck, her little face buried against my cheek. I can't stop smiling. I have family at last, love and the warmth of belonging. No one will take that away from me again. No one.

NEFERTITI HAS CHANGED IN THE PAST six years. The lithe mischievous girl is gone. A woman who has borne, and is bearing, children is in her place—confident and poised. It is her strength that will make her husband's dream come true. She wears her crown with authority. I have seen strong men tremble when displeasure sparkled from her eyes. I have seen weak men become strong when she has smiled at them.

Today, her cheeks are glowing and her eyes shining.

"Can she stay here with you for a few days?" she asks.

Would any other temple in the land be asked to act as nursery to a five-year-old child? I remember my own childhood as the oracle, the Nameless One, and shudder to think of any child exposed as I was to the long and tedious rituals, the gloom, the oppressive darkness. At Merytaten's age I was already cased in gold, and forced to sit statue-still from dawn to dusk, punished if I so much as moved a muscle or blinked an eye. In this temple she will run about and play in the sun's light, and at noon she will rest in a shaded garden.

"We are going to look at the site for our new city," Nefertiti says excitedly, and then, because she thinks I will be hurt not to have been asked to accompany them, she adds: "As soon as we are ready to put down the boundary stelae you will be called." I nod and smile, and swing the child around. What is a city to the mystery of the spirit that lives forever! A city can be razed to the ground, and generations may walk unknowing on its dust, but a living being—ah, yes—a living being! Now, there is something worth thinking about. . .

The new city is to be on a plain bounded by the river to the west, and a natural amphitheatre of limestone cliffs to the east. No city has ever been built there before—no temple, no palace. The powerful priests of Amun own not a grain of its sand, nor a sliver of its rock. It was a childhood dream of Amenhotep and Nefertiti to live in that place one day, having reunited there after a long separation, he returning south after years of study in the City of the Sun, and she, sailing to meet him from their father's southern estates. Their two boats had come in sight of each other just as the sun partially emerged from cloud, casting long and brilliant rays to the earth, the fan-like shafts turning the bare plain to a magical, luminous gold. It had been one of those unforgettable moments, charged with emotion. They were a long, long way from the rigorous disciplines of the temple college at Yunu, and the rigidity of court ritual and protocol. They had picnicked there for a whole day and had never felt so happy. It was on that day that they knew they would be lovers.

In the third year of their marriage they had laid down three stelae marking the place, and had started planning and building. Now, in the sixth year, they will mark its boundaries more precisely with a further eleven stelae. They will ride in their chariot from point to point, followed by crowds of their people, marking their intentions in stone. He changes his name to Akhenaten: "the servant of Aten": names his city Akhetaten: "the horizon of the Aten": "the threshold from which the Eye of the Sun's Disc looks upon the world": and for Nefertiti he chooses the name: Nefernefruaten: "beautiful are the beauties of the Aten".

"*Long live the Horus, Strong Bull, Beloved of Aten; the Two Ladies, Great in Sovereignty in Akhetaten; the Golden Horus, upholding the name of Aten; the King of Upper and Lower Egypt, Living in Truth, Lord of The Two Lands, Nefer-kheperu-Ra Wa-en-Ra; the Son of the Sun, Living in Truth, Lord of Diadems, Akhenaten: Great in his length of days, who giveth life for ever and ever.*

"*The Hereditary Princess, Great of Favour, Mistress of Happiness, gay with the two feathers, at hearing whose voice one rejoices, soothing the heart of the King at home, pleased at all that is said, the Great and Beloved Wife of the King, Lady of the Two Lands, Nefernefruaten Nefertiti living for ever.*

"*As my father the Aten lives, I will make Akhetaten for the Aten my father in this place. I will not make him Akhetaten south of it, north of it, west of it or east of it. And Akhetaten extends from the southern stele as far as the north stele measured between stele and stele on the eastern mountain likewise from the south-west stele to the north-west stele on the western mountain of Akhetaten. And the area within these four stelae is Akhetaten itself: it belongs to Aten my father; mountains, deserts, meadows, islands, high ground and low ground, land, water, villages, men, beasts and all things which the Aten my father shall bring into existence eternally for ever. I will not neglect this oath which I have made to the Aten my father, eternally."*

On an obelisk of red quartzite that sparkled in the rays of sun, Amenhotep inscribed a prayer from the ancient days to the sun-gods, which for him had been the turning point in his long struggle to understand the gods. The words were not exceptional in themselves, but because they came to him at the moment when he was ready for them, they unlocked a door that for him would never close again:

"May You wake in peace, O purified, in peace,
May You wake in peace, O Horus of the East, in peace,
May You wake in peace, O soul of the East, in peace,
May You sleep in the Night-bark,
May you wake in the Day-bark,
For You are He who oversees the gods,
There is no god who oversees You."

He causes this to be set up where the great temple to Aten is to be built.

"For You are He who oversees the gods,
There is no god who oversees You."

How many times has the Spirit-from-whose-source-all-else-flows spoken: the words sounding in the minds of those who have ears to hear, like flute call or silver lute, but when translated into the language of time becoming like a drum crashing on the wrong beat, or a sistrum shaken to the wrong tune. Already I can see that my friend's clear and flowing vision will inevitably harden, as he is forced to flex his muscles against opposition, and as I look into the bright eyes of his children my seer's eye sees the shadows of the future, though as man I refuse to admit it.

5

THE NEW CITY

THE OFFICIAL MOVE TO THE CITY takes place two years after the boundary stelae are put down, and it reminds me of the great bird migrations I have witnessed, when countries to the north of us are touched by the cold, dark hands of winter. So many boats and barges have been requisitioned that the river must be groaning under their weight. Canopies flutter like bright wings about the royal party and their chosen priests, courtiers, craftsmen and the women of the harem. I am in the foremost boat, with the co-regent and his queen and their daughters. Merytaten, under the restraint of my arm, leans over the side to count the fishes, little Maketaten sitting on a high ebony stool beside us, asking no questions but staring at everything with greedy eyes as though she were seeing it for the last time. Ankhesenpaaten has the youngest daughter on her hip, and is walking her up and down the deck trying to quieten her cries. The baby is obviously frightened by the disturbance of her quiet routine, and the crowds of strangers which, even on the royal boat, crowd round her. There is a feeling of tremendous excitement, as though this is the day of our birth, and we have been privileged to enjoy it with all the knowledge and awareness of being adult. I remember my journey to Waset, and how each thing I saw had opened my eyes a little further to the wonder and beauty of being alive. Now it is as though that in itself had been only a pale shadow to this new adventure, the richness of this new experience. I feel Merytaten move excitedly as she catches sight of the silver glint of scales under the blue-silver water, and I know that seeing through her eyes, sharing them through our love for each other, is even better than I could ever have imagined or dreamed of in my lonely imprisoned years. How much else is there that I have not dreamed of?

Nefertiti comes close up beside us as her eldest daughter calls out her joy, the scent of the oils on her body stirring me. I try not to look at her, my heart filled with a desperate loyalty to my prince, but the beauty of Aten Himself could not outshine Nefertiti Nefernefruaten, and when her cheek is so close to mine I can think of nothing else. Something in me resents Nefertiti, and something in me longs for her. Everything about her speaks of her love for her husband and yet—and yet she plays with me with her eyes, and her shoulder touches my arm unnecessarily as she leans over to kiss her daughter. I point out the fish which has already slid away from where Merytaten is pointing (or is it a totally different fish?); Nefertiti smiles, amused at the effect her closeness is obviously having on me, and mercifully moves away. I lift Maketaten to my shoulder and, holding Merytaten's hand, I take them both to the stern to see the canopies and the sails of the other boats, which stretch as far as the eye can see, a green island neatly dividing them, sacred ibises streaming away from them over the fields, white gulls flurrying and diving for scraps behind them.

My prince has arranged that we should arrive at noon, and the new city lies white in the heat, the air as thick as water, vibrating before our eyes. Canopies have been raised over the landing stages, and the co-regent's party, at least, is protected from the fiercest of the sun's rays while the proclamations of arrival are read, and my prince and I put the offerings we have brought on the new altar overlooking the river. Then, as we are carried to the Great Palace the other boats draw in to the quay, and bales and boxes and barrels are unloaded, overseers shout, servants complain, workmen on the half-finished buildings shout greetings and insults, whistling at the girls. Behind them come the people who have been chosen for the new city, the families who no doubt will become the aristocracy of the new order, the first families of Akhetaten, loyal friends and their servants, all the merchants, scribes, gardeners, brick-makers, stonemasons, tally-men and tax-collectors that will be needed to serve them.

I will live in the Great Temple, but my quarters are not yet completed. I am given a room in the palace overlooking the garden. Whole trees have been brought from the east and from Nubia, and channels have been dug from the river to water their roots and feed the lily ponds. I will be able to watch the lilies open as a free man. My heart rejoices at how unexpectedly life can turn about, and I am glad that I did not succeed in killing myself in the House of Many Thresholds.

THESE ARE HAPPY DAYS, FULL OF hope for the future. The rays of the god Aten hold us under his protection and no harsh event yet happens to disturb our dream.

Akhenaten's first coronation, as Amenhotep, the co-regent, had been threefold—at Men-nefer, at Yunu and at Waset. He performed all the rituals that were at the time expected of him.

At dawn he stood at the entrance doorways of the three greatest temples in the Two Lands dressed only in a simple kilt. As the hours went by he had moved step by step through each, gradually being invested with golden sandals bearing the images of fallen enemies on the soles, sashes and jewelled aprons of elaborate design signifying the various stages of the sacred rituals, exquisite collars of gold and precious stones, each gem symbolizing a different aspect of the divinity—malachite for fertility and natural growth, lapis lazuli for ultimate sanctity, turquoise for the aspiration towards the divine, the richest, deepest colour of the stone the most precious and reserved exclusively for royalty. Carnelian stood for the busy world of phenomena that cannot be ignored, and amethyst for magical transformation. All were designed in new and potent combinations unique to the new pharaoh, each signifying his particular statement, his promise, to the god he is to represent on earth. Reading back Akhenaten's coronation collars now it is clear that even then the stress was on the gold of the sun and its life-giving rays: even then the Aten was given the most attention, though the other gods still featured.

The final apogee of the coronation after many different rituals of purification with oil and water and incense, was, or course, the crowning itself. The throne chair was designed to the new king's specification, but the crowns, the tall white one for the southern lands and the red for the northern, have been unchanged since the earliest times. The totem plants of north and south, the lotus and the papyrus, were ritually tied by the High Priest of Hapi, the Nile god, before the throne, the scene reflected in carving and paint on the lower part of the platform on which the throne was set. Khemet's strength is in its unity—the unity of north and south, of Life and After-Life, of Pharaoh with the gods and Pharaoh with his people.

When Akhenaten moved to his new city he had a special coronation hall built and designed a special ceremony for it so that he might be crowned again according to the rites of the Aten alone.

The hall was roofed except for one round hole above the actual throne. All the scenes depicted around the walls were relevant only to Aten-worship, and the ceremony was so timed that the king had completed the circuit of the walls and all the prayers and incantations necessary, all the laving with oil and water and fumigation with incense, by the time he came to sit upon the throne. At that moment the noon sun blazed down through the gold-edged hole in the ceiling directly on to the throne and enclosed him completely in his rays. The blaze of light on all the gold he was wearing and the gold dust on his body almost blinded us. It seemed indeed that the king had actually become the Light of the Sun.

In the early years of Akhetaten that followed this spectacular affirmation, the Aten seems very close and real. As I watch the king's children swimming in the pleasure lake, laughing and shouting joyfully to each other as though no shadow would ever touch them; as I watch the queen turning her elegant head to listen with a smile to anything I choose to say, and see the king himself raise his arms above the altar in the temple, his face illuminated from within by a genuine spiritual conviction, I believe we have entered a new and golden age that will have no end. The priests of the Aten are chosen for their spirituality, not for their connections with powerful and privileged families. The king listens to petitioners with attention and passes wise and sensible judgement. Although he is a god, he does not keep himself isolated and remote from his people. He and his family are seen daily. Every building of importance is decorated with scenes of family love. He is setting an example of love for his people to follow, and it seems they are following it for there is a sense of joy in Akhetaten, of peace and plenty and contentment, that I have encountered nowhere else.

DURING THE LAST YEARS OF THE old king's life my prince becomes more and more preoccupied with how he will reorganize the country under the new god. He has his father's blessing in this, though I suspect the old man doesn't realize quite how far his son intends to go. The health of Amenhotep Neb-maat-Ra has deteriorated even more in spite of his attempts to placate Sekhmet. He is grossly overweight, and has some infection of the gums that makes his life a misery. One by one he loses all his teeth, and banqueting, which used to be such a pleasure to him, becomes a nightmare. When all the expert physicians have been consulted, and all their methods have failed to help, the medical papyrus that was such a marvel to king Khufu in the ancient days is brought out. But the king still suffers. When one of the Mitannian princesses comes to join his harem to cement relationships with her father, he requests that she bring with her the miracle-working statue of Ishtar from Nineveh, his own gods having failed to heal him. My prince is furious with him when he hears about this, and if his mother, Tiye, had not intervened, he would have smashed the famous idol to pieces, causing a very dangerous situation to develop. The Asian colonies of the Two Lands are restless enough without any further provocation.

AS THE OLD KING BECOMES MORE and more disgruntled and miserable, Queen Tiye tries to interest him in the new city by bringing him to watch the building, hoping that the bustle of activity and the gleaming new walls and tiles will remind him of the vigour of his youth when he himself broke away from Waset and built her a new palace at Per-hay, well away from the city. She hopes the lake the young people are digging at Meru-aten, to the south of their city, will remind him of the extraordinary feat he undertook when he dug her a lake in fourteen days, to comfort her because the priests of Amun had not given her the part of Amun's consort, Mut, in the great Opet festival. But his life is a burden to him, and not even his grandchildren can lighten his heart.

FOR THOSE WHO HAVE MOVED TO Akhetaten, there is a feeling that all the world is fresh and new, and any dream is possible. Wherever you look beautiful new buildings stand proud. Even the poor quarters of the town are clean and well constructed, with good drainage and ample room to breathe. Inscriptions everywhere are full of joy and praise, the concept of conquest and war apparently forgotten. The sculptors' studios ring with the sound of chisel and hammer, eager talk and laughter. The young artists rejoice in the freedom they have been given to break old rules and experiment with naturalism.

The royal family seem to be everywhere, easily accessible and full of enthusiasm for everything that is skilful and innovative. Even those portraits which are more like caricatures than genuine likenesses (and there are many before the sculptors master their new techniques), are passed by them, Nefertiti laughing heartily, Akhenaten telling himself that man-as-he-is is more precious to god than man-as-he-pretends-to-be. He is a little rueful sometimes when he gazes at some particularly uncompromising statue of himself, knowing that this is how posterity will see him, but the pleasure he feels at the liveliness of the work, and the fact that he is doing away with pretence and pretension, at last dispels the feeling.

Gentle-faced Son of the Sun, pacing the flowery halls and passageways of your palace, sleepless in the night, heart bursting with all the great dreams for your people. You see them as purged and purified of all false expectations, freed from superstition and fear, released from heavy obligations to greedy and corrupt priests. You see all the people of the world, from boy working the water-bucket at the irrigation canal to the noble sculptor modelling the divine features in plaster and chiselling them in stone, united in joy and love, the one light shining into their hearts, the one light making them see. From the first cry of the child at birth to the last sigh of the dying man you hear only one theme—praise of the great force that drives them all to fulfil one mighty and magnificent purpose.

Akhenaten believes the world is a perfect place, made imperfect by the separation between people, the divisions and rivalries, the struggle to assert the part against the whole, the petty and temporary self against the great and eternal Self. He wants to draw all living beings together into his own body as it were, and with that body, now transformed into a pure and holy channel, mediate the Light of the First and Last, the One and the Only, so that all may be nourished by it, all sustained and ennobled and transformed by it.

As he stands in the great temple, open to the sky, and lifts his arms to the Aten, he is lifting the arms of all mankind, he is lifting every heart, every dream, every aspiration. With such a common and overwhelming purpose how can brother steal from brother, brother envy brother, brother murder brother?

The palace is built for light. There are more window spaces along the upper walls than there ever have been in any building before. Light pours down and illuminates with dazzling brilliance the painted scenes of fish swimming among water lilies, birds among trees, gazelle peacefully cropping. There are more garden courtyards, stair-wells open to the sky, and chambers open to the flow of people to and fro than in any other palace.

For Akhenaten the Aten has no shadowy secrets, no dark side, no hidden and dangerous elements. "Love the Aten through me," he says, "and all that will follow will be pure and beautiful as it was meant to be at the Beginning."

He sleeps little, his thoughts crowding and teeming with all his plans to change the human race. Many a night he bursts into my sleep-chamber and, talking volubly, his face alight with his vision, he pours out his ideas, pacing back and forth, back and forth, hardly aware that I am wearily propped up on an elbow watching him, longing for him to go so that I can go back to sleep. Often I am ashamed of my impatience, of my unworthy doubts, of my lack of faith that the human race can and will change.

"Don't you see?" he says, "it is because we have had so many different gods, each with its rival demands, that we are always in conflict with one another. When we have one overwhelming and overriding belief and are all working with one aim in mind, conflict will cease."

"Ay," I think. "It is a fine dream, but how long will it be before the conflict starts again between those who think the Aten should be worshipped in this way, and those who think it should be worshipped in that? How long before one thinks he is nearer to the Aten, and another that *he* is?"

I, WITH MERYTATEN AT MY SIDE, am a familiar sight, she growing in stature and beauty with each new moon, I, gradually unfolding like a flower in the warmth of her love. My feelings for Nefertiti become more and more ambiguous. I watch her manipulate her husband and know

69

that it is her word that is law in the city, though Akhenaten thinks it is his. When she drives her chariot through the streets, her eyes sparkling, enjoying the speed and the feeling of the power of the reins in her hands, passers-by are honoured to be covered with the fine yellow dust from her wheels. She is an ambitious and a clever woman, but that is not necessarily a bad thing. Akhenaten the dreamer needs a partner with practical drive to implement his dreams, and when they are seen together hand in hand, arm in arm, cheek to cheek, their love is apparent to everyone. Is it jealousy then, I ask myself, that prevents my wholehearted acceptance of her? My friendship with Akhenaten is close, and it is she who always breaks up our long philosophical discussions. If this is jealousy, I am not sure whether it is because Akhenaten has Nefertiti, or because Nefertiti has Akhenaten.

HOW LIGHT THE BREEZE THAT LIFTS the fronds of the tamarisk this dawn. I walk along the path beside the river still in shadow while the Aten rises above the mountains of the east, its long and generous rays touching the roof tops of Akhetaten and bringing the rich green fields of the farm lands on the west bank into life—drawing the young shoots from the black earth, opening the buds on the fruit trees, unfurling leaves. Birds are flying high, setting off in myriads for the grain fields. Soon the boats, heavy with food for the city, will be plying across the river; mingling with the forests of masts already bobbing at the quayside.

Palm leaves rustle gently above me, catching the breeze like sails. I look at the gardens of the great houses as I pass, those that come down almost to the water's edge. This is the house of the foreign minister, "Chief Mouthpiece of Foreign Countries"; here that of the royal scribe and steward. The chief sculptor's garden is a tangled mass of vines and creepers over trellises and trailing untidily but beautifully over sycamore and peach; very different from the chancellor's garden next to it, carefully laid out in rectangles, no plant daring to leave its appointed place or drop a petal on the well swept path. Servants are out watering the gardens, preparing them to withstand the heat of the day. I hear one calling to another; one whistling monotonously the chorus of a popular song. But all in all the sounds of the city have not really started up yet. The whole world seems poised between sleeping and waking, and I almost hold my breath waiting for the day's cacophony to break out, the eyes of the world to open, and the sun's light to blaze into every heart.

In that pause suddenly something happens to me. One moment I am looking at the walls of opulent houses painted with colourful and elaborate designs, with lush and fecund gardens backing on to the river, the next I am looking at a desolate desert plain, with low and scattered ruins of featureless mud-brick—a peasant's shack is the only building I can see where the great temple to the Aten was a moment before, a goat tethered to the stump of a column that was once encased in gold. I rub my eyes, horrified. And when I open them again, the living city is there once more in all its glory, Akhetaten, the horizon of the sun, the beautiful capital of my king.

I no longer feel like strolling beside the river. There is a chill on my heart and I hurry towards the temple. What is the meaning of the vision? Surely the god will not let this happen? Surely Akhetaten will endure forever as Men-nefer has, as Waset, and the pyramids of the ancient kings? Surely the favoured one will not be deserted thus? I reach the temple, scarcely acknowledging the greeting of the porter at the gate and hurry to the place where I had seen the goat sharpening his horns against the broken column. The column is whole, rising to the sky, every part of its surface rich in allegory. There is the king, there the queen and their daughters, all reaching up their golden arms to the golden rays of the Aten which is offering them the golden sign for eternal life. I sigh. Shadows pass over the mind from time to time. Sometimes they presage something, sometimes they are meaningless waifs and strays from the home of idle thoughts. Perhaps it is only because I am so happy in this lovely city that I dread its passing. I shake myself and go to prepare for the morning ceremonies. Today I will be careful to say everything, do everything, with meticulous attention. How precariously we are held in the hand of God! How necessary it is continually to be aware of his munificence in allowing us to exist, and to pray for the continuance of his favour.

Akhenaten joins me. His face is troubled.

I bow to my king and ask him what has disturbed him.

"I had a dream," he says. I wait, knowing that he will tell me; knowing also what the dream had been.

"I dreamed," he says and pauses, as though the memory is too painful.

71

"Ah my friend," he says at last, his voice breaking with emotion. "All this was gone." He waves his hands to indicate the colonnade of mighty columns surrounding the sacred courtyard, and the many altars that stand beneath the sun.

I take his hands in mine and we stand in silence, suddenly afraid of extinction.

He is the first to recover.

"Buildings may pass and jackals may devour the dead," he says, his voice stronger now and unfaltering. "But the god remains, and in him we have our being."

What indeed is this city of painted plaster and shining artefacts that we should dread its passing so? "But O," I think, "is it not pleasant here? Let the end not be yet, O Lord. Let it not be soon."

6

THE TEMPTATION

IT IS NOT ONLY IN THE new city that temples are raised to Aten. Through-out the land, beside the old gods, Aten takes his stand: his altars open to the light, his cipher, the globe, with long rays reaching out to touch everything into life, with hands to bless the royal family offering eternal life, and through them all their subjects. On the whole requests for new temples for other gods are refused, and maintenance grants to existing temples cut. It is to pacify the growing concern of the powerful priests of Amun, that Amenhotep Neb-maat-Ra orders a temple to Amun to be built in the south, but he knows, and they know that this is not enough. When mysterious fires break out in the storerooms containing the precious oils and vestments in the new temple of Ra-Harahkti (now dedicated fully to Aten) in Waset, I am sent to investigate.

THIS JOURNEY IS NOT LIKE THE other. Then, at the first sight of the great and beautiful city my heart had raced to be part of it. But now it lies like a dark shadow on the land, the smell of fear in its temples, and a miasma of hate issuing from the minds of its priests. I had been relieved to leave it and I now dread to return. The sun shines as brightly here as on Akhetaten, but the quality of it seems different. It has a harshness, a cruelty. It is a breeder-of-flies and corruption rather than a giver-of-life and renewal.

As I disembark I fancy a group of men are watching me closely from behind some bales of linen-flax. They whisper, and one of their number glides away. I am greeted with eager courtesy by a deputation of young priests from the Temple of Aten. I can sense under their formal words a desperate holding-back, a sense of urgency that is made to take second place to protocol and politeness. I would relieve them of this were I not so aware of the watching eyes. Sacrilege had been committed in our temple, the fire had unmistakably been caused deliberately, and unthinkable blasphemous words had been scrawled on some of the walls. I must not let anyone see that we are worried or shaken. Calmly, I return the greeting, and calmly walk beside them through the streets, through the great portals of the temple complex, skirting Amun's sacred lake, white with geese, to the temple my prince has raised to the Aten. Quietly I survey the damaged chambers, and see where the servants have washed out the offending words. Thoughtfully I look across at Amun's house. If Aten is seen to be humiliated with no redress will he not lose his credibility with the people? How should I avenge his name? Time has already passed and Aten himself has not moved to punish those who have offended against him. The priests of Amun will be laughing, preparing their next attack. My prince is anxious that no spells are used.

"The days of superstition and fear are over. The only magic in my kingdom will be the magic of life itself." It would be so easy to put a curse on them, I think, tempted. But if we want to clear out the dark side of magic from our land and free its people from the fear of it, we must not use it, no matter how tempted we are. From every deed a thousand spring; and every time we act we are responsible for the future.

My colleagues are now openly distressed, and interrupt each other to describe the horrors of the night of fire. I question them about every detail, hoping to be able to pin the act on someone specific who can be brought before the king's justice. There is no question in anyone's mind that the Amun priests are guilty, but they have been too clever for us. There is no evidence.

Someone has disturbed the geese on the lake, and the noise they make sounds like derisive laughter. My young colleagues look at me and each other, waiting for the noise to die down before they speak again. I wonder if the sound has chilled their blood as it has mine. Without our noticing their approach we have been joined by two priests of Amun, one tall, the other short, both with faces like masks.

They express concern that we have suffered in this way, softly declaring that times are changing and respect for holy matters is not as it used to be.

I bow, but beg to disagree.

"There have always been vandals, tomb-robbers and heretics, and there have always been those who respect and honour the true and sacred mysteries." I look at them pointedly. "Both reap what they sow, whether it be in this world or the next."

It is their turn to bow. "True," they say piously. "Too true," but they betray not the slightest flicker of guilt. And then they deliver an invitation from Na-aghta. My heart sinks. I dread meeting him again. I tell myself it will be different this time. This time I am strong and free, I have the co-regent of the Two Lands as my friend. This time they can do nothing to me. But all the horrors of my early years return, and I shiver. The tall priest of Amun notices this and for a moment his mask-like expression slips, and I see a snake glint in his eyes. Ah, Aten, Mother-Father of us all, give me strength in this confrontation.

They bow again and leave. My young priests who have been silent and outraged throughout this exchange begin to talk, too fast, and all at once.

"You must not go!"

"You will not go—surely?"

"It's a trap."

"They will do anything to shut us down and drive us out. We have as much right to be here as they—but they resent us."

"We have lost several of our priests to them."

"How do you mean "lost?" I managed to get a word in at last.

"They've left Ra-Harahkti. They've left the Aten. They've gone to be priests of Amun."

"Some were already Amun priests, and they've gone back. They've been intimidated."

"How? How intimidated?" I think I might find some guilt here to lay at their door.

The young priest who had spoken last, the first shining hairs appearing on his chin, looked embarrassed.

"How? How exactly intimidated?" I repeated sternly.

"It's difficult to prove it," he mumbled.

Another broke in. "We find venomous snakes in our sleeping quarters."

"Scorpions in the chests in which we keep our clothes."

"Could these not have found their way in naturally?"

"Not so many. Not so often. Not in such closed chambers and closed chests."

I frown.

"We find bad spells on slivers of stone or scraps of papyrus wherever we go."

"But there is still no proof that it is the priests of Amun who are doing these things. Surely they would not stoop to such petty harassment?"

An agitated chorus assured me that everyone present believed that they would.

THE INVITATION IS FOR TODAY. I have had a night's sleep since I arrived in Thebes—or shall I say a night has passed in tossing and turning and praying, and now it is the dawn. I perform the rituals at the rising of the sun, feeling strength and confidence growing with each incantation:

"You who oversee the gods, whom no god oversees: help me.
You who were before all things and will be beyond all things: help me.
You who understand all that there is, there being nothing beyond your understanding: help me.
Light of the Overworld. Light of all the Thresholds.
Light of our sleeping and our waking: help me. . ."

I set off for the Temple of Amun confident in my god. But Na-aghta is no fool. He does not have me brought directly to him. His tall messenger leads me through the temple itself, beneath the huge and overpowering columns of the papyrus hall, down long corridors, dimly lit by clerestory slits, few and far between and high in the wall, through sanctuaries and chapels where flickering flames in braziers and lamps throw fearsome shadows of the god Amun before me and at my back. Everywhere images of the gods Akhenaten is rejecting stare down at me accusingly. I am uneasy. My old loyalty to them, my sense of their reality, fighting my new found confidence in the Aten alone. "What if. . .?" I start to think, but refuse to accept the development of the thought. These images are what the Amun priests have made. They are not the shining spiritual Beings my ka has encountered.

There is a dreadful silence apart from our own footsteps—and no sign of a living man. Occasionally I think I hear someone behind us, but when I turn to look there is no one there. It could be the echo, or it could be that there is someone following us who keeps out of sight. Where are all the people who normally serve the temple, the lithe dancers and singers, the priests and novices, the scribes, the cleaners, the cooks, the tithe collectors and administrators? The whole place seems deserted—yet I sense a dark and brooding presence.

We leave the temple at last and start winding in and out among a labyrinth of passages in the priests' quarters. I am tense and nervous, and on the point of violent anger when finally my silent companion knocks with his staff three times at a door. It creaks when it opens, and I am waved before him into a chamber only dimly lit with tapers. It must be deep in the building and has no means of admitting natural light. Na-aghta is there. Huge reliefs of the triad, Amun, his consort, Mut, and their son, Khonsu, are carved on the walls behind him. The taper light flickers, and his shadow moves grotesquely over them. He has succeeded in frightening me. A pulse beats in my neck so insistently I am surprised he doesn't see it and comment on it. I hear the door shut behind me, and all the terrors of my childhood return. Sweat begins to run down my face and body, part of it due to the close, suffocating heat of the room, part to my fear. But I have learned something in my years of freedom and keep my head held high, meeting his eyes boldly. He is standing, and he is taller than I am.

"My Lord Priest, Prophet of Amun," I say, forcing my voice to be steady, "I am grateful for your courtesy in inviting me here. I presume it is for the purpose of offering an explanation and an apology for what happened at the Temple of Aten-Lord-of-all-Horizons." Something of my courage has returned as I remember the prayers I had fortified myself with before I set off.

His expression is coldly amused.

"My Lord Priest, Prophet of Aten, I assure you I have no explanation for anything that happens in your precinct. If your inferiors are careless, that is a matter surely that has to be dealt with within your own temple."

I am silent, but meet his eyes steadily. I remember how Ma-nan used to control me, and am wary.

"I have invited you here," he says smoothly, "because I think it is time we discussed matters to our mutual advantage."

"You mean the rule of Maat, the felicity of the rule of Wisdom and Justice in our country," I say equally smoothly.

He bites his lip very slightly and I think, perhaps, I have surprised him.

"Of course," he says with a shade of impatience, and I feel I have the edge on him for the moment. "It has not escaped our notice," he continues, recovering his composure, "that our royal co-regent Amenhotep—"

"Akhenaten," I correct him pointedly.

"Akhenaten," he acknowledges with a slight twist of his mouth, "is giving increasing support to this minor god—"

"We speak of no minor god," I say quietly. "The God Aten has existed before and will exist after. It is he who spoke in the great void and it is his eye that is the consciousness of all things."

Na-aghta's eyes flash.

"These things are claimed for our Father Amun. It is Amun who is the Creator of all things."

"His coffers fill while the bellies of his people empty. Is that the sign of the Father?"

"My lord, take care," he says; and his voice is as hard and sharp as the cutting edge of a sword. Behind him I sense something move. In the dim light I strain my eyes. A shadow detaches itself from the other shadows and a figure joins the high priest.

It is Ma-nan.

It seems to me all the blood drains out of my face, and I clench my fists to prevent my hands shaking. He looks at me, up and down, for what seems an eternity. My throat is constricted and, try as I will, I can bring out no words.

"Greeting, Nameless One," he says mockingly, noting my discomfiture. For a moment I almost fall under the old spell. I have not called on Khurahtaten for help for a long time, but I call now. I know I have not the strength even yet to stand against the man who caged me all those years.

A voice speaks softly behind my back, though there is no one there. "You have names reaching back to the Beginning. Have courage."

"I am named Djehuti-kheper-Ra," I say, and this time my voice leaves my throat and fills the dark chamber powerfully. "You have no more power over me."

"Was Djehuti-kheper-Ra the name your mother cried at your birth?"

"No. It is the name my king has given me."

"What words did your mother cry?"

"You know as well as I, I do not know my mother."

"Nor your father?" The tone of his voice shows me that these are not idle questions. He is leading to something.

"Nor my father," I say, my heart pounding. Is this the moment? Is it now I will learn the names of my mother and my father? Is it now my life is to be placed in history—to have a before and an after that men will record?

There is a terrible silence in the chamber as the two men stare at me, and I hold back the questions that I ache to ask.

"I could give you the names of your mother and your father," Ma-nan says at last, very, very slowly.

I say nothing.

Khurahtaten my friend, help me! What is it to know the names of your mother and your father? He will not give them to me for nothing. *Fall not into his trap. . . fall not. . . fall not. . .* I know it is Khurahtaten's voice urging the caution in my ears.

"I don't wish to know them," I say at last, and all the pain of my childhood wells up in my heart. I begin to tremble uncontrollably, tears pouring from my eyes. Through them I see the triumph in the eyes of the two men before me. They know what it has cost me to say what I have said, and they smile.

I turn and stumble from the room. I wait for no one to usher me through the labyrinth of passages. I am staggering like a drunk man as I hurry away from my tormentors. They know—and they know I know—that they have me trapped. I'll not have a moment's peace now until I have the names of my mother and my father.

I hear footsteps behind me and I start to run. I feel I cannot bear to face anyone. I see a door, and with a desperate burst of energy I fling myself at it, and drag it open. Then I slam the door shut behind me and stand panting heavily, leaning against the heavy wood. I turn my right ear to the timber, and strain to catch any sound made by my pursuers.

My heart is beating so loudly at one point it is difficult to tell whether the sounds I hear are the thud of footsteps outside in the corridor, or the drumming of my own heart.

I have no idea into which chamber I have stumbled.

It seems to me at last that both the excessive beating of my heart and the noises in the corridor have died down. I glance round to take my bearings and suddenly freeze—the hairs on the back of my neck rising.

By the flickering light of torches I see that I am in the sanctuary of Sekhmet. Towering above me is the huge black basalt statue of the goddess with the watchful head of a lioness and the body of a woman. She is seated, and in her one hand she holds the ankh, the sign of life, and in the other the rod of her divinity: but it is her eyes that terrify me. I feel her presence. The statue is alive with her. She is looking directly at me with the wary, totally absorbed stare of a lion watching its prey.

I back against the door and fumble at the catch. To my horror, I find that the door is locked and I cannot get out. Whether the catch snapped back as I slammed it shut, or whether someone locked it from the outside once I was in—either knowing that I was inside or unaware of it—I can't say; but I am trapped in a chamber almost entirely filled by the fearsome goddess whose rage nearly destroyed mankind, whose hot breath blows the desert storms, and who has the power to tear down mountains and devastate cities. I press my back hard against the solid wooden door, as far away as I can get. The statue appears totally still and calm, yet I can sense the powerful energy of her—the tension of a great cat poised for the kill.

At first I am too frightened to think, my body running with sweat. The chamber, apart from anything else, is unbearably, suffocatingly hot. I try to bring myself under control. My king has taught me that there is only the one, the Aten. If so, she, the Great Destroyer, is but the fierce and violent instrument of his anger. I ask myself if I have reason to believe that I have drawn that anger down upon myself, and I know I cannot answer truthfully that I have not.

I begin to edge around the huge plinth on which she rests, hoping against hope that there might be a small door at the back of the sanctuary. Sometimes there is one for the oracle to enter, but not often. The space between the wall and the side of the goddess is so narrow, and I am so clumsy with nervousness, that I inadvertently touch her foot as

I squeeze past. For a moment all the breath is knocked from my body and a blinding pain shoots through me. Gasping, I fall back, and it seems to me as though lightning is playing about her form, crackling in jagged rays from her finger-tips, clothing her in an ever-changing aura of fierce and rippling light.

I fall to my knees and find myself gibbering with fear, pleading with the gods, any and every one. The words come out jumbled; tumbling like discarded trinkets from a dusty box, but from behind them something is trying to get through to me—the Nameless One, the first, the only true one. . . Suddenly I know to whom I should be praying, to whom I should be calling out.

The light around her fades and the menacing blackness of the stone from which her image is carved returns.

I stand up. I look into her eyes. I cease to fear. I cease to tremble.

She looks back calmly into my eyes. She is no less magnificent, no less powerful and real, but now I see another aspect of her: the Protector; the fierce Defender. It is no accident that in the ancient teaching of Men-nefer her husband is Ptah, the craftsman, the creator, he who fashioned the ten million things of this earth upon his potter's wheel. It is no accident that from this union of the Creator and the Destroyer Nefer-tum was born, rising from the lotus. The teaching tells how this child, poised between the two, pulled from either side by energies too great to bear, wept, and from his tears mankind was born. The destruction she brings is never wanton, never random. She and her husband, Ptah, together create and destroy matter for ever, the balance between the two necessary for existence. If the balance is upset—and man can do it if he chooses—then only are her powers dangerous and inimical.

I respect her. I stand before her in awe, meeting her strength eye to eye. No longer afraid.

"Hail, Sekhmet, lady of the gods, who holdeth her fan. The lady of the scarlet garment; the mistress of the white and red crown; the great magician in the boat of millions of years, lofty when she rises in the abode of silence; the royal wife of the lion; the mother on the horizon of the sky, the joyful, the beloved, who destroyeth the rebels collected in her fist. . . Hail!"

It is she who tells me to try the locked door again. I know, before I touch it that it will now open—and it does.

As I leave the Temple of Amun the sunlight smashes into my face and almost blinds me.

I AM FORCED TO RETURN TO Akhetaten without having settled the matter of the fire satisfactorily. There I find rumours rife that the priests of Amun are working with spells to destroy us. A series of accidents in the city make the superstitious very nervous, but Akhenaten goes from place to place, calling the people to him, speaking like a father, telling them that spells can have no effect against the strength of the Aten.

"Think of our city surrounded—by a high invisible wall with every gate guarded. Inside the city there are gardens and pleasant homes, people living at peace and in joy. Is this not how it is, my people?" he calls out, suddenly raising his voice. The answer is immediate and enthusiastic. There are indeed pleasant homes and many gardens in Akhetaten, and people living peacefully.

"This is how it is, our father, our king!"

"In such a city, enclosed by such walls, no enemy can reach us."

The people cheer.

"*But—*" he adds warningly, and the people are silent as he lowers his voice, making it deep and sombre—"but if someone from inside opens the gate, then may the forces of our enemy enter and destroy us." There is a murmur of fear.

"The walls of our faith may be invisible—but they are strong. The gates of our faith may be impregnable—but if a traitor opens them, we are lost."

He looks down at the faces of his people.

"Who is the traitor who will do this, my people?"

No one answers. They look uneasily at each other. What does he mean? "*Doubt is the traitor!*" he shouts. "*Fear is the traitor!*"

The people sigh and groan and go away to their homes determined to be strong and steadfast in their faith.

But—of course—that is not as easy as it sounds.

The Princess Maketaten becomes gravely ill, and there is no doubt in many minds that it is the work of the hostile spells from the Amun priests. Physicians from the famous college at Yunu are called to her side.

When they fail to help her, her father and I as priests of the Aten try what the priests of Hat-Hor have tried from ancient times. We lay her on the couch in the chamber of dreams and leave her alone and in silence with the lamps of the going-out and the coming-in, of the wishing and of the dreading. Through a hole in the wall we watch as she gradually falls asleep, becoming one with the great ocean that was before all things. We see the pain on her thin face as she turns from side to side, as though to break free of the wings of Horus that hold her to the head-rest. Then the fighting stops; and gradually the Peace of the Great One that is beyond all understanding enfolds her, and she sleeps as all things slept in the heart of God before the separation into this and that, here and there, then and now.

All night we keep vigil from outside the chamber, monitoring every movement of her eyelids, every twitch of her limbs, praying that we will be given wisdom at the time of interpretation. In the morning more lamps are lit, the lamps of the waking and the remembering, and her father and I move in and sit beside her, speaking the words of asking in the manner prescribed by the ancient texts. Before she wakes she answers us, words floating to the surface of her mind and drifting off like smoke. We have to register them quickly before, like smoke, they fade and disappear. The interpretation of her dreams is given us by our god in answer to our prayers. She sees herself as a cormorant tied by a thread to the wrist of a fisherman. . . longing to be free. She sees herself as the fish caught in its beak. . . longing to be free. She sees herself as the fisherman taking the fish from the bird's beak, held himself by a thread to the shadowy figure of hunger behind him—he, too, longing to be free.

"You are free," whispers Akhenaten, leaning close to her, his tears falling on her soft, pale cheek. "You are the king's daughter. . . beloved of Aten. . . you are free. . ."

She sighs, and opens her eyes. She looks at us deeply puzzled, as though we are strangers, and then she reaches out her arms to someone we cannot see, and her face lights up in recognition.

It is then we know that she is ready to leave us and there is nothing we can do about it.

* * * *

83

THE FLOWER CITY OF AKHETATEN BECOMES a place of weeping. There is not a man, woman or child who has seen the princess since she came to live in the horizon of the globe, and has not thought her lovely.

Merytaten is inconsolable and turns to me for comfort, but I desert her and leave for Waset. I tell myself Maketaten's death is Na-aghta's doing, that he has induced her dreams and led her away from us: but deep inside I know that this is nonsense, that the child has been ailing since birth and was never intended to wear the cloak of this life for long. I tell myself the lie because I want an excuse to confront Na-aghta and Ma-nan.

Without invitation I storm through the complex of buildings that surrounds the sanctuary of Amun, stride through the echoing corridors, and halls misty with the smoke of incense. I surprise a group of slender temple-dancers at their practice and cause the musicians to falter. Archivists walking from one chamber to another with papyrus rolls fall back staring, one dropping a long roll that unravels in front of me like a carpet. Novices call after me. At last my way is barred by the same tall man with the staff who had led me such a devious route before.

"I demand to see Na-aghta," I say boldly, knowing that I am insulting him by not giving him his full title. I am hot with determination, my only fear that I will be forced to wait somewhere and have time to cool down.

"Demand?" he says coldly.

My anger makes me think I have courage.

"Demand!" I reply fiercely.

He stares at me balefully for a long moment or two and then nods, turns and leads the way.

Na-aghta is busy in the store-house berating the master of granaries. The man is trying to explain that it is the fault of the co-regent that the place is not as full as it should be, and stops in mid-sentence, embarrassed when he sees me. Na-aghta turns to see who it is, and looks momentarily astonished. But only momentarily.

"This man," my guide says scornfully, and I notice he uses none of my titles, "demands to see you, my lord Priest, honoured Prophet, Beloved of Amun." Na-aghta has already composed himself.

"Greetings, Priest of Aten." His intonation is insulting.

I flush, but say nothing. I am still holding carefully to my anger. He looks at my red face with amusement. I am half aware that the master of the granaries is thankfully sliding away. My guide is gripping his staff like a weapon, ready to defend his master, physically, if need be.

"Have your unruly followers been setting your store-rooms on fire again?" Na-aghta asks with mock solicitude.

Suddenly it seems to me crazy to accuse him of killing the Princess Maketaten. It had seemed so plausible when everyone was murmuring around me. Now my good sense returns to me, and leaves me washed up like a fish on dry land. What am I to accuse him of? What demand! I know what I want—but I cannot say it.

He is a man of great subtlety: a formidable opponent. He knows why I have come. Smiling, he indicates that I should follow him. I do so. The arrogance with which I had entered the building is leaving me, and my stride becomes less sure, my back less straight. I am taken to an inner chamber and told to wait.

I sit on a leather and ebony chair and wonder why I have been such a fool. But gradually, as the confusion of my thoughts settles, I know that I was right to come. Whether he caused the death of Maketaten or not is not the issue. The issue is that he is still powerful enough to inspire fear, and make people believe he is capable of killing a royal princess in the safety of her home many leagues away. I know that Nefertiti herself believes it, though her husband strives to dissuade her. Of late it has worried me a little that she seems to be dabbling herself, privately, in spells.

I know that I will ask Na-aghta, and Ma-nan if he appears, who my father and my mother are. The question has been tormenting me, as they knew it would, ever since the day I learnt that they could tell me. I reason that I am becoming useless to my prince because I am so preoc-cupied with this question. My sleep is suffering, and so is my health. I can settle to nothing. As a child it had haunted me continually, but since I have gained my freedom, and my name, it has hardly crossed my surface-mind. Bitterly I resent their raising of this old ghost.

Na-aghta returns—with Ma-nan. I stand at once, and bow politely to him. Long years of hate are held in check. I want to know—I need to know—what only he can tell me. When I have the information I will concentrate on outwitting them for my prince. I know that Ma-nan is ille-gally in the country. Na-aghta could well be arrested for harbouring him.

The two men stand before me and we wait, each for the other to make the first move.

It is I, the fool, who speaks first.

"You told me that you had certain information for me."

The two men look at each other and smile, and look back at me. "If that is still the case, I am now prepared to listen," I say.

Ma-nan prowls like a restless lion, circling me, looking at me.

"You are a man now," he says with deadly sweetness. "You are the friend of kings. Do you remember how I nurtured you as an infant, cared for you as a child?"

"I will never forget," I say grimly.

"You repaid me with ingratitude," he says silkily.

"I admit I have never repaid you as you deserved," I reply, pleased with the ambiguity.

Na-aghta is enjoying the game, but keeps out of it.

"Why should I do you a favour?" Ma-nan purrs.

"You offered—I did not ask."

"You are asking now."

I wonder if I can walk out—not knowing—once again; and I know that I cannot. He knows that I cannot. He waits for me to ask what I should offer him in return, but I manage to hold my tongue. At last he grows impatient.

"I miss my own country. I miss the Two Lands," he says.

"You are in your own country. You are in the Two Lands," I say.

"You know I cannot walk freely in the streets. You know I cannot sail on the river."

"It is not in my power to take off the sentence of banishment," I say. "But it is in my power to report that you have broken the king's command." Perhaps I can blackmail him into telling me what I need to know.

"The Heretic's command," Na-aghta says suddenly, turning the game about.

I look at him, shocked.

"That is treason," I say sharply. I know I should rush straight out of the temple, call the king's guards and have these men arrested before I become any more involved. My prince would thank me for it. He is looking for an excuse to crush the prestige of the priests of Amun.

But a maggot is beginning to gnaw at my heart. A maggot that, if not killed, could devour my whole body. The two men know it is there, and play with me.

"What will you do for me if I tell you who you are?" I am silent. I am in agony.

"I want to return to my country as a free man."

"That may be possible to arrange," I hear myself saying. I think I sense Khurahtaten in the room but I refuse to look at him—refuse to listen to him.

"Amun must have the lands diverted from him to Aten, returned. Aten must be declared subsidiary to Amun."

"That is not possible." My voice betrays my disappointment. Akhenaten will never agree to this. I am lost. Years of torturing curiosity await me.

They look at each other, and I can see that they are considering whether they haven't perhaps demanded too much as a first step. Na-aghta nods almost imperceptibly at Ma-nan. Khurahtaten is shouting in my ears, but I will not listen. I am sweating. *Go away!* I cry in my head. *Go away! I don't need you. I know what I am doing!*

"You think the co-regent will not agree to our terms?" Na-aghta asks smoothly.

"I know he won't," I say miserably, hopelessly enmeshed now, and not even trying to win the game.

"But if he is no longer the co-regent? If he does not become king?"

How could I have fallen once again into the clutches of Ma-nan? I remember Akhenaten's words about the traitor who opens the gate, and inside I am weeping. I have never been greedy or ambitious—why now? Why now? Khurahtaten, is it too late? But he has gone. I am on my own.

"Tell me who my parents are," I demand, a terrible conviction that I already know growing within me. But whatever the answer, I know I have already gone too far to turn back.

Ma-nan smiles and closes his trap.

"Your father is the Pharaoh Amenhotep Neb-maat-Ra, the beloved son of Amun, the father of all gods. Your mother is his wife-daughter, Sitamun."

It is said.

There is a long and terrible silence as the two men study my reactions.

"You lie!" I say at last in a dry, dry voice. "If I were the son of the king and his daughter. . ." The silence in the chamber becomes painful. If? But why—why, if this is so, am I not living like a prince. . .? Am I not the co-regent myself? Sitamun's blood is of the royal line: as eldest daughter of the king she is the royal heiress. I have seen portraits of her as God's Wife of Amun, the wings of Mut's vulture head-dress close about her ears. Tiye's blood is common, even though her husband's love has given her the title of First and Great Royal Wife, and her son is declared his heir. I remember Tiye's eyes—the way she looks at me. It is because of *her* I have been denied. It is because of *her* I was given no name, hidden like an unclean thing.

"Tell me. . ." I say brokenly, humbly, to my old enemy.

He smiles.

"Need I tell you? You are no fool. You know the ambition of the queen for her own flesh and blood."

"But—" I was thinking of Sitamun herself. Was she so over-awed by Tiye that she allowed herself to be taken as wife then kept in obscurity among the foreign princesses as though she were no more than they? Childless as far as any one knew; dying young. I had never seen her, except perhaps in a dream, weeping, standing behind her father-husband and his wife, Tiye.

Somewhere in my heart words I can hardly comprehend are beating. *Akhenaten is my brother! Akhenaten is my brother!*

It seems to me that the great void is very, very near. I could reach out and pick up the crook and the flail—or I could reach out and pick up a festering bag of maggots.

"*Enough*," I say sharply. "Your story is preposterous."

I turn on my heel and stride out of the room. Instinct must have shown me the way through the labyrinth of corridors, because I am almost blind with tears. Only once a sound makes me turn my head and, through an open doorway, I see the old king's favourite general, Horemheb, the one whom Akhenaten feared and respected so much in his youth.

LITTLE MAKETATEN IS HARDLY IN HER tomb when we receive news that Akhenaten's father (my father!) is seriously ill, and not expected to live more than a few days. Events are happening too fast. I have not had time to work out exactly what I am going to do about the information I now carry like a great lead weight about my neck. I have told no one as yet and hope that I will have the strength never to tell anyone.

When the call comes from Akhenaten to visit the deathbed of his father, the request comes for me to accompany him.

"I always remember," Akhenaten says thoughtfully, "how angry he was when I asked after you that time we saw you at Men-nefer when you were still an oracle." My heart beats faster. Is my relationship going to be made known at last without my having to declare it myself? I pray that it is. The secret I am keeping is almost destroying me, as Ma-nan knew it would. *How cunning they are,* I think. If I take the bait I will reinstate Amun in gratitude to them. If I do not, I will still never have another moment's peace of mind, and my friendship with Akhenaten, the friendship on which he has grown to depend so heavily, will be changed and soured. Nefertiti has noticed the change in me already and has asked me on several occasions what the matter is. Each time I deny that there is anything. Each time she has looked less convinced.

Since my return from Waset, Merytaten has been estranged from me. I know it is because I deserted her when she needed me after the death of her younger sister, but I am in no mood to be subtle and tender. I am moody and awkward and keep myself to myself, until it is she who seeks me out and, putting her arms around my neck, pleads with me to forgive her, although it is I who have been at fault. We cling together, and in that clinging I vow that whether I tell of my royal birth or not, I will have Merytaten to wife—though how this will be possible for a "commoner" I do not know.

We all go to Per-hay, Akhenaten and Nefertiti, their daughters (only five now, since Maketaten's death), and Akhenaten's infant son, Tutankhaten, by one of his secondary wives, Kia.

I have not been in the king's private chambers before and am impressed, if a little disturbed, by the heavy opulence around me. Our city is light and bright and sparkling. His room is painted crimson and gold, the furniture black ebony, the screens the same. The statue of Ishtar that he had borrowed from Ninevah dominates one side of the room. Some say that Ishtar is just another name for our Isis; but I must say I find her presence in this place alien and oppressive. She has been no help to our king, though in her own land she is famous for the miracles she has wrought. I ponder on this. Taking over a divinity from another people, without understanding how her very being is dependent on the deepest thoughts and aspirations of her people, is like taking a palm tree to a cold climate, and expecting it to grow. Her life's blood is the active belief of her people. Here the king is believing in her at one remove as it were. He has heard she has wrought miracles—but his heart does not know it as her people know it. Thinking about this made me wonder if Akhenaten will be able to change the beliefs of his people overnight as he hopes. He has not taken into account the fact that belief has a life of its own, and that the energy generated in this way is powerful in itself whether the object of the belief is genuine or not. How much more powerful, I think, awed, would a belief be if it were grounded on truth! With such a belief a man could raise the dead or walk on water.

Queen Tiye, her face red and swollen with weeping, and her brother, Ay, the king's close friend, adviser and master of horse, sit on either side of his bed.

Amenhotep Neb-maat-Ra the great king who has ruled the Two Lands for nearly forty years, is barely conscious. I think of the statues I have seen of him, the beautiful young man in full vigour, carved in stone that will endure forever. He was handsome when I first saw him, though thicker in the waist even then than the sculptors made him. Now he is an ugly hump of flesh in the bed, his breath rasping, his festering mouth dribbling. But Tiye sees him as he was, a lover tender and fiery, a good-humoured ruler, enjoying fine things.

We gather round the bed, directed by the thin sharp finger of the chief physician. I hear a disturbance at the door and Horemheb strides in. The physician protests and tries to wave him back. Tiye looks up sharply and indicates that Horemheb may stay.

The chamber is hot and crowded. The flies are already gathering, the servants swishing at them with ostrich-feather fans. Little Tutankhaten looks as though he is going to be sick and Tiye, ever in command, indicates to Ay's wife, Tey, Nefertiti's stepmother, that the smaller children should be removed. There is bustle and noise for a moment as they are ushered out. I hear Tutankhaten throwing up in the antechamber and slip my hand into Merytaten's. Her face is very white and her hand is trembling. She is scarcely more than a child, but is expected to behave like a grown woman.

It looks as though the disturbance has penetrated the old king's coma. His eyelids flutter and Tiye leans forward eagerly. Without looking up, Tiye crooks a finger at Akhenaten, and he moves forward to lean beside her and to stare in his father's face. They have not been close—the son competing always with his dead brother for his father's affection. In a sense, Akhenaten has been impatient for this moment, anxious to go further with the installation of Aten as sole god than his father would allow him; but there are things for which he will regret his passing. Horemheb pushes himself forward and whispers something in the king's ear.

The sick old man opens his eyes and gazes round himself, bewildered, as though looking for someone. His eye falls on me and stops there. Horemheb whispers again, and Tiye tells him sharply to be quiet and move back.

As he reluctantly moves back he looks hard at me. Nefertiti has not missed a thing. Tiye puts her firm brown hand on her husband's chin and turns his head so that his eyes meet those of Akhenaten. The co-regent, guided by Tiye's other hand, leans forward and kisses his father's forehead.

I am at a loss to know what to do. Horemheb is willing me to step forward and make myself known to my father. I can feel it. But my loyalty to Akhenaten is too strong, and I am resisting. Merytaten leans her head against my arm, and for a moment a longing to be acknowledged as a royal prince, and therefore acceptable as a husband for Merytaten overwhelms me. I forget what it will do to Akhenaten. I take a step forward. Tiye raises her hand and Ay moves forward and cuts off my path to the king. I see the dark and furious look Horemheb gives her, and know that he is not an enemy I would like to have.

The king is dead, and I have not been declared his son.

I too look at Tiye—my eyes for the moment filled with hate; hers with bitter triumph.

FOR THE NEXT SEVENTY DAYS WHILE the old king's body is being embalmed, the country is officially in mourning, but behind the scenes the preparations for the regent's coronation as full pharaoh go ahead.

Everyone has his or her part to play in both the funeral and the coronation, and there is hardly a moment when I leave my prince's side. He seems to be relying on me more than ever to support him in his plans, and I haven't the heart to let a hint of what has been going on in my mind disturb him. If the old king had declared for me. . . But as he did not, I decide to keep silent: determined that my secret will go with me to my death.

Tiye, always the power behind the throne, is still in charge. She insists that her son marry one of his own daughters to make sure there is no question of doubt about his accession to the throne. Nefertiti, like herself, is not a fully legitimate female heir, and she knows that Horemheb, in a powerful position as head of the army, has objections to Akhenaten's accession because of his enmity towards the army's god, Amun. I am terrified that Akhenaten will choose Merytaten, his eldest daughter, and I spend a night in the desert battling with myself, the star Sopdt witness to my suffering. Horemheb has tried to see me several times, but each time has been prevented either by my own evasive tactics or by Tiye.

Akhenaten chooses his third daughter, Ankhesenpaaten, and I find Merytaten weeping in the garden with relief.

We kiss as lovers kiss, and both know that we cannot live without each other. She begs me to ask her father if she can be my wife, but I tell her the time is not right. There is the funeral to get through and the coronation. Then, perhaps. . . when things have settled down. To ask and be refused—that I couldn't bear. She can't see that refusal is a strong possibility. Nor can she know the turmoil I am in. At one moment I tell myself how sweet it would be to take Ma-nan's bait and to be pharaoh: the next I remember what the cost to my brother would be. I have no longing for worldly power as some men have, and am content to work in the spirit for the renaissance of the spirit.

HOREMHEB IS SENT BY AKHENATEN ON the advice of Nefertiti to the frontier, where the vassal countries, knowing that the old king is dead, try their strength. Within a short while of his presence there letters begin to come, offering loyalty to the new pharaoh but demanding expensive favours in return.

Suppiluliuma of the Hittites, one of Egypt's old antagonists, writes:

*"To my brother, the king Naphuria Akhenaten, thus speaks the
Great King Suppululiuma of the Hittites. I hope you are well. I hope
your wife, your sons, your nobles, your horses, your chariots are
well. I myself am well, My wife, my sons, my nobles, my horses and
my chariots are well.*

*"I send you gifts as much as any great king should send to another.
Gifts of silver, of cedar and lapis lazuli. I send boxes of precious
stones and unguents, and women for your delight. In return I
expect gifts as much as any great king should send to another. Gifts
of furniture, of ebony and ivory, of sweet oils and wines, of fine
linen and gold. Your father has ever been a brother to me. May the
gods see that you and I too are brothers.*

*"Hostile forces mass at my southern frontiers. Shall I not expect that
my brother will send his armies to help his brother?"*

A hundred years or so ago Men-kheper-Ra, the third of the Thutmosid kings, had ridden his war chariots through most of the kingdoms of
the Middle East. Those that he did not conquer and make into vassal
states, he negotiated clever alliances with to Egypt's advantage. The
Egyptian empire was strong when Akhenaten came to the throne and
the kingdoms of the north, of the Hittites and of Mitanni and Syria
played careful diplomatic games, anxious to keep her support and
goodwill. Many of them had princesses hostage in the royal "House
of Women", secondary wives of Amenhotep Neb-maat-Ra passed on
to his son, Akhenaten, at his death.

I see some of the letters that pour in to the royal archives, but not
all. Many of them request help. Many complain of help not given. All
are filed away carefully. No help is sent to Suppiluliuma. I do not even
believe the gifts are sent. My brother believes that the frontier states
will settle down as soon as Horemheb has explained that the double
crown of the Two Lands is in safe hands and that the Aten, the great
circle of Divine Light, encompasses them all.

He has never liked Horemheb, but respects him as his father's favourite and most trusted general, and would have invited him home for
the funeral had Nefertiti not persuaded him otherwise. The young
queen seems under a great strain and has lost much of her kittenish

enthusiasm for life. Her face at times is quite drawn, as though she has had very little sleep, and she frequently treats me with coldness. I find myself beginning to fear her, though sometimes I wonder if I am not doing her an injustice. If she loves her husband and is loyal to him, it would be natural for her to be wary of anyone she believed to be a threat to him. I don't know how she could possibly know of the matters Na-aghta and Ma-nan had discussed with me. Perhaps it is just shrewd observation. Or perhaps. . . I suddenly start and all the colour drains from my face. Perhaps she and Horemheb. . .? Never! If anything, she hates Horemheb. Has she not persuaded her husband to leave him at the frontier, so that he will miss the funeral and the inevitable manoeuvring for power that will accompany it? The other possibility is Tiye. She certainly knows who I am, and she might well have told her favourite niece and daughter-in-law, so that they could work together to protect Akhenaten from the threat they believe I pose.

7

THE ICONOCLAST

AFTER HIS LATEST AND MOST IMPORTANT coronation it is not long before Akhenaten makes public pronouncements that the mystery of the One God is to be represented by the disc of the sun and by no other image. All other images representing the manifold aspects of the One God, which have formerly been called "gods" and have been worshipped as such, are to be recognized as secondary attributes of the One God, which they always were, and nothing more. Any priest who claims otherwise is to be deprived of his office; and if he further persists in his folly he is to be outlawed, and declared nameless. Swiftly, the king's soldiers fall upon the priests of Amun-Ra at Ipet-Esut, and expel by force all who resist within the temple precincts. Workmen are deputed throughout the land to hack out all references to Amun as the supreme deity, and to substitute images of the new pharaoh, his queen and their symbol of the Aten, the sun's disc with its rays ending in hands holding the ankh, the symbol of eternal life, above their heads. Mighty Waset, deserted by the rich and powerful families who had followed Akhenaten to his new capital, becomes a quiet backwater. Dispersed throughout the Two Lands her disaffected priests find niches for themselves, biding their time.

BUT I NEVER FEEL HAPPY ABOUT the desecration of the holy names. No matter how often I tell myself that distortion and corruption must be wiped off the face of the earth and a new, pure form of religion must take its place, to see the image of a god smashed and the name chipped from a temple wall makes me sad. There was something there that had once been good, something that was needed, something powerful and numinous. Misinterpreted and misused—an opportunity has been wasted, a message lost.

One temple in particular causes me difficulty and almost loses me my friendship with my brother, my king.

It is rare for Akhenaten to leave Akhetaten and visit Waset, but one day we go together to the west bank there to supervise the work of purification. Akhenaten inspects his father's magnificent mortuary temple first. The work had been completed before our visit and wherever we go the name "Amun" has already been hacked out, even from "Amenhotep", his own father's name.

Silently Pharaoh walks the colonnades and chapels beside the bowing, obsequious mortuary priests, checking that the names of Amun have been changed, that the images of Amun have been removed. Even in dark chambers where natural light never penetrates, the king orders torches to be held up to every nook and cranny.

I am glad to leave and, impatiently, wait in the gardens while my companion pauses before the huge colossi of grindstone that stand at the entrance. It seems to me the old king is still keeping watch over his former kingdom. I wonder if Akhenaten feels uneasy under the fixed and powerful gaze of the gigantic carved faces. I wonder what he is whispering under his breath as he stretches his thin neck and tilts back his head to squint up at his father's stone head blazing in the sun's rays.

He turns on his heel suddenly and strides towards me. We say nothing to each other as we climb into the waiting chariots and ride off to the next temple he has set his heart on attending to personally.

Against the great arc of the cliffs at Serui, the rock wall that holds the tombs of the kings secret from the gaze of the living, Men-kheper-Ra, the third of the Thutmosid kings, the empire builder, the warrior, had built his temple to Amun. The long avenue that leads to it is lined with statues. On either side, two much larger temples lie deserted. The one to the left is from the ancient days, the mortuary temple of Mentuhotep, almost completely ruined, a small chapel at the back, where the actual tombs of the king and his wives lie, all that is left in good working order.

Priests still attend the mortuary cult among the ruined splendours of the ancient temple.

To the right, built on three huge terraces, another temple, almost dwarfing its neighbours, shimmers in the heat-haze. It has always been a puzzle that Men-kheper-Ra had built the second, smaller temple on this site and abandoned this much larger and more impressive one. It is clear that there had once been a garden with ponds and fish and singing birds, but the water has dried up, and the canals that fed them have long since silted and overgrown with reeds. Some of the old trees still live and a few gardeners tend them, for they are rare incense-bearing trees brought by Men-kheper-Ra a century before from the distant land of Punt over the great ocean.

The trees are still tended but not the temple. No priests come forward to greet us. Its great doors stand open, its walls crumbling, the paint that must once have enriched the surface of every wall is flaking off. Sand has drifted in to lie against the pillars and the walls behind them. The tracks and faeces of desert foxes and jackals can be seen.

I had thought Akhenaten would not trouble himself with a temple that was already dead and deserted before his birth, but for some reason when we have finished with the smaller building still in use, we turn in through the open gate of the one the warrior king had abandoned. I have not been within the precincts before, though I have passed by several times and admired the beauty and the fair proportions I glimpsed there. This temple seems different from any other I have ever seen. It seems to have grown from the earth, rather than having been built upon it. I explore with increasing excitement the long cool colonnades that run parallel to the cliffs. For the first time l have the strong feeling that the name "the Two Lands" does not refer only to the north and south of Khemet—but to the Land we can see and the invisible Land behind it that sustains our spiritual existence as the other sustains our physical. There is a strong and powerful charge of spiritual energy still active in these precincts.

I seem to be crossing a threshold into another realm. My skin prickles. My breath comes fast. I have stood in many, many temples in my life, but never have I felt quite like this.

I look round. With my eyes I can see a neglected and derelict building, but I can feel a living and a vibrant one. It seems to me I can hear chanting—women's voices high and clear from the direction of the Hathor chapel to the left of where I'm standing. They are faint and haunting, but unmistakable. And then, in a moment, gone. I rush to look inside the chapel. But there is no one there. No footprints on the even film of sand.

I look at Akhenaten, wondering if he has heard it too, wondering if he is feeling what I am feeling. But he looks unaware and is directing his workmen to their tasks.

I want to be alone and move away from the others. I can see the hated name of Amun in every inscription. I can see his image a hundred times repeated.

And then I notice something else. Some iconoclast has been here before us—but not to eradicate the name of the god.

I begin to study the inscriptions with greater attention, particularly those that look as though they have been deliberately damaged. In each case it is the name of a pharaoh and not a god that has been hacked out. The cartouches of the first three Thutmosid kings are left undamaged. Or are they? Sometimes it looks to me as though there were a name in the cartouche that has been removed and the Thutmosid name engraved on top of it.

Sometimes the workmen had been careless and remnants of a different name appear beneath the new one. Men-kheper-Ra must have usurped this temple from someone else. I am intrigued. The early kings of our dynasty were great heroes. They had expelled the hated Hyksos invaders from our land and extended our borders well into Djahi. They had established the rich and powerful empire Akhenaten had inherited. Surely no one would dare obliterate any of their names and de-sanctify their mortuary temple?

And then I notice as I go deeper into the temple and find inscriptions hidden in the shadows behind doors or pillars, or too high for the iconoclasts to notice, that another name occasionally appears. *"Hatshepsut. Maat-ka-Ra. Female Horus of Pure Gold. Sovereign of the Two Lands. King of North and South. Son of the Sun. Beloved Daughter of Amun. Living in Splendour Forever."* The epithets used are half male and half female. I forget why I am here and search feverishly through the building for clues to the identity of this mysterious sovereign. The name of the queen of the third Thutmosid king was Hatshepsut Meryt-Ra, but the epithets and other names of this "Daughter of Amun" were quite different. It is clear "she" was a "king", not a "queen".

Not only is my interest fully aroused now but I am beginning to feel very strange. I am trembling. I am elated as never before. It is as though the rest of the world has ceased to exist and I am no longer flesh and blood, but a bodiless ka floating from place to place in this vast complex of buildings, led by a kind of inevitability to find the few poor scattered fragments of a name that no longer means anything to the people of the Two Lands, but is beginning increasingly to mean a lot to me.

"*Hatshepsut, Maa-ka-Ra. Hatshepsut. Maat-ka-Ra.*"

Even when I can no longer see the hieroglyphs spelling it out the names roll through my head like thunder. I begin to notice that it is everywhere in the building—"Daughter of Amun"—underlying the Thutmosid names. A female pharaoh! "The female Horus of Pure Gold."

I can hardly breathe for my excitement. What story lies behind the ruined temple? What powerful feud had driven the third Thutmosid king to take these measures, to abandon this magnificent structure and build his own beside it? He must have hated this Hatshepsut. He must have tried to wipe her and her memory from the face of the earth. I visualize him usurping her place, hacking out her name, trying to use her temple as his own. I wonder if he too could hear her name ringing through these colonnades and courtyards and chapels. I wonder if he too could hear chanting when there was no one there to chant. Did he feel as I feel now—on the edge of some overwhelming revelation—and decide to flee rather than face up to it?

But I do not flee. I cannot. I am held to the place by a feeling so strong that it almost makes me lose consciousness. I find myself climbing the ramp of the third terrace as though I am sleepwalking. I find myself passing through the gaping hole where the third door had once been as though I am being compelled by an invisible force. As I pass through I swear I hear the great cedar doors crashing closed behind me, the bolt being drawn. But there is no cedar door there, though there might well have been in Hatshepsut's time.

I cross the third courtyard and see the procession of Amun as though it is happening at this very moment, though my reason tells me I am looking at a painted relief carved on a wall. I see the glint of Amun's golden barque, the sweat gleaming on the shoulders of the men who carry it. I hear the praise-singers and feel the cool swish of the fans of palm-leaf and ostrich-feather.

I enter Amun's sanctuary—knowing exactly where it is—knowing that I have been there before. I fall down on my knees with my forehead on the ground. I see nothing—but experience an immense and awesome presence. I feel the hot breath of anger on the nape of my neck. I have been here before. I have offended. I was part of the mighty drama that had destroyed this temple, wiped this pharaoh's name from the records of the Two Lands. I begin to babble, pleading for forgiveness, though I still cannot remember what I have done.

At that moment I hear a sound behind me. It is not the roaring in my ears of the god's anger—nor the shouting and chanting and praying of the dead—but the ordinary sound of a living human voice shouting.

Bewildered, I lift my head.

The sanctuary is a ruin. I am surrounded by cold stone and shattered images. Rocks from the cliff have fallen on the roof and cracked it, letting in a thin shaft of light. Sand and dust have come with it and cover the floor.

Akhenaten is behind me and his face is distorted with rage.

"What are you doing?" he screams.

Clumsily I rise to my feet and stare at him, struggling to come back to the present, to remember who I now am. In my heart there is a sad, sad feeling of loss. . .

And then Akhenaten seems to go insane. He has a hammer and a chisel in his hands and he begins to hack at all the references to Amun he can find in the sanctuary. I can hear his workmen below on the other terraces doing the same thing—but they are only carrying out orders, chatting and whistling among themselves. But Akhenaten is striking the rock inscriptions as a murderer strikes at a victim. I have never seen any man so possessed by hate and anger. His strength is prodigious. His eyes are glazed and unseeing.

I draw back—shaking—and leave his side, running down the long ramps, looking neither to the left nor the right. I cannot stop him and I cannot stay to watch. I pass through the broken gate and run towards an old quarry on the cliffs to the right. As though I know where I am going I make straight for a dark gash in the rock. Tears are streaming from my eyes and the feeling of loss is overwhelming. I climb a slippery heap of chippings and pull aside some old rubbish and timbers that are over the hole in the cliff. Like a child who has a favourite hiding place when it is in trouble, I scramble into the dark cavity, the entrance to a tunnel. This is familiar. This is known to me in the same way as all the rest of the mysterious temple. But if someone had questioned me I would not have been able to give sensible answers. My heart is pounding with love and desire and frustration and pain—but for what or for whom I cannot say. The tunnel is blocked a short way in and there is no way I can pass further though I tug at the boulders with my bare hands and my blood mingles with the dust.

At last, exhausted, I give up and return to the sunlight. I sit beside the entrance, panting, dust and blood and sweat running down my arms. I look across at the terraces of the temple Akhenaten is desecrating, the huge, impassive cliff that towers behind it dwarfing us all. What are we doing? The sky above the cliff, above Akhenaten, above me, is vast and without limit. How small and ridiculous we suddenly seem to be pitting our passions against these images. We know nothing of "the gods". We know very little about anything. We are like ants spending a whole day trying to move a crumb over an obstacle when, if we but paused to think, we would have found a better way.

I begin to return to my ordinary consciousness. I am Djehuti-kheper-Ra, Pharaoh's brother, and I have been behaving in an extraordinary way. The feelings that had driven me to act as I did now seem unreal and bizarre. I can scarcely remember them. I know only that I do not want to enter that temple again. I no longer remember the name I found hidden among the inscriptions, the name Men-kheper-Ra had tried so hard to obliterate. Let the ancient story lie, I think, if it means enmity between me and my brother.

When Akhenaten at last leaves the ruined temple he does not look at me. I offer no explanation or apology, but ride beside him silently. His face is drawn and tired, as covered with dust as mine. We part at the palace as silently as we had ridden, going our separate ways.

But when we next meet, it seems he has come to terms with the experience in some way, and treats me as though nothing has happened.

This is the last time he personally attends to the elimination of Amun's name in the Two Lands.

* * * *

101

MY DREAMS AT NIGHT ARE OFTEN disturbed by dark images, Ma-nan's familiars, howling round my bed, he himself with eyes as black as jet, standing in the doorway offering me the two crowns. Many a night I stand up and pace the room to escape my dreams, asking myself what I would do if I were king. My gentle admonitions have increasingly little effect on my friend and brother. He cannot see that under the surface of the victorious edifice that he has built for Aten, the ground is not firm, and the slightest pressure from a determined enemy could bring it tumbling down. Because men smile and bow, and obey his commands, he believes they understand and accept his teaching. Many a time I visit the house of a labourer as a healer-priest, and find small effigies and talismans of the traditional gods that have been hastily and inexpertly hidden at my approach. I never report this to the king, because I find lately that he tends to punish such lapses. His dream of freeing his country from fear by bathing it in the light of truth has not taken into account two things: one, the natural tendency of humans to hold to old, familiar ideas as firmly as an infant holds to its cot cover; and two, the corrupting influence of power. He does not seem to notice that by the suddenness of his new decrees and the warnings he issues at any breach of them, he has not rid his people of fear, only changed the source of it. But perhaps I am being too critical. Certainly in his city of Akhetaten there are very few shadows. What is happening in the rest of the country, as his officers enforce his new laws, we do not know, for in Akhetaten we live in a golden age. All that is beautiful is encouraged: art, singing, music, dancing; festivals celebrating each year of the new king's reign; festivals of rejoicing at each of the royal birthdays. Breaking once again with tradition, tombs are started for the royal family and high officials, in the mountains to the east of the city—where the sun rises. Death is to be a journey of the day—not of the night.

I AM SITTING IN THE SHADE of a sycamore tree in the garden of my house. It is noon, and the city is sleeping. Even the dog, lying under the lee of the wall, is too lethargic to do more than open one eye and cock an ear as a figure walks softly past him. When he sees who it is his tail wags momentarily and then falls back on to the warm flagstones again.

I know her step, but pretend I have heard nothing. Soon her soft hands are over my eyes and I can feel the curves of her body on my back. I lean my head against her breasts. She kisses the top of my head but still keeps her hands firmly over my eyes. I know I am supposed to guess who she is and I go through all the names of her sisters. And then I start on other names, as though I have had many lovers. She drops her hands angrily—but before she can move away I twist about to take her by the shoulders, and swing her round till she is close against my chest and my lips can reach hers. After her lips I kiss her eyelids and her ears.

She jerks her ear-lobe away and I see the marks of my teeth still on the flesh.

"Who are these other women?" she asks sharply.

"Are you not my only lover?" I ask, and, by trying to keep my tone light, I make it mocking. I regret it at once. I have stupidly spoiled a beautiful moment.

She is flushed, angry. She starts to move away. I take her arm more roughly than I intend to pull her back to me.

"Let me go," she says fiercely.

"No," I say, "not while you are angry with me."

"Why should you worry if I'm angry with you? You obviously have other women who are not."

"I have no other women. Believe me. You are my only love."

"It is no wonder you refuse to speak to my father about our marriage. You have no intention of marrying me."

"I will speak today. This very day. I love you. There is no other woman—Merytaten—beloved of Djehuti-kheper-Ra."

She stops struggling to pull her arm away and looks at me cautiously.

"You will speak to my father? *This* day?"

"Yes," I say recklessly. Suddenly time seems very, very short and I curse myself for having wasted as much of it as I have.

Her anger disappears like darkness when the Aten appears. She flings her arms around my neck and kisses me breathlessly.

"Now! This very moment!" she cries. "Before you change your mind."

The dog Bel has seen the commotion and decides to join in despite the heat. He rushes round and round us barking and wagging his tail. There are tears of happiness in Merytaten's eyes. I can feel them welling in mine too, but my joy is mixed with fear.

* * * *

103

ONE DAY I AM IN MERYTATEN's chamber by myself. I have arrived at dawn, expecting to find her, warm and rosy from sleep, ready for me. But the room is empty. The fine coloured linens have been flung carelessly off the bed, as though she has risen in haste and left, without calling her women. The imprint of her body is still on the remaining bed-clothes and I stand for some time looking down at it, visualizing how she would have looked as she woke and wondering what had made her leave so early. More than likely she is walking by the lake, I think. She has always loved the dawn more than any other time and infinitely prefers saying her prayers to the Aten in a natural setting rather than in the formal atmosphere of the temple.

The room is full of her—flowers in alabaster vases, rows of elaborate wigs on their stands. I cross the room and stand before the table that contains her cosmetics—ground lead to darken her lashes, ground malachite to shade her lids, powdered henna for the colour red, and powdered gypsum for whitening her already fair skin. There is a range of exquisitely shaped glass jars of perfume, the stoppers resembling the heads of birds. Everything has been neatly laid out by her serving women, the only thing out of place is the mirror, resting untidily on the edge of an unguent casket as though picked up and put down before she raced out of the room to catch the sunrise.

I pick it up idly and look at its polished surface. It is almost round, like the sun on the horizon, but richly golden like the sun at noon. In it I see the reflection of my own face. I have seen reflections and images of myself before and should not be surprised at what I see. But this time I can hardly bear to look at my own face yet I cannot look away. Behind me stands the figure of Hathor, whose sacred mirror I have in my hand. She is compelling me to look at myself, and, behind the superficial good looks, the full mouth so like my brother's, the deep and searching eyes, I see other faces, some not as noble as I would like to be, some self-seeking and hypocritical, some pretending to an enlightenment they do not have, some frightened, some arrogant, some impatient and careless. This is one who has great potential, the mirror is telling me, who has the weight of many lives behind him, who is favoured by the gods—yet this is one who procrastinates, who finds excuses not to fulfil his mission, who seeks the comfortable way, who basks in praise and shuns criticism. My eyes fill with tears of shame and I can no longer see the image in the mirror. Is Hathor smiling behind me? Does she see the tears of shame as tears of self-pity? Does she interpret them as just another attempt on my part to escape true self-knowledge?

The door is flung open and Merytaten comes into the room, her face alight with the magic of the dawn she has just experienced. She rushes at me and flings her arms around me.

"What? Admiring yourself in my mirror?" she laughs and puts the lotus-handled polished metal disc down on the table top. "Is it not enough that I tell you every day how handsome you are?"

I kiss her, glad that she has not seen me as I truly am, wondering how I am going to live with the knowledge I have just gained about myself.

"Put shame away, it will destroy you," Hathor whispers at my side. "Put pride away. It too will destroy you. Step out of the mirror into the real world without shame, without pride. Do what you have to do without worrying how the image of it appears in the mirror." I turn my head and look over Merytaten's shoulder half expecting that Hathor is still in the chamber with us. But I can see no one beside ourselves.

8

THE TOMB ROBBERS

In Waset one day on business for my pharaoh, I am informed by the superintendent of the Royal Necropolis in the valley beneath the shadow of Meretseger, that he believes a gang of tomb robbers is at work in the remote southern arm of the valley. Previously it had not been thought that there were any royal burials there and the Medjay, the valley police, were not in the habit of patrolling the area. But one night a guard in the main body of the valley had become curious when he thought he saw a glimmer of light half way up a cliff face and had gone off with a companion to investigate. The two men did not return. Their bodies were found two days later buried under a pile of loose chippings. A careful search of the southern valley revealed that there were indeed trails of recent footprints in the sand. They petered out where the rock took over from the sand, but a broken alabaster cup had been found in a crevice, the break still sharp and unweathered. They followed scuff marks on the rock, an occasional fragment of ancient artefact or scrap of torn clothing, until they came to a narrow ravine where they found a few crude steps carved out of the steep rock sides. They even found the burnt-out remnants of a torch flung carelessly into a hole.

My visit coincides with the superintendent's decision to try to apprehend the thieves and I find him deep in discussion with the Medjay about the plan.

I insist on joining the group that is to visit the site that night.

They try to dissuade me, but I am adamant. I carry Pharaoh's seal. They cannot refuse me. But I can see by their expressions that they think I will be a liability.

I have always had a particular hate for tomb robbers. I know Akhenaten believes the elaborate spells depicted on the walls of the old tombs, designed to help the soul of the deceased through the trials and difficulties to be encountered in the Duat, have lost their significance in the blazing and purifying light of the Aten, but to the kings who were buried according to these ancient rites they were very important. And I, who believe in the efficacy of spells, hate the thought of tampering with them. In the tombs being carved into the cliffs behind Akhetaten, the ancient Book of Awakening, an essential in any burial for thousands of years, is replaced by hymns to the Sun and icons of Akhenaten and his family. Though embalming is still practised, the talismans that used to be bound into the mummy bandages to protect each part of the deceased with magical power are now omitted. Only the image of the Sun and its rays offers protection. I am not sure this is wise. There might not be power in the actual turquoise, gold and jet of the Horus Eye that is laid upon the body—but there is power in the thought of the one who lays it there, and in the belief of the one who prepares to wear it through eternity.

THE SUPERINTENDENT OF THE NECROPOLIS, THE chief of the Medjay, two strong Nubian guards and myself set off in the late morning and make our way down the valley that branches off to the south, away from the main area usually guarded by the police. We cannot be sure the robbers will return but we intend to find the tomb and take up our positions in and around it. We will either wait until they come, or find enough clues left by them to apprehend them later. The tomb itself must at any rate be examined, re-consecrated and re-sealed. I am curious as to whose tomb it will prove to be. Since I have discovered who my parents are I have been eagerly studying all that is known about my ancestors. My experiences in the temple of the mysterious Pharaoh Hatshepsut have further intrigued me and set me examining old records. I can find her name nowhere, but many anomalies in the texts indicate that there was a pharaoh between the second and third Thutmosid kings. I long for this tomb to be hers. That it was hitherto unknown to the necropolis staff makes it a possibility though not a certainty. Many kings took great care to ensure their tombs were secret and never recorded, knowing that the treasure buried with them would be a strong temptation to robbers.

The morning begins to heat up—the high walls of rust-yellow rock holding the air absolutely still in the sunlight. We climb a ridge and are faced by a further climb to the ravine the Medjay suspect holds the entrance to the robbed tomb. As I struggle to find a foothold on the steep rock I wonder how the heavy objects of a royal burial could possibly have been brought up this way. Yet it is clear that they were. I wonder at the dedication of the robbers, who come at night no doubt carrying the same objects down again. We all hope as we sweat our way upwards, that with such difficult terrain, we will find the tomb still largely intact. It is a forlorn hope however. Tomb robbers are not easily deterred. The pickings in these tombs are so rich and the men who rob them care nothing either for natural or supernatural hardships and dangers. We remember the two young men who were murdered and look anxiously over our shoulders at the silent columns and walls of rock behind us, wondering if we are being observed.

At last we reach the dark hole in the cliff excavated by the robbers. It is a doorway that had been carefully hidden behind boulders. Flash floods had brought down further debris to disguise it, but something must have alerted the robbers to the presence of a tomb. They have taken no precautions to hide it once again, believing no doubt that it would be safe from discovery in this remote place.

The superintendent and myself light our torches and crouch down to enter. The three Medjay are to be left on guard outside.

I don't know to whom my companion is praying, but I speak to Akhenaten's god and ask for protection. The corridor inside is steep and slippery with chippings, disappearing into the darkness below. I turn my ankle on the rubble and mutter an imprecation. The robbers have cleared a narrow path, which we now thankfully use. As we go deeper in there is the strong smell of stale air, and a pleasanter smell, perhaps of cedar and funeral unguents. I am not happy with dark and confined places after my childhood experiences as an oracle and begin to sweat with fear, and wonder if I dare turn back. My retreat is blocked. The official prods me on. The place is suffocatingly hot. The corridor becomes steeper. I almost slide and bring myself to a halt only inches away from a deep pit. I hold up my arm to prevent him from hurtling past me into the void. This pit, a feature of most tombs, symbolizes the dark and fathomless Unknown dividing life in the flesh from life in the spirit. When the deceased has passed this point in the descent into his tomb, there is no turning back. The robbers have laid a palm log across the top and worked their way over it, as we do now. The log moves under my weight and it seems to me my heart stops beating. I stare into the blackness below that the light of my torch cannot penetrate and feel real terror—not of any physical danger, but of the Unknown and Unknowable Mystery over which we are poised every moment of our lives.

My companion is holding his torch high, waiting at the side for me to finish my precarious journey across the pit. I glance up to where the flame illuminates the ceiling above us. It is painted with a myriad golden stars. I pull myself together and reach the other side, holding my torch upright and steady for him as he had for me.

Beyond a doorway lies a chamber painted throughout with countless numbers of deities. Beyond this is a carved burial hall with two huge square pillars holding up the ceiling painted, as before, with golden stars. On the surfaces of the white plastered walls and on the broad faces of the columns, the journey of the soul and all that it will have to face in the Otherworld before it can reach the point of justification and the return to life, is depicted in black outline. I notice the magnificent Litany of Ra among the inscriptions.

The huge red sarcophagus seems undisturbed, but the grave-goods, the priceless possessions of the king, are scattered everywhere, many broken and discarded. Life-size cedar-wood statues of guards that had no doubt stood at the entrance to the chamber are lying face down on the floor, their coverings of gold-foil ripped off, their eyes of precious stone dug out. The broken planks of cedar that must once have formed the walls of shrines to enclose the sarcophagus, lie in splintered heaps—their covering of gold-leaf untidily pulled off. Some objects have been smashed against the walls so that the precious stones embedded in them could be more easily removed. The long difficult climb down the ravine must have deterred the robbers from carrying anything too bulky or too heavy.

That the lid is still on the sarcophagus makes us think that the robbers will surely be back—for they will want the numerous talismans of silver, gold and precious stones that must have been ritually placed into the bandages close to the king's body.

Our torches are flickering in the stale air and I am beginning to feel nauseous. I have never been inside a sealed tomb before. Those still being worked on by noisy workmen have quite a different atmosphere. This place is heavy with magical spells. My mouth is dry. Every shadow seems to move, every breath I draw could be my last.

While my companion examines the sarcophagus I gaze in fascinated awe at the drawings on the walls. They represent the finest mystery teachings, the secret knowledge handed down from initiate to initiate since the ancient days, copied on these walls by scribes who know very little of their meaning, sealed against the eyes of the living, understood fully only by the dead. . .

I have been trained in the Mysteries but never tire of seeing the different ways they can be depicted, the different ways they can be symbolized. I count off the names of Ra in the litany—hundreds upon hundreds of them. These are the ones known to man. There will be many more known only to the gods and one known only to Ra himself. In the names lie the clues to an understanding of his nature. Here are the ciphers of the ancient myths—the gigantic, nightly, yet eternal, conflict between Existence in the form of Ra and Non-Existence in the form of the monstrous snake, Apep. Here are the holy and hidden aspects of a life that never ends, depicted in images than can do no more than hint at the reality they are supposed to represent. As my eye follows the story, my heart begins to take it up, and I forget where I am and why I am here. I am passing through the trials. . . pitting my strength against the danger and the enemies. . . reaping the reward's of survival. . . rejoicing at the sudden illumination of ancient and perennial truths.

Suddenly I am drawn back into the flesh with a start. The chief of the Medjay has arrived. It seems we have been in the tomb longer than we thought. Outside the sun has set and half the night has gone. The guards have seen the glow of several torches down in the valley and they are sure the robbers are approaching. The two men have been left hidden near the entrance and the chief has come to warn us.

We have a hasty consultation. We know now from the inscription that the sarcophagus holds the body of Men-kheper-Ra, the third Thutmosid king. He is one of the great heroes of the Two Lands, and his tomb must be one of the richest in the valley. We hate to think what the robbers might have already stolen, and are determined that they will not rob the body itself in its nest of golden coffins.

The chief has given his men instructions to remain hidden until the robbers are well into the tomb and then to follow them in. With luck we, hidden behind the square columns of the burial chamber, and they, blocking the door, will trap the intruders neatly. I wish I did not feel so frightened. I am not a man of action and I'm shaken and disturbed by the strong magical charge of the tomb. The superintendent and the chief of the Medjay seem untouched by the strangeness of their surroundings and look as though this is all in an ordinary night's work for them.

The torches are extinguished.

We begin the long wait.

There is no sound or sight in the heavy darkness. I am tormented by memories of my youth—of waiting in dark places, menaced by Ma-nan's furies. But Ma-nan's furies are familiar to me. Those that lurk in this darkness are not.

What kind of man was this king? What priests shook their rods of power in this place and cast the spells? There is a malevolence here. Men-kheper-Ra had been a warrior. Killing came naturally to him. His ka must be stained with the blood of thousands. I care nothing for the honour he is held in by his descendants for I hold no one in honour who so little respects the lives of others.

I can feel his ka in the chamber with us and draw back, shivering. But I can feel something more than this. I can feel that there is something between us—a personal hatred—a personal vendetta. There is something from the past drawing him to me, and me to him. My hand holding the heavy handle of my unlit torch is so wet with sweat, it slips from my hand, and I hear the exclamation of the chief of police, chiding me for making a sound when the robbers must surely be nearby by now.

I long for their arrival. At least they are flesh and blood, I strain my eyes into the darkness, wishing that I could see something—anything—however fearsome.

I begin to feel a constriction in my throat and believe invisible hands are around my larynx squeezing the life out of me. I tear at them with my own hands and try to cry out for help from the others. I don't care if the robbers are alerted. The robbers are nothing to the evil force that is choking me. I wish the robbers had already opened the sarcophagus and broken up the talismans and taken on themselves the potent spells and curses. . .

What is this hate between this king and me? What have I done?

Suddenly there is light.

Three rough, muscular men stand in the doorway holding torches above their heads. They stare into the chamber seeing only the gold that gleams in the flame-light.

My throat is released. My eyes leap to the sarcophagus, but there is nothing to be seen. It is lidded and undisturbed as before. There is no one in the chamber but the three law-enforcers, and the three lawbreakers.

We wait, scarcely breathing, hidden until they put the torches down and start work with the tools they have brought to lift the lid of the sarcophagus. I see a shadow at the doorway and at the same moment the chief of the Medjay shouts and we all leap forward, the two Nubians at the door, the superintendent, the chief of the Medjay and myself.

Desperate for action after the fearful tension of waiting, I find myself beating at one of the robbers with a heavy piece of timber I have seized from the floor. I beat and beat and beat. He has been caught unawares and has lost his footing. He begins to bleed and gibber for mercy. I go on beating.

Suddenly I feel a hand on my arm and spin round fiercely—ready to attack again. It is the superintendent, his face alarmed, telling me to stop. It is all over. We have captured the robbers. I look around, dazed. The other two robbers are bound and lying at the feet of the police, apparently unhurt. The one I attacked is dead.

I stand looking down at him in horror. I cannot believe I have done this. I fall on him, pleading with the gods to give him back his life. He falls from my hands like a bundle of empty clothes.

I cannot make him live again.

WE CLIMB DOWN THE RAVINE AFTER we have resealed the tomb, carrying the dead man between us. Pebbles slide under our feet. The sun is rising.

The names of Ra ring in my ears. . . "He whose Brilliant Eye Speaks". . . "He who is the Renewer of the Earth". . . "He who is the Master of Becoming". . . "He who Gives Light to the Living and the Dead". . . "He who is the Eternal One". . . "He who is the Lord of Light". . .

Do you see me, Flaming One? Do you see the guilt in my heart? Will I ever expiate this crime?

Ah, Traveller of the Invisible and Imperishable Sky, help me. How easy it is to know thy names, how difficult to live according to thy laws!

9

THE SLEEPING SPELL

"My lord," General Horemheb stands very straight before the king, and I can see the veins on his neck and in his hands. He is frustrated and angry, but keeping himself under control. Nefertiti stands behind her husband's chair with her arms around his shoulders, and her chin resting on his head. Her eyes never leave Horemheb. His never leave the king. I can feel their awareness of each other like a tangible but invisible thread between them.

Akhenaten is looking relaxed, enjoying the embrace of his favourite wife. The presence of his friends and family give him confidence in the company of the man who has always made him uneasy. Tadukhipa, his young Mitannian wife descended from his own grandmother's royal line; Ankhesenpaaten, his daughter-wife; Nezem-mut, not as beautiful as her sister Nefertiti, but nevertheless a good friend, and I—all surround him. Merytaten is not present. She is sad because I have not yet kept my word and spoken to her father about our marriage.

"My lord, forgive me if I speak my mind. It is the mind of a man of honour, a loyal and trusted servant of your father—"

"I am the king now," Akhenaten says easily. "Are you *my* loyal and trusted servant, General?"

Horemheb's colour deepens. "Of course, my lord. . . I mean only—"

"I know what you meant, General. I respect you as my father respected you. You have my permission to speak as freely as you wish."

"I have been honoured to serve both your father and yourself, sir, as Commander-in-Chief of your armies, as judge of your criminals, as ambassador to the vassal states of your empire, as superintendent of your tribute collections. . ."

"I know your titles, General. Speak to me of your mind. A man's mind is more interesting to me than a hundred thousand titles."

"I meant only that the mind of an ordinary man may be confused and undisciplined, but that the mind of the holder of such titles may not be."

"Speak," Akhenaten says, still unruffled, his right hand going to his left shoulder to take hold of Nefertiti's, turning his head slightly to let his lips rest upon her slender fingers for a moment.

Do I sense the tension in the handsome general increase? I love my friend the king, but he seems more and more insensitive to the undercurrents of feelings around him. He is even taking Nefertiti's love for granted these days, never doubting that she and everyone around him is equally as excited about the abstract beauty of the new philosophy, equally obsessed with the intricate working of the eternal light within the heart.

Horemheb is concerned with the immediate. The great empire built up by Thutmose III and maintained, after a fashion, by Akhenaten's father, is beginning to disintegrate. The Amorites and the Hittites are on the move. Loyal vassals are pleading for assistance to resist them, and not-so-loyal vassals are taking the opportunity to break away. The rich flow of tribute which has been pouring into the Two Lands since the time of Thutmose III, bringing with it general prosperity, and private luxury for the royal household and the priests of Amun, is beginning to dry up. Horemheb speaks now, long and passionately, on the need for a strong hand to hold the reins of the empire, the need to enforce the tribute laws, the need to send troops to teach the rebels a lesson.

"You hold in your hands the crook and the flail, my King," Horemheb says. "You have used the crook. Now it is time to use the flail."

Akhenaten listens to him patiently, his eyes becoming thoughtful, his chin in his hand, Nefertiti's arms pushed aside.

"And what if I believe that the Aten shines on all men and its light seeks all men's hearts, and only the Aten may join men of different nations together?" he asks quietly.

116

"The Aten has given the nations into the hand of Pharaoh, my lord, the Aten has put them under the heel of the servant of Aten."

"Oh, really?" says Akhenaten, raising an eyebrow. "I thought you believed it was Amun who had done that." Horemheb flushes, and I see his knuckles white as he clenches his fists. He bites back what he wants to say.

Akhenaten looks at him amused, relaxed for the moment, and then his face shadows, his eyes narrow.

"My grandfather, and his father before him, were misled by the false god Amun," he says, and now there is a dangerous edge to his voice. I have noticed lately that my king is subject to inexplicable and violent changes of mood, sudden rages that come out of a clear and cloudless sky, the frustration of a far-sighted man looking to the horizon, while his fellow men look no further than the walls that surround their own houses. "Conquering and slaughtering and enslaving is not the way of the Aten. If foreigners are unhappy under our yoke, set them free. We should not have taken their lands in the first place."

"My lord, whether we should or not is another question." I begin to admire Horemheb's self-control. I know he is murderously angry, but his voice barely falters. Akhenaten has asked for plain speaking from his senior officials, and Horemheb goes as close as he dares. "Your grandfathers won for you a great empire, and you owe it to them and to your subjects to hold it firm and strong, that no man may harm a hair of the head of any man in it."

"What is an empire but people who have been conquered and exploited? There were many hairs harmed when we took it."

"A king looks to his own people and takes what they need. This play between nations is expected. The Hyksos conquered us because our kings were weak, and their people needed tribute and land. It was only when Amun put strength in the arm of the great Ahmose that he could drive them from our land and harry them to the far reaches of the world. No one blamed the king for this. All rejoiced. His name will live for ever as the saviour of the Two Lands. It is up to us to use our strength, the strength *he* gave us, to protect the honour and respect he won for us, otherwise the mangy curs of every nation will piss on us."

"I piss on the "honour" and "respect" you speak of," Akhenaten says bitterly. "They are the smiling masks over the festering sores of fear and

117

hate—the legacy of Amun. If the nations truly respected and honoured us we would not need to fear that they would pull away from us now."

For a moment I think Horemheb will strike the king. Nefertiti must think so too, because she moves swiftly forward between them.

"My husband is an idealist, General," she says smoothly. "He dreams. He has visions. But though they may seem impractical to you, because you are accustomed only to see with the eyes in your head, I assure you that to one who can see with the long sight of the spirit they are very real and very practical."

Horemheb's eyes smoulder, but he bows stiffly to her and to the king. I know that he does not understand. To him physical presence is all that there is. The ba and the ka, the spirit that reaches throughout eternity and is aware of its oneness with all that is, and the soul that is the pupa of the spirit, still aware only of itself as individual, are to him empty concepts, for experience has not yet shown him their reality.

HOREMHEB IS KEPT AS AN ADMINISTRATOR, when he longs to be a general. The despatches from the empire are placed carefully in the records office and the Aten is made entirely responsible for the peace-keeping.

Akhetaten is further from the Middle East than the old administrative capital Men-nefer and letters take longer to reach the king. This, with his lack of interest in foreign affairs, slows down the correspondence dangerously. Letters begin to be less friendly. Time passes and further letters are often sharp and accusing. Vassal states rebel or are invaded, and the much-feared Egyptian bowmen are either not sent at all or sent too late. One vassal even dares to threaten the might of the Two Lands in his frustration: "if ants get hit do they not bite back?" he writes.

I pace through the lovely gardens of the Great Palace and feel uneasy. It is not that I think Horemheb is right, and we should send troops to kill people, but I believe peace-keeping is a positive strategy, perhaps one of the most difficult, complex and important strategies a ruler has to consider. It involves close and careful knowledge of the ways of the people, constant listening to their needs, guidance and help with everything that will be for their good. A happy and contented community, steadily based on a set of enduring and co-operative values, will not easily turn to disaffection. As for invaders—intricate and cunning diplomacy, if timely, can work wonders. Amenhotep Neb-maat-Ra knew everything that went on in every country that could possibly pose a threat to his empire. His spies were posted everywhere, their despatches read meticulously. Trouble was attended to long before it became trouble. Foreign princes were enticed to the colleges of the Two Lands, foreign princesses married into his House of Women. A continuous stream of bribes—Nubian gold, Sinai turquoise, fine linen, and exquisite furniture—flowed to the Hittite, Amorite, Mitannian kings and the rulers of the vassal states. Over the long years of his reign Amenhotep had developed the strategy of peace as skilfully as ever Thutmose III had developed the strategy of war.

Akhenaten is interested in neither. He believes that once the country is united under one true and incontrovertible religion, once every man, woman and child, has put its faith and its future in the far-reaching hands of the Aten, a great peace will come. With Khurahtaten's teaching in my heart I believe this too but I am ill at ease with the way he is making the transition. At first we talked about a gradual weaning, a gradual education. But the recalcitrance of the priesthood, unwilling to give up their livelihood and their privileges, and the stubbornness of the people in holding to time-worn superstitions, has made him impatient. And impatience clouds the mind. He is using force to topple the old temples down, stringent laws to forbid the worship of old and comfortable gods. Trusting no one to interpret his vision for him, he has made himself the sole companion of the Aten, the sole interpreter of the God's wishes.

In vain I suggest that though Hat-Hor, Isis, Ptah and the others may not be the supreme God, they represent at least aspects of the supreme being. They have a part to play in the gradual awakening to full spiritual consciousness, just as within a school different teachers work on developing different capacities in a child, some discarded as it develops beyond them, others taking their place to carry the child further. But my friend, my brother, my king tells me that the "teachers" I speak about can no longer be trusted. . . their teaching has lost its potency, their priests teach the ancient myths by rote, and no one looks to the original meanings.

"Dead myths are like stones tied to the legs of a man thrown into water. Cut the thongs that bind them to him, and let him swim freely, seeking the sun's light."

"But the sun's light may be too strong to look at directly," I say quietly. "Are not myths often the only way we can seek it out and gaze on it?"

"Ah, living myths," he says. "*Living* myths, my friend."

I bow. There is a truth in this.

AKHENATEN HATES TO LEAVE HIS NEW city, but he needs to supervise the building of the new temples he has ordered throughout the Two Lands. I am the only man he completely trusts, and he asks me to leave Akhetaten and travel to distant places for him. Basking in his love I still cannot bring myself to tell him what Ma-nan and Na-aghta have told me about my parentage: and without revealing that, I cannot ask for Merytaten's hand.

AWAY FROM THE PROTECTIVE AMBIENCE OF Akhetaten prospering in the hope of a new age, I find a sense of gradual dissolution. It is as though the boy who normally keeps the bullocks walking their endless circular path has fallen asleep, and the cogged and creaking wheels that draw the life-giving waters for the irrigation ditches are slowing down, the water now the merest trickle. The temples that have been the hub of the cities and the villages are lying for the most part deserted, weeds already cracking the paving-stones, wind-blown sand seeking the inner sanctuaries. City and village life continues, of course, but it seems to me there is a lassitude about getting things done, a feeling that no one would care or notice whether a new building were built, or an old one repaired.

I consider the dilemma of rulers. Rigorously enforced rules destroy initiative and clip the wings of those who are capable of soaring to great heights, but complete lack of order has the same effect, for they become so bogged down in the ruin-field created by their less inspired fellows who mistake freedom for licence to destroy, that they might well lose heart and give up trying. One of the old gods Akhenaten still has respect for is Maat, the goddess of Cosmic Order, of balance, of justice and truth. A pharaoh who rules with Maat keeps the balance between freedom and law. This Akhenaten intends to do. But in these outlying places, away from the charismatic inspiration of his presence, his administrators, confused by the removal of a neat and easy set of laws to administer, tend to bend everything to their own advantage irrespective of whether it is just or not. The old, old human tendency to go to one extreme or the other, instead of looking for a sensible compromise, is in evidence wherever I go.

I am followed by people complaining about the way the officials are exploiting them, the way the young are running wild.

"They care for nothing," the middle-aged fathers complain. "When I was young I worked from sun-up to sun-down and was proud of my work, but now they hang about on street corners in gangs, their only interest is chasing girls and beating each other up."

"The streets are not safe any more," mothers complain. "Our daughters are afraid to go out."

How sad, I think. *How sad that such breadth and beauty of vision should be lost like a flash storm in the desert. Ah, my friend, my brother, my king, you go too fast for your fellow man. You destroy the old order before the new has taken root in the heart.*

Everywhere I go, I listen and watch and note. I send letter after letter to the king, advising him what should be done to carry his vision out into the world beyond the shining walls of Akhetaten, but when he replies, he answers nothing in my letters. He speaks of family matters, or of how he has held a festival for Aten and the entire population of the city has joyfully attended. He speaks of a hymn he is preparing for the tomb of Ay, his father-in-law. In a letter I receive at Yunu he quotes from it, (though he warns me the final version will be more polished).

"Beautiful is your appearing in the horizon of heaven, you living sun, the first who lived! You rise in the eastern horizon and fill every land with your beauty. You shine and are high above every land. Your rays, they encompass the lands so far as all that you have created. You are Ra. You are far off, yet your rays are upon earth.

"When you go down in the western horizon, the earth is in darkness as if it were dead. They sleep in the chamber, their heads wrapped up, and no eye perceives the other. Though all their things were taken, while they were under their heads, yet they would not know it. Every lion comes forth from his den, and all worms that bite.

121

Darkness. . . the earth is silent, for he who created it rests in his horizon.

"When it is dawn, and you rise in the horizon and shine as the sun in the day, you dispel the darkness and shed your beams. The Two Lands are in festival, awake, and standing on their feet, for you have raised them up. They wash their bodies, they take their garments, and their hands praise your arising. The whole land, it goes about its work.

"All creatures are content with their pasture, the trees and herbs are verdant. The birds fly out of their nests and their wings praise your ka. All wild beasts dance on their feet, all that fly and flutter—they live when you arise for them. . .

"Ah, beautiful is the rhythm of your setting and your rising. Each day a renewal and re-affirmation."

But I know that the day and the night my king sings about is not only, as it appears to be, the day and the night of the sun I see before me now.

I TRAVEL THE LENGTH AND BREADTH of the Two Lands, from the turquoise mines of the eastern desert where I order a temple to Aten on the site of the old dream chambers where the miners used to seek inspiration and instructions in the dream state from Hathor and Horus, to as far west as the great lake, She-resy, the home of Sobek, the crocodile god, and the ancient labyrinth of Amenemhet-Enkh where all the numerous gods of the Two Lands had their shrines under one vast roof. I visit the busy ports in the northern delta where the trade-ships plying the Great Green bring beautiful slender vases from the Mycenaean islands, Phoenician silver, and timber from Kepel.

In the far south, in Nubia, I travel on pack donkeys deep into the interior, sometimes on rocky tracks so precipitous and narrow I think each moment will be my last. Everywhere I carry the message of the Aten, who shines on all. Everywhere I put the king's seal on plans for new buildings to his honour and authorize defacement of the old gods in his name.

* * * *

IN HIS BEAUTIFUL CITY AKHENATEN DESCRIBES on more than one stele the special relationship he has with his God.

"You are in my heart, and there is none other that knows you except your son, Neferkheprure, Sole-one-of-Ra, whom you make to comprehend your design and might. . ."

I return to Akhetaten in time for the distribution of honours. The streets are crowded with people trying to glimpse the Son of the Sun and his family. They fall back as I stride through, many recognizing me as the king's closest companion, and High Priest of Aten. As I approach the palace and the Window of Appearances that spans the royal road, the restless movement of people jostling to get a better position, the hubbub and chattering die down. The crowds within sight of the Window are silent and orderly, bowing in awe before their divine king. Each charioteer is beside his chariot, a groom holding the horses, while he makes obeisance. The fan bearers are in neat rows, the bowmen, the servants of the royal household, the officials from distant cities and their retinues. . . All are bent almost double, their faces lifted to the rays of light coming from their king, as flowers lift to the sun, their hands, with palms towards him, raised in respect.

I take my place among the priests of the Aten as discreetly as I can, responding to their murmured greetings with a nod and a smile, bowing with the rest. Our position is a good one and I have a clear view of the Window. Akhenaten and Nefertiti are naked apart from their crowns, but their skin has been rubbed with gold dust and they gleam like the sun. I have not seen my king go this far before, but I know it has been in his mind. He wants to make a point—and is making it. From his hands flow gifts: jewels and menat collars, goblets and exquisite jars of precious unguent. Bek, his chief sculptor, is receiving gifts, I see, and the goldsmith, Pa-ren-nefer. Merytaten, among her sisters, her gold limbs shimmering in the sunlight, leans forward to hand over a slender alabaster vase to the wife of Bek. My heart stirs to her beauty, and the beauty of her mother, holding her youngest child in her arms.

Akhenaten sees me and indicates that I must approach. Embarrassed that I am still in my travelling clothes, I move forward, bowing with every step. His eyes seem glazed when I am near enough to look into them, but it may be the effect of the decoration he has around them drawn with kohl, with malachite, with lapis lazuli. . .

He hands me gifts with his golden hands, and I feel no connection between us. I cannot believe this is my friend. There is such remoteness. It is as though he is inhabited by his god. Behind his shoulder, I see Merytaten's lovely eyes alight with joy that I have returned.

After the ceremony, when everyone has dispersed, I go into the palace. Merytaten runs to me at once and flings herself in my arms, the gold dust from her body rubbing off on me. I have been away a long time, and in that time she has matured a great deal. It is almost a woman's rounded breast that presses so eagerly against mine. I kiss her as I would kiss a woman, and for a while everything else disappears.

For the moment we are aware only of each other—but the moment has to pass. Akhenaten puts his hand upon my shoulder, and from his expression I see that he does not approve of my obvious passion for his eldest daughter.

When we are alone he speaks of it.

"I love you as a brother," he says gently, "but. . ."

"I am not fit to marry your daughter," I finish the sentence for him.

"You are fit. Certainly you are fit, if she were not the eldest princess of the royal household. Take one of the younger princesses with my blessing. But Merytaten has to marry my heir."

"I love Merytaten."

"She is beautiful and wise. We all love her. But she must marry royally. She must marry Tutankhaten." There is a long silence between us. I weigh the words I am about to say very carefully.

"What if I were indeed your brother?"

Akhenaten laughs.

"What if Horemheb were pharaoh!"

"The king your father had another son, by a wife more royal than your own mother."

Akhenaten's face clouds suddenly.

"What are you saying?"

"I am the son of your sister, Sitamun, and your father."

Why does he take the news as such a threat? His face is dark and angry.

"You lie!" he says. "My sister had no son."

124

"She had me."

Akhenaten would like to dismiss my claim as nonsense, but he is beginning to remember his father's strange attitude towards me. He is remembering that Amenhotep called me to his death-bed, and that he was about to say something to me when Tiye stepped between us. He is remembering that she turned his father's head away from me and towards himself.

I can see that he is disturbed and needs to think.

I bow.

"I am not claiming the crown, my lord. It is your blessing I want, for the love I bear Merytaten."

"Merytaten belongs to Tutankhaten. He is my heir," Akhenaten says stubbornly. The thoughts I have given him are too new. He has not assimilated them yet.

"You speak a great deal about breaking down the old rigorous rules, my lord. You speak of love being the most important judge of whether an action is right or wrong."

"Love, yes. Love being uniting the heart with the Aten. Not lust of the flesh," he adds harshly. There is something in his tone that makes me realize that he is not just speaking about Merytaten and myself. I have noticed, since my return to Akhetaten, a certain estrangement between Nefertiti and himself. They are still seen arm-in-arm in public, but in private I have felt the tension between them. There have even been bitter jests about their youngest three daughters not being his. I have noticed other things too. The wonderful feeling of hope and excitement, the belief in a new age, is just beginning to lose momentum. . . just beginning to turn sour. There are little satiric carvings of the royal family as monkeys being passed around, and unkind graffiti scrawled on walls. The figure of the pharaoh depicted naked, with all his natural imperfections exaggerated, upsets some of the old school who feel it degrades the idea of the divine king to see him as no different and no better than other humans. Nefertiti's beauty is more to their taste, more in the tradition of the divine pharaonic images they are accustomed to, and on more than one occasion I wonder if they are not turning to Nefertiti more than they are to him, and if he is sensing this and resenting it. She is a shrewd and intelligent woman, and I have never felt completely at ease in her presence. It would not surprise me if she were deliberately cultivating interest in herself at his expense. It would also not surprise me if the rumours were true that her youngest three daughters are not Akhenaten's. Are they Horemheb's? I look at them hard, but can see no proof one way or the other. The image of Nefertiti herself is reflected in their features. Horemheb himself has no children with his own wife.

"My love for Merytaten goes deeper than the flesh, my lord," I insist.

Suddenly Akhenaten sighs deeply.

"Sometimes, Djehuti-kheper-Ra, I wish I did not carry the burden of the double crown." He is silent a long time after this, and then he says, but not with as much conviction as before: "Tutankhaten is my heir. Merytaten will marry him."

"And what if I am your brother?"

"You are the brother of my heart whether you are my father's son or not, but I will hear no more talk of you and Merytaten."

I am silent. I will wait. Another time he may listen, and give his blessing. I am not the only one to have noticed that his moods are erratic and changeable.

I am surprised he did not make more of my announcement that I am his brother. Perhaps it does not come to him as unexpectedly as I had thought it would.

I bow and take my leave.

MERYTATEN AND I ARE UNITED NOW in everything but the king's official blessing. There is a pleasure-palace in the south of Akhetaten at Meru-Aten, where we spend much time walking in the gardens, rowing on the lake, and lying together in her chamber.

"If I bear your child, he will let us marry," she says. I kiss the lids of her eyes and her hair and her breasts and say "Yes", but know that the one will not necessarily follow the other.

My tongue seeks out every secret part of her, and my seed flows in her like the great river itself.

We grow careless, forgetting that just because our love-making is so intensely private to us it can be put to public use. Ma-nan and Na-aghta have not given up, and I receive a message that if I do not arrange to meet them at a certain house in Waset on a certain date, it will be the worse for someone I love. My heart is cold. I tell Merytaten that if I fail to keep the appointment they might bring our secret meetings to the notice of the king.

"What does it matter?" cries Merytaten. "I want them brought to the notice of the king!"

"He has the power to part us."

"No one has the power to part us."

"Ah, my love—if only that were so."

"I'll come with you, and tell them what I think of them."

I have not told her all about Ma-nan and Na-aghta, nor about the secret of my birth. She knows only that the two men are threatening me in some way. How can I explain to her who has lived all her life in the warm glow of the Aten, the way these men have found to rouse the darkest side of me? I tell her now a little of my youth and the terror in which Ma-nan held me, but I can see she doesn't understand why I allowed myself to be so held.

I tell her she cannot come with me, it might be dangerous.

"We will send some of my father's soldiers to arrest them," she says at once. "The priests of Amun have no power any more."

How little she understands how men who have once had power go to any lengths to keep it. They may change their masks, but rarely their hearts. Even I in some dark and guilty corner of my heart still harbour the temptation to reach for the crook and the flail. Ma-nan and Na-aghta can give them to me. Or if not them alone, then Horemheb, who appears to be in league with them. My conscious mind has totally rejected their offer and my conscious attitude to my king is totally honourable: but that little maggot still gnaws where no light reaches. I suppose I hope that somehow I will be able to have Merytaten and the throne, and still keep an honourable friendship with Akhenaten. A co-regency perhaps.

Anger at myself and fear of the danger we are in causes me to seize her fiercely, kissing her so hard and deep she struggles to draw back, her eyes suddenly alarmed. I hold her thighs and thrust into her so savagely she cries out. When I am done it is my turn to be ashamed. What kind of loving is that, I ask myself. It is no more than a cry of fear, a desperate attempt to fuse us together so that we may never be parted. But—and I look at her hurt and angry eyes—have I not brought about the opposite of what I wanted? For the first time, I look into her eyes after love-making and know that she has not been with me.

"I'm sorry," I say humbly, my voice breaking huskily.

She looks at me for a moment, puzzled, and then draws me close into her arms again.

"It's all right," she whispers. "You must have had your reasons."

I kiss her very, very tenderly now and touch her where she needs to he touched—but gently. She winces at first, but then sighs, and slowly, slowly I bring her to the point where everything is loosened, everything flows, and sweetness of feeling is beyond words.

I GO TO WASET WITHOUT HER.

The mighty priest of Amun, who had lived in luxury like a king, greets me in a house like any other house, a small entrance courtyard, a small, dark, cool room leading off from it; no more than three or four rooms in all beyond that.

He is alone: I, ill at ease. Since I received the message I have discovered in my own experience the reason why oracles are supposed to be celibate. My mind is in turmoil. All the levels of my love for Merytaten are active. I feel her in my body, in my mind, in my soul. I cannot reach to the level where I am spirit. I cry to Khurahtaten for help, but I have lost the skill of going into the silence. I have lost the means of reaching him. I cannot feel anything but anxiety that she will be harmed, that I will have brought harm to the person I love most in life.

Why? I cry bitterly to Nut, as she stretches over me, dark and vibrant with stars; the little boat I am on pushing through the black water, the cool night wind filling its sail. *I am trying so hard to bring about good in the world. Why. . . why. . . why does it always turn into evil?* I know my words are unreasonable. I know the wording of the question is wrong. Only the arid desert, where it is flat as a paved floor, has no shadows, and even there, though it cannot be seen, the darkness bides beneath each grain of sand. Light and dark is the pattern of life. It is so. I cannot change it. Rather should I ask: "Now that this evil has come to me how should I transform it into good?"

My love for Merytaten might be distracting me from using my skills as oracle, but it has given me other advantages, confidence in myself as man for one, and a greater understanding of what it means to be human. I had in the past perhaps been too concerned with reaching directly after spirit, almost ignoring the fact that I am also body and soul. I look at Na-aghta's bitter, triumphant face and know that the twist on it comes from something that has happened to him in his life that he has not been able to accept and transform, and has nothing to do with me.

Na-aghta, friend, I think, *let it go before it destroys you.*

I no longer feel nervous. I know who I am and what I am doing.

"You threatened me, Na-aghta?" I say, giving him no titles.

"You and your king have tried to destroy me," he replies coldly.

"No," I say. "No man can destroy another. It can only be the man's gift to himself."

He scowls.

"Don't preach at me, priest. I know the games you play."

I acknowledge his words with a bow, but my eyes are wary. It is true that if he destroys me it will be only with my own connivance, resigning myself to the dark, abandoning hope—but my love for Merytaten is strong, and shouts from my whole being. If he were to touch her, immortal as she is, I know I would have no strength or courage left, no capacity for transformation, no life worth living. Ah—there is my weakness!

He smiles. He can read my mind easily.

"You can save the princess if you wish," he says smoothly, smiling, knowing what he knows.

I look at him, but say nothing. Waiting.

"The infant Tutankhaten is too young to rule. . . but you are of the right age and of the royal line."

"The Two Lands has a king," I say sharply.

"I am a seer," he says slyly. "I have knowledge that the king will not live long."

"You lie. You are no seer. If you have that knowledge it is because you plan to murder him!"

"Watch what you think, my lord. Every thought is an action."

"Watch what *you* think, sir. Your thoughts are treason."

"Who will call me to account?"

"I will."

"You forget the princess."

"I left the princess in good hands. She is with Nezem-mut, her aunt."

Na-aghta smiles mockingly. "Nezem-mut is General Horemheb's future wife."

"Never," I shout, shocked, and now no longer confident. If I had not been so concerned every moment of the day to be with my love I would have noticed a net of intrigue tightening round the court. Looking back now, I see it. Is Akhenaten aware of it? I doubt it. It is I who should have warned him. It is I who should have protected him. At this moment I am bitterly ashamed of my obsession with Merytaten.

"I offer you the princess as wife. I offer you the Kingdom of the Two Lands," Na-aghta says softly.

I can hear my heart beating.

A few years ago it was enough that I walked about in the sunshine and had a name; now do I covet so much more?

He notices my hesitation, and waits.

I hear a faint sound behind me, and turn to find Ma-nan, dark-cloaked, standing in the doorway. I wonder if I will get out of this room alive if I refuse. This would not worry me so much if Merytaten were not under their dark shadow. Perhaps, I think, perhaps if I let them kill me, they will spare her. After all, they will want her blood-line to legitimise the next of their candidates. Something moves on my left. I swing round and face a giant cobra with a golden eye. It is raised to strike but pauses, as though held in thrall by Ma-nan's dark powers. To the right, another sound, and there I sense a form so loathsome that the devourer of hearts so frequently depicted in tombs would seem beautiful in comparison. It is the shadow of slime, the slime of shadow, formless yet moving to take on every disgusting form I can conceive of. For a moment I fancy I glimpse Merytaten's exquisite body being sucked into it, hear her desperate cry for help.

"Enough!" I shout. It requires a tremendous effort of will to convince myself that the images are only illusion. But I succeed, and they vanish instantly. I am alone with the two men, but I have seen enough to know what they can do to Merytaten if they *choose,* and I know that her resistance to them may be considerably less than my own. Or will the innocence of her heart protect her where the guilt of mine cannot?

"I can't give you my answer now. I need to think about it," I say, believing that in this way I will be able to leave the room and warn my king.

"We'll hold the princess until you have decided," Na-aghta says. "If you warn Akhenaten, she will die."

"And not easily," Ma-nan adds darkly.

I round on him.

"What do you hope to gain from me?" I shout. "I am a priest of Aten and will uphold its worship even when I am king."

"We do not ask that Aten be abandoned," Na-aghta says quietly. "Only that Amun, our father, be reinstated."

Will I do that? Will I? What makes them think this? It is true that my vision is not always the same as the king's: but then, is any person's the same as another's? I have thought more than once that if I were king I would somehow integrate the old religion with the new, rather than try to abolish it altogether. I would make adjustments, change emphasis, bring to the surface the forgotten deeper meanings of the ancient images.

Suddenly I feel deathly cold. I realize it is not because I have a different vision they want me as pharaoh, but because they have established power over my mind and body. Even now I find I cannot move my limbs. I am slipping back under their control.

"Khurahtaten!" I call. No sound from my lips. Only my mind forming the word of his name, my heart the love I bear him. He is here. I know he is. But he cannot reach me. I have put barriers up against him in my arrogance. Through my desire to stand alone, I now stand alone.

Ma-nan is forcing his ugly images on me, surrounding me with ghouls. I can feel a scream of terror rising in my throat—and then. . . and then it comes to me that if they can do this, *so can I.* A dark and fearful horde of images come racing to my mind, and with a bitter inner violence I project them outwards. I see Na-aghta blanche, and then Ma-nan stagger. A fierce joy possesses me. *I too can play this game.* I too can make people cringe in terror, plead for mercy. The thrill of it makes me forget all else. The sense of power, of revenge, is intoxicating. I want to go on and on. I want to kill them with this new and deadly weapon I have discovered in myself. And indeed I might have done so, had they been defenceless ordinary people. . . but after the first shock they rally and for a long, tense moment we stand at stalemate—in empty darkness—impotent and powerless to hurt each other.

It is I who crack first. I can feel my concentration slipping. I can feel the return of fear. I fling myself at the door before it gets out of control. I use all my strength, and burst out into the close, hot streets of the city. I shoulder people aside as I run. I think of nothing but of getting away.

131

It is only when I am on the boat returning to Akhetaten that the full significance of what I have done dawns on me. Ma-nan has won. I have become no better than he. I can always in the end run away from Ma-nan—but will I ever escape the dark stain that is now on my own heart?

The boat cuts through the waters of the great river. I weep: filled with shame.

ON MY RETURN TO AKHETATEN I find that Merytaten has been taken ill. The physician cannot decide what is the matter with her, and Nefertiti and the king are by her side, deadly afraid that she will be taken from them as little Maketaten had been. When I hear the news I am in despair. This is the work of my enemies surely. With a chill heart, I hurry to her side. I have no confidence that I will be able to help her, now that I have taken the darkness into my own soul.

She is lying very still, very pale.

"She has no fever," the physician tells me. "It is almost as though she has ceased to live, and yet cannot die." I lean over her, calling her name, thinking without hope that perhaps her illness could have been caused by her fears for me, and now that I am safe returned she will instantly recover. It is indeed a false hope. She does not move. Even her eyelids are still—no dreams disturbing the no-man's-land where she has gone.

"It is enchantment," Nefertiti says anxiously. "There is no other explanation possible."

My eyes give me away.

"What do you know of it?" she demands.

I cannot answer her. How can I tell them what has passed between those demon priests and myself, and what will save their daughter's life? I am aware that the room has gone very quiet, and everyone is staring at me. Akhenaten's eyes are full of such pleading misery, it almost breaks my heart to see them; the high colour of anger is beginning to stain Nefertiti's cheeks.

"What have you done to her?" she cries.

"Nothing. I have done nothing. I swear it!" How easily the lie is spoken. I am blind, deaf, dumb on all the rich and varied levels of my being. I have forfeited my inner strength; the help of Khurahtaten; the help of my god.

132

Seeing that she suspects me of causing Merytaten's illness, and seeing the emotions in my face, Akhenaten begins to suspect me too, and in his suffering seizes my arms and shakes me, thrusting his face close to mine.

"I told you you could not have her. Is this your work? Is it?"

He is not as strong as I, but his passion makes him strong, and my guilt weakens me. What have I done to this beloved friend who asked me to leave his daughter alone? It is because I love her she is lying here. It is because I love her that she will die.

"I love her," I cry out at last, and the suffering in my voice will surely convince them that I am innocent. "I could not harm her. I would not harm her. If anyone's it is the work of—" I pause. Behind the queen I have just noticed her sister, Nezem-mut.

Nezem-mut may be as plain as her sister is beautiful, but I have always liked her. Surely, surely it cannot be possible that she would—but Na-aghta has said that she is to be the wife of Horemheb. If I could do what I have done, who knows what dark passions surge in Nezem-mut's apparently calm breast. I find it significant that as soon as I look at her she turns her back, and goes to stare out of the window. I can feel her agitation without even seeing her eyes. Is she caught in the same spider's web as I?

"Nezem-mut," I say in a low voice, so low that no one hears, not even Akhenaten who is almost on top of me. But Nezem-mut hears. She turns, her face red and swollen with tears.

"This is the work of the priests of Amun," she bursts out, almost choking on her sobs. The eyes of everyone in the room are drawn to her now, and I am as instantly forgotten as the loser in a race. I see her caught in the charged beams of their attention, and pity her distress. She is torn, racked, tortured. She loves Merytaten, I know. Who would not? But Na-aghta and Ma-nan, possibly even Horemheb, must have used her in some way, as they have used me in the past and are using me now.

"Why do you say that?" asks Nefertiti, her eyes blazing like black fire. Her sister flings herself at her feet, beating her head on the ground. I rush forward without thinking and put my arms around her, lifting her up. I don't know what I intend to do. Perhaps I am afraid that if she confesses I, too, will be implicated. I don't know what I think. The power of the dark priests is in the room. Of that one thing I am sure.

Akhenaten suddenly loses control completely. In his mind at this moment there is no doubt that Nezem-mut is right—his daughter's illness is due to the malevolence of the priests of Amun. The hate he bears them knows no bounds. He forgets everything—the vision of his god of light, his belief in peace and love and understanding. . . He turns and rushes to the door shouting for the vizier and the captain of his guards.

"Arrest every priest of Amun you can find, and if they resist, kill them!"

He has tried to obliterate the dark side of magic by teaching that God is light: tried to break the occult stranglehold of the priests by stressing that the one and only god's healing, protecting, helping rays shine down upon the royal family, and through them are transformed and dispersed throughout the world: tried to control just this kind of corrupt and dangerous use of natural forces. He knows now he has failed; and in his failure he has probably lost his second daughter.

Inside the room, it is as though time has been frozen. The physician is poised beside a brazier where he has been burning herbs. Nefertiti and I are close to Nezem-mut, who has her hands to her face, even her tears apparently arrested in this long and brittle moment. On the couch with its golden lion paws and the golden lion head behind the ivory and ebony head-rest, Merytaten lies, exquisite, pale, totally motionless, fine linen covering her from foot to breast. It seems to me I see the wings of a bird folded around her, shimmering with light as though the sun is reflected off rippling water. I remember my own experiences in the House of Many Thresholds, and wonder if her ka is hovering in the room, listening to us, watching us. . . trying to speak. . . I curse myself for allowing myself to become so embedded in fear and darkness that I cannot reach her.

Break free! I cry deep in my heart. *There is a way. You are a child of light. Call on the Beings of Light to help you!*

And then it seems to me the shimmering light around her intensifies—but even as I begin to hope, a sound breaks the silence of the room, and I spin round in time to see Nefertiti strike her sister a second time across the face. The atmosphere in which Merytaten might have achieved her freedom is shattered. I seize her mother's wrist angrily, and hold her back from a third blow.

"You both know something," she spits out. "I can feel it. Tell me!"

I find that I am holding her arm, and the arm of her sister. It is as though we form a triangle, and I can feel the force of Nefertiti's will driving through us, taking us over. She, too? I am alarmed. As her husband's partner in both religious and state matters she has achieved much that is on the side of light, and I doubt if Akhenaten could have achieved as much alone. But she has always had a restless energy that could just as easily be harnessed for evil as for good. I, at least, am aware of what I have done and will guard against it in the future—but she is not so quick to analyse her motives and her feelings, and may go too far.

With an effort I break the contact.

"We know nothing," I say wearily. "We suspect it is the work of Na-aghta of Amun."

"Why? Why do you suspect *him* of all the Amun priests we have displaced?"

"He is a man of great force, and great determination."

"And what else?"

"Personal hatred of the king."

"And what else?"

She is no fool. Her eyes bore into mine. Nezem-mut has taken advantage of the respite from questioning to kneel beside her niece's bed, holding the pale hands and sobbing, praying to all the gods of the Two Lands for help in restoring her.

"You hear?" shouts Akhenaten suddenly. "She calls on demons at a time like this!"

"Not demons, Majesty, she calls on them only as aspects of the One God—the many hands of the Aten. . ."

"So! You change my teaching!"

"No, Majesty. I only draw out of it what is already there."

"I have forbidden the names of the old gods to be invoked. I have forbidden their mention in this city, in this land."

"As gods, yes, but surely as aspects of—"

He strides to the door and calls the guards. His face is distorted with rage.

Within seconds Nezem-mut and I are marched away as prisoners. Stunned and horrified, I look over my shoulder to see the outer shell of my love still lying unmoving on the bed, the lovely, flickering winged light gone, only darkness surrounding her.

10

THE RELEASE

DARKNESS SHOULD NOT WORRY ME, BUT it does. There is no measure of time here, where Ra is not seen to rise or set. I cannot see the stars. The moon has become a myth of pearl, pregnant with secrets. How brief my freedom was, how sweet and fragile. Did I dream Merytaten? Did I dream her limbs intertwined with mine, the trust in her eyes, the sudden laughter and the sharing of thoughts? In this bare room I ponder on many things, not least that my king of light, my dreamer, poet, mighty channel of God's will on earth, should make such errors of judgement. Are his eyes now so blind with light that he does not see the darkness under each grain of sand, let alone in his own heart? God is Light, yes, but also Maat and Djehuti and Ptah; Osiris, Isis, Horus; Hathor and even Set. Justice and Order, Wisdom and Truth, Creator of Form, Giver of Life, Resurrector of the Dead, Challenger and Destroyer. We may have gone wrong in worshipping each aspect of God as though it were a separate being, forgetting the whole when we worship the part, but is he not committing the same error, choosing light as the sole attribute and dismissing all the others as subsidiary? Who are we to divide the One into the Many, but who is he to choose one of the many and give it the status of the One? His revolution will fail because it is not grounded on the whole truth, but only on a part of it. In my darkness I see the shape of his defeat and weep. But need I weep? Whatever happens he has made men question what had become dead ritual, and no matter how those who overthrow him try to erase his name from the record, he will live forever, and whenever the flow of communication between god and man becomes choked with weeds and debris, men will stir to his voice again, and try to unblock the channel, free the flow.

And I, will I be remembered? Will I remember? This darkness gives me a taste of death, without the resurrection. Strange how different this room of stone feels from the House of Many Thresholds. There is no going out or coming in here, only abiding despair. I waste precious time in misery and bitterness, until a fine, small voice at last makes itself heard.

Passing in and out of my body
my soul sees
what I do not see,
hears what I do not hear.
When he sings
the birds listen.
When he weeps
the Great Ocean
absorbs his tears.
When he teaches me
I learn.
When I am tired
he lifts me.
What perversity
makes me
want to stand alone,
a dry stick
in a field of corn,
a dry stick
cracking in the wind?

What perversity indeed? I turn around from wasteful darkness and reach for my strength. My king, my brother, my friend is in danger. I can feel it. That he should leave me here is proof that he is allowing himself to be manipulated by dark forces. Whether they are outside himself or within makes no matter. I compose myself, and work on my old techniques for reaching out beyond the limits of my physical body to that world which is in neither time nor space.

If I had not allowed myself to be tumbled on the beach by every emotional breaker, I would have been able to swim out to the deep ocean much earlier and draw from it the wisdom I need. Now at last I have the strength to do it. My counsellor; my guide, Horus-Khurahtaten, is here in answer to my call. Together we will see what can be done.

SOUL-FLIGHT IS EASY WHEN THE HEART is right and the world is stripped away. My dark room becomes a sycamore branch, on which my soul-bird pauses before taking off. The falcon and I soar, the yellow dust of Set's desert flowing from our wings like smoke, Osirian green glancing off our feathers like sunlight.

At first the freedom intoxicates me. What could I not do as soul, untrammelled by the body? But the eye of Horus is on me and I know the task I have been set is all that I will have time for now. . . is all that I am ready for.

Things are at first confusing. How many would-be soul-travellers report back untruths, for no other reason than that they are unused to seeing with the eyes of the soul, and even more unused to describing what they see in the limited and limiting vocabulary of the physical world when they return?

DEEP IN MY HEART LIE THE images of the great spirits that my people call the gods. Generations of belief have put them there, and I find my thoughts fly to them now as the easiest way to understand what I am seeing.

It is at first as though I am floating through the world as I know it; unseen, but seeing. And then it is as though I see the same space my world is occupying inhabited by innumerable other beings, usually invisible to me, flowing through each other like the cross-currents in a river, apparently not aware of each other, yet affecting each other nonetheless.

Then I am in regions for which I can find no analogy.

Is it the voice of Djehuti, the god for whom I am named, I hear deeply vibrating in my heart, my earth-ears catching no whisper of the words, yet my earth-tongue already struggling to give shape to the sounds that are not sounds?

"I am Djehuti, he who is the writing reed of the inviolate god, the lord of laws, whose words are written and whose words have dominion over the two worlds.
. . . I am Djehuti who prepares tomorrow and who foresees what will come afterwards. I have dispelled darkness, and driven away the storm."

The chant, that is not a chant, is taken up by another. Hathor—whose breath is the scent of the sycamore in flower, whose blood is the green sap of the world, whose breast-milk sustains us as our limbs grow, whose music brings joy to our hearts. . .

Then Isis, whose fierce love protects us; who mends the broken, nurses the sick; whose mother-heart will never let us perish no matter how we are beset by enemies; Lady of the marshes, who solved the secret of the tamarisk tree and brought her husband back to life. . . Even Apep, the dark serpent, the destroyer, trembles at her name. . .

I have hardly time to adjust to the strangeness of the realms we are passing through when Khurahtaten calls to me, his voice a falcon cry. Now we are above the desert cliffs to the east of Akhetaten. Below us the dry dust swirls and eddies where workmen have made paths to the tomb of my pharaoh; the mountains crouch; the gullies, where storms have washed away the sand, lie serpent-like far below. The shadows are sharp and black in contrast to the blazing light of the sun.

Why are we here? I wonder. *I want to speak with my brother the king in his palace.* A sudden chill thought strikes me. Is he dead? Is he dead already?

"No," says Horus-Khurahtaten quietly. "There is still time."

We plunge like the birds we are, and steeply the rock faces hurtle by, rock on rock, layered through time like man's reaching and failing. In a dark gash of shadow a deeper shadow crouches—the entrance to the tomb Akhenaten is having built for himself and his family. The sad little daughter, Maketaten, is already lying there.

If he is not dead, I think, *why are we here?* But there is no time for further questioning: we are inside the tomb, our wings folded, passing like smoke through the mighty corridors. The entrance, a dark slit in the rock of a mountain, had seemed, like man, nothing very much, but inside, again like man, chambers and corridors filled with powerful and symbolic meanings, reaching deeper and deeper into the bedrock. At the time of my going to prison the tomb had not been finished, and I can see that it is still unfinished. Strangely, it is deserted; the usual clamour of hammers, and men moving about and shouting to each other, absent.

Rock-silent the huge central corridor takes us to the chamber where the king will lie in death. On the plaster walls the reliefs are half-finished; some painted, some not; the artist's and the workmen's tools still lying around where they have been put down. The flickering of light that illuminates these details is unexpected. The main chamber is not deserted, as the corridor was.

Within it, at the centre, Akhenaten is lying on a workman's wooden bench: standing behind his head, Nefertiti.

Startled, I look closer, and am relieved to see the shallow rise and fall of his chest. On his forehead where the uraeus usually rests, lies a large, translucent amethyst crystal faceted at both ends. The flickering flames of the tapers and torches in the chamber shining through the crystal cause ripples of purple light to play upon his eyelids.

My spirit companion and myself pause at the doorway, and make no sound. The two in the chamber do not notice us.

I feel uncomfortable. I am witnessing a very private rite, and am torn between thinking that I should leave at once, and anxiety for my friend and king. I myself, through Khurahtaten, have learned a great deal of esoteric crystal-lore, but even I would not lightly dare to do what Akhenaten is now doing. Nefertiti is holding a second crystal above her own head, also amethyst and also double-ended and the light of the wall-torch shines through it. I notice he has his right hand on his breast, where a scarab carved from amethyst rests. She plays the beam of light that shines through her crystal alternately on the amethysts that lie on his forehead, and on his heart, as though she is trying to stimulate some active response from these centres. I know what they are trying to do. Of all the seven colours of light, the purple ray gives the vibrations closest to pure spirit. To find three such large amethysts with no break or flaw, double-ended, identical in size, is rare and, once found, very powerful, echoing the mighty *Three In One* of the universe:

141

the Creator, the Creation and the active force of the divine spirit that infuses everything and keeps it going.

Nefertiti speaks the secret words from the old texts with confidence, as though they are not new to her. I see by Akhenaten's expression that he is deep in trance.

I fear for them, knowing that there are laws pertaining to this work, and that to break any one of them is to lay oneself open to great danger. One of the most important is purity of motive, and I sense that this one, at least, is being broken. Nefertiti and Akhenaten are trying to free their daughter from the horrifying spell she is under, and that in itself might justify the method they are using had that been their only motive. But they are also seeking to find a revenge spell that will destroy Na-aghta.

"*Stop!*" I cry—but, of course, my voice cannot be heard.

Is it possible that, for a second, Nefertiti hesitates? But if she does, it is only for a second.

I recall the time I, too, used the three amethyst crystals, the Horus violet ray, to reach the knowledge beyond knowledge. . . the voice of my teacher murmuring in my ears.

"Is your motive pure? To help and not to harm?

"Is the will concentrated? You are the potter's hands; if you tremble, the pot is ruined.

"Is your thought clear, do you know what you are doing, and why you are doing it?

"Are you working with love? Remember, if there is a grain of hate anywhere in your heart it will deflect the shaft of Light and bring about evil, and not good."

Nefertiti's voice is full of hate.

I try to bring my own will to bear on my friend and king, to counteract hers.

"My lord, be aware. . . be aware of what you are doing. The energy you seek can illumine men's hearts. In that seeing, they can change. Use this energy, not for revenge but to illumine the hearts of the priests of Amun that they see—and, in seeing, change their ways." Akhenaten stirs, and his eyelids flicker.

Nefertiti looks at him sharply. She is still not aware of our presence at the doorway, but feels something is wrong.

142

I call out again, and she looks swiftly round the room, her eyes flashing from beneath winged eyebrows like brilliant lightning through storm cloud. Ah, but she is beautiful! The strength of my will falters. Have I misjudged her? What the priests of Amun have done to Merytaten deserves to be punished! I myself long for vengeance. Do I not want to hurt them as they have hurt me? I remember the burning skewers in my feet as a child. I remember the beatings, so carefully delivered that no marks showed, when I was being displayed in the temple. And now the subtler tortures of the mind. . .

I feel the whiplash of Khurahtaten's anger on my cheek and stop my thoughts in time. He indicates that we must leave and I know that if I cannot help my friend I had better go. To join my hate to his would be disastrous.

I AM ALREADY BACK IN DARKNESS, and I am alone. Bitterly, I think how easy it is to hate one's enemies, how difficult to forgive.

Gradually wisdom returns and I take hold of the two truths that had nearly slipped from my grasp. One: that there is nothing, no one, that cannot change, transform. The second is that that which is man beyond his nine modes of being—beyond the three groups of three: body, soul and spirit; heart, intelligence and power; shadow, double and name—that which belongs to man even beyond the Duat, to the first thought, has all the energy it needs for moving mountains, transforming hearts. The magic tricks we use, the three amethysts, the green Osirian heart scarab with its gold thread holding it to the chest of a dead man, the amulets, the elaborate word-spells vibrating the etheric: all these are no more than the counting beads a child uses before it has a clear mental image of numbers.

Akhenaten knows this. This is why he has been trying to stop the trade in amulets, trying to forbid the use of spells, trying to educate the people to reach for a direct relationship with God. He sees himself as the last trick they will need before they are ready. He has spoken to me many times of the moment when he will step back and let the people "touch the rays", as he calls it, themselves.

Ah, Akhenaten, brother, king, why do you seek revenge through spells, like any back-street sorcerer and fallen priest? You have such greatness in you. Magic may be used for good. . . perhaps; but magic used for revenge is hardly worthy of a god-king touched by the rays of Aten.

How many days after this I stay isolated in darkness, I cannot tell. Some days I feel ill and despairing; on other days I feel strong, and thoughts come to me worthy of my training as oracle and priest. I try to use the time for learning, and in the darkness pretend I am dead, and entering with the sun into the twelve divisions of the night. With the sun, awakening to life each mansion of the Duat that we enter, bringing joy... I smile to think that as a child I had taken the twelve mansions literally as the hours of the night. Now I see this mighty myth, inscribed on the tombs of kings, in all its rich profundity... the huge wheel of Time in which the sun itself is born, lives and dies, is born, lives and dies: the body lying forever with earth-eyes watching the pageant, knowing that everything is renewed, is renewable, while the soul flies in and out of the tomb... in and out of the pageant... free.

Suddenly, the door of my room clangs open, and sunlight shatters like glass in my eyes. I bury my head in my arms, the light causing me pain.

I know someone is standing in the doorway, and I know it is my king, but I cannot yet bring myself to stand up and face him.

He waits for me to adjust. Slowly, slowly I lift my head, and blink at him. He is a black shape against a blaze of light. My eyes hurt, and I close them again. He comes forward and takes my hands, helps me to my feet.

"My brother," he says gently, "forgive me."

Now I struggle to open my eyes. *Brother?* He has accepted me as his brother?

He puts his arms round me and holds me close. I can feel the tears on his cheeks.

"There is nothing to forgive," I say quietly; and mean it. I have known anger. I have made mistakes.

"Merytaten...?" I breathe her name, but dare not put the question into words.

"The same," he says sadly. "But I have come out of my madness, and I know what we must do."

I remember the ritual of the three amethysts, and fear his meaning.

But my eyes are open now, and I can look into his. He is right: the madness of fear and anger is gone. He is calm.

He takes me out of the prison, his arm around my shoulders. My gaolers fall back, and press their foreheads to the ground as he passes. I am returned to the palace and given fine foods to eat, clear wines from the delta vineyards to drink. I can eat and drink very little. I want to sleep.

I sleep.

When I wake a harpist is beside me, playing, and a singer from my temple, with lotus flower on head and in hand, is singing. On a chair by the window my brother is sitting, gazing thoughtfully out at the garden. How beautiful this room is, I think, noting the flowering papyrus tiles on the walls, the ceramic fishes on the floor, the gold and ivory and ebony of the delicately made furniture, but most of all, the sunlight. Everywhere, the sunlight.

The king turns at once when I wake, even before I speak, and comes to embrace me. Then he dismisses the harpist and the singer and sits beside my bed. I lie back, enjoying the luxury of the soft bed thongs after the hard floor of the prison.

"When you were imprisoned," he says, and he speaks calmly, as though he knows that what has been done cannot be undone—but that I have forgiven him. "I nearly betrayed everything you and I have worked for." I say nothing, but am relieved. Perhaps my warning thought had reached him after all.

"I tried. . ." His voice falters.

"I know," I say gently, sitting up and swinging my legs round so that my feet rest on the floor. We look deeply into each others eyes. Tears begin to gather in his.

"Don't," I whisper, putting my hands on his shoulders. "Brother, don't."

"I nearly—"

"I know. But you did not. In the end, you did not." I kiss him, as a brother kisses brother; not as a subject, king. It could not have been easy to turn the power he had against himself and not his enemy, forcing his own transformation from resentment to forgiveness. "Now that we are together," I say, "and we are no longer crippled by hate and fear, we will surely be able to save Merytaten."

"I know it," he says simply.

I wonder about Nefertiti. Has she accepted the change in him? As

145

though in answer to my thought, he tells me that Nefertiti and he have faced a crisis together and come through it closer than before. He tells me he has had a premonition of his own death.

"What our enemies have done to Merytaten is nothing to what they can do to me," he says calmly. "I am going to knit my family together closer than it has ever been."

My heart beats faster. Does this mean Merytaten and I will be united at last? My thoughts wander off, seeing the wedding feast, seeing our chamber, our quarters in the palace full of light and beauty. We will make love in the full light of the Aten—no longer finding it necessary to hide in the shadows. I am smiling—but he is still speaking.

"Nefertiti is officially to be made my co-regent so that if something happens to me there will be no break in the flow of energy from the Aten," he is saying. "Ankhesenpaaten is bearing a child, but he will be too young to rule for a long time."

I can hear his voice flowing past me like a river. He has called me "brother"! What place has he in mind for me in this pooling of family strength? I would have thought his brother would be a better choice for co-regent that his wife. And what of Tutankhaten, his and Kia's son? Is it not foolish to cast him aside even before he knows that Ankhesenpaaten will bear a son? What court jealousy and intrigue will this not stir up?

"Nefertiti has borne me no sons," he speaks on, and I hear his voice now as though it is coming from a great distance. "Her daughter will bear me a son that will be greater than both of us. Divine blood will flow in his veins, pure from the Aten. His strength will be the strength of Nefertiti Nefernefruaten and myself, united and multiplied."

And if he fails to beget a son with Ankhesenpaaten—will he turn his attention to another of his daughters?

"My brother," I say, trying to keep my voice steady. "My king. If Tutankhaten is not to be pharaoh, there is no reason why I should not marry the princess Merytaten."

He does not reply, but rises and turns away.

"Merytaten is still in thrall," he says. "We must go to her."

He claps his hands and servants enter. Clothes are brought for me befitting a prince and I am led to the chamber where my love still lies. I am shocked at how thin she is. Her skin is as waxen as the petal of a white lily, and as fine. I can see her bones like crystal underlying it.

We sit on either side of her, one hand holding hers, the other holding each other's, so that we three are linked. Quietly, we prepare to relax. No words are spoken. It seems as though this time we know exactly what to do.

Above us we visualize the disc of the Aten and from it the rays of brilliant light coming down to us as Akhenaten has had it depicted on so many walls and sacred papyrus scrolls. But now somehow it seems as though it is here with us in this room as a reality and its power is filling us and is all around us. We see the hands at the ends of the rays holding out the sign of life to her lips and nostrils. We see them touching her eyelids and entering her body to infuse every organ with health. We ourselves feel the power coursing through our veins. Our hearts no longer ache for Merytaten, anxious and afraid. We are filled with the conviction that she will be healed and that if only we had sat down calmly beside her and called down the healing rays of the great Aten disc before, she would have been released sooner.

We are now using the ancient and potent symbol as it was meant to be used—as a visible focus for the energy of our own hearts in unison with the energy of the great creative and driving force of the universe. . . the will-thought before which there was no other.

We can feel her hands growing warmer. We can see colour coming to her pale cheeks.

We could have done this before. I think sadly, *if only we had not been so full of fear and hate.*

It seems to me that the three of us are floating. The room seems to have dissolved. Now I can hardly feel her hand in mine; but I can hear the beating of her heart in my heart. It is almost as though bubbles of light are floating up around us, and everywhere the light is becoming stronger and stronger. I know we have broken the spell. I know that we are all free.

How long we would have drifted like that in pure bliss I do not know. The opening of the chamber door brings us back to earth.

It is Nezem-mut, pale and thin from her imprisonment, but her face is full of relief to see Merytaten sitting up in bed, holding our hands, the three of us laughing like children.

147

11

THE FIRST DUEL

QUEEN TIYE DIES AND THE COUNTRY goes into mourning almost more for her than it had for her husband. For so many years she has been a force in the Two Lands. Small, wiry, energetic, no longer beautiful, but always fascinating, her voice has been heard in almost every decision her husband made in his last years. I have never seen the best of her, but I know Akhenaten is devastated by her death.

"The umbilical cord is finally cut," he says sadly to me. I am surprised that he has recognized how closely he has been tied to her. I stand beside him as he watches her belongings being taken to her tomb, and see the expression on his face as her bed is carried past, her favourite chair, her fans, her mirrors, her wigs. On huge stone scarabs throughout the Two Lands Amenhotep Neb-maat-Ra, her husband, had declared his love for her and his determination that, though she was not of royal blood, she would be accepted as the Great Royal Wife and mother of the future heir to the double crown. She was the daughter of his Master of Chariots, Yuya, a commoner, yet so close to the royal heart he was already interred in the Valley of the Kings. Everyone knew that if Tiye crooked her little finger the mighty Amenhotep, ruler of a vast and wealthy empire, would come running. It had been a measure of the power of the priests of Amun that they had crossed her once, choosing one of Amenhotep's other wives to play the god's consort at the Festival of Opet one year. Some said it was a deliberate act of defiance on their part because they felt she was diverting the king's attention and bounty from them and because she had caused one of their number to be humiliated and disgraced when he had dared to question one of her decisions.

Well, her son had tried to destroy the priests of Amun, and she had not objected. I had always felt that she would not be one to forgive easily. In recent years she has spent much time at Akhetaten and supported her son as she had supported her husband. She was a familiar sight seated on that very elaborate chair that was now being lowered into her tomb, in the little sunshade kiosk built for her in the huge, hot courtyard of the Temple of the Aten.

The little boy Tutankhaten stands beside his mother, Kia, and makes no attempt to hide the tears that stream down his cheeks. He has been very close to his grandmother. In some ways closer to her than to his own mother. Akhenaten is fond of Kia, but Tiye had found her boring and irritating and taken every opportunity to denigrate her and keep her son from her. Tutankhaten spent a great deal of time with Tiye at Per-hay, liking nothing better than to go boating on the lake with her and listen to her stories. As she grew older and no longer had her husband to occupy her time, her memories became very important to her. For some reason there was a remarkable bond between the boy and the old lady and he never tired of hearing her tell about "the old days" when Amenhotep and she had travelled the Two Lands and beyond to foreign lands as well. Tutankhaten listened wide-eyed to the tales of strange gods and strange ways and vowed that one day when he was king he would be as widely travelled as his grandparents.

Tiye died without knowing that Tutankhaten might never be pharaoh. Akhenaten had made the decision when she and her grandson were away visiting the northern palace at Men-nefer. It had not been a deliberate attempt on his part to go against her wishes or deceive her. It had been a spontaneous decision made during a time of great stress and confusion, but once made he was sure it was the right thing to do and she would eventually come to accept it. I was not so sure and was awaiting her return to Akhetaten with interest. But she died of fever in Men-nefer and it was only her body that was brought back to the south.

It seems the capricious arrest of myself and Nefertiti's sister has brought to the surface a great deal of resentment that had been festering unnoticed before. The manifest power of the priests of Amun in striking down one of the sun-god's own children (and for the second time) in her own home, many leagues from Waset, has caused dismay and awe. All the things Akhenaten had neglected, all the enemies he had made by trying to push aside the traditional in favour of his own private vision, has added fuel to the fire that is beginning to crackle in the Two Lands. He needs help desperately, and he can trust no one. The head of his army, Horemheb, has been seen visiting the outlawed priests of Amun, and shows a sullen resentment when given any orders by the king. Akhenaten is surrounded by courtiers who flatter, but whom he knows keep lines of communication open secretly to the enemy. Some of the artists and officials who have worked with him are loyal, and Ay, his father-in-law-uncle, the master of his chariots, and his father's close friend, remains at his side, though on the strength of this friendship with his father gives him many a straight talk on how his policies are bringing about the ruin of the Two Lands.

Akhenaten points out that his father himself had noticed that the priesthood of Amun was becoming too powerful, and had tried to curb its power and strengthen that of the priests of the Aten.

"But he used diplomacy, not force," Ay says.

"I am not using force," Akhenaten replies.

Does he really believe that depriving people of their livelihood, destroying their beliefs, arresting them if they demur, smashing down their most sacred monuments, is not force?

I sigh. Change through diplomacy and education takes so long! But it lasts. Yes, it lasts!

The next months are hectic. It has been announced that Nefertiti, Great Royal Wife, who has always been regarded as an equal to her husband, is to be formally declared his co-regent. Elaborate preparations are made for her coronation, and we are too busy to think much about Ma-nan and Na-aghta. Merytaten's love further distracts me. Pharaoh seems to believe that he has solved the problem by strengthening the royal Aten throne. Perhaps even I think the danger to Akhenaten's life has been averted by Nefertiti wearing the blue crown. The priests of Amun probably know that she has been turning more and more lately to spell charts that are forbidden, and has some views that are different from her husband's. Like me, she verges on a compromise these days, though there was a time she would not have considered anything but total commitment.

Perhaps the powerful and disaffected priests hope that Nefertiti Nefernefruaten will be able to modify, if not change, Akhenaten's policies, and will transfer their attention to her, away from me.

She takes the throne name: Smenkhkare, which means: "establishing the spirit of the source of light".

Akhenaten declares me prince, and accepts me openly as his brother, but he tells no one of my relationship to his sister Sitamun, for that would reflect badly on his own mother who deprived me of my place in my father's house and broke his wife-daughter's heart. The great Queen Tiye's memory is precious to her son and to her people. I respect this, remembering all that she did that was good. I wonder privately, however, if Akhenaten would have defied her if she had opposed the displacement of her favourite grandchild, Tutankhaten, by the unborn offspring of Ankhesenpaaten. I try not to resent the fact that I too have been displaced.

I MAKE IT MY BUSINESS TO seek out Nezem-mut, though it seems to me she is trying to avoid me.

I corner her at last in the courtyard of her quarters, feeding the fish. She is kneeling on the paving stones at the edge of the water and so cannot retreat as I come up behind her.

"We have to talk," I say quietly.

She continues to trail her fingers in the water, tickling the silvery bodies that flock around them. She does not look up. She is the thinner for her recent experience and it seems to me her mouth is permanently shut tight in a thin line, a small muscle in her jaw occasionally twitching.

"Nezem-mut," I say gently. "I have not come to fight with you. But there are things I need to know."

She straightens up slowly; very slowly. At last she is standing beside me, but she still does not meet my eyes. She is looking down, still at the fish swirling round and round in the water, snapping at the handful of grain she has thrown in. The water-lily leaves are fairly pushed aside in the excitement. Perhaps no one remembered to feed them when she was "away", I think, surprised at the way my mind is running on, occupied with the problems of the fish, when something else, so momentous, is clamouring for my attention.

"I had nothing to do with Merytaten's illness," she says defensively.

"I know," I say. "But. . ."

"I did not know anything about it."

"I'm sure you didn't. I'm not accusing you, but. . ."

"You do accuse me!" She looks suddenly up into my face and her own expression is tormented. "I've seen the way you look at me. I've seen the way you pursue me."

"Believe me," I say. "I'm accusing you of nothing. It's just that I heard that you intended to marry Horemheb and. . ."

"Marry General Horemheb!" she exclaims, and I am sure there is genuine astonishment in her face.

"Have I been misinformed?" I am almost equally surprised. I had believed Ma-nan's statement completely, and when she behaved as though she knew more than I did about Merytaten's condition when we were both accused, I had thought it was confirmed.

"Who informed you?" She is standing straight up now, her thin face as tense as before, her eyes guarded and angry—so like Nefertiti and yet so unlike. *Beauty is in proportion,* I find myself thinking irrelevantly. There is something in the way her features are arranged that make them miss being beautiful. But perhaps it is not the features at all, but the fact that there is no light in her face. It is always guarded, always tense and suspicious. I realize it must be difficult for her to live in the shadow of her exquisite sister, but surely there is no need to "shut down" like this.

"It doesn't matter," I say.

"Tell me," she demands. I don't know whether to tell her everything about Na-aghta, Ma-nan and me. I had been so sure she already knew. "There is nothing between the general and me," she repeats sternly, with emphasis. "I want to know who is spreading rumours."

"How did you know who was responsible for what was happening to Merytaten?"

She turned away from me and walked a pace or two.

"I did not say it was the general."

"I know."

"Then why do you accuse me?"

"I do not accuse you," I repeat impatiently. "I accuse you of nothing—though. . ." I pause, remembering it was when I said Merytaten was safe among her family that Ma-nan implied she was not because her aunt Nezem-mut was going to marry Horemheb. Was this just one more instance of Ma-nan's trickery—a ploy to frighten and manipulate me? Was it a complete fabrication or was some plot afoot to marry Nefertiti's sister to the general and make him king if I would not become their puppet? But surely it would serve the general better to be married to one of Akhenaten's daughters. They carry the royal blood line. Nezem-mut does not. She is certainly nobly connected—her father the brother of Queen Tiye and her sister pharaoh's Great Royal Wife. But Horemheb from a family of commoners would surely need more than her to take the throne.

Nezem-mut has turned again and is looking at me haughtily.

"I know you, Djehuti-kheper-Ra. I've seen you playing for power."

"I love Merytaten. If that is playing for power. . ."

Did she mean only this?

She pursed her lips.

"The king has said you cannot have her. Why do you persist? What game are you playing with the priests of Amun?"

"I would ask you the same question."

"I play no games. I observe. My spies have seen you closeted with the priests or Amun many times."

Spies? Always spies. Everywhere spies. Even when Akhenaten tries to keep an atmosphere of openness and trust around him.

"I have seen General Horemheb "closeted", as you say, with the priests of Amun more than I," I retort sharply. "What do your spies make of that?" And why have your spies not told you that the priests of Amun are planning that you shall marry Horemheb, I silently add. The general has no children by his present wife. Has he truly made no approaches to you, the sister of the queen? "If anyone is playing games for power it is he."

I cannot penetrate the veil across her face. She has retreated even further into herself and no hint, no clue, tells me what she is thinking. One of Nefertiti's younger daughters comes running towards us and Nezem-mut takes the opportunity to escape any more questioning.

After this I observe her closely whenever Horemheb is mentioned. She is old not to be married and I've often wondered why Akhenaten has

154

not arranged it. One theory I put to Merytaten is that it is because she is enjoying her privileged position in the palace so much she doesn't want to give it up to take a subordinate place in some nobleman's household. She seems totally absorbed in her sister's children and the gossip of the court. Merytaten's theory is that she has loved, or still loves, someone who is hopelessly unobtainable, and refuses to settle for second best. It crosses my mind to wonder if her secret obsession is the general and mention this to Merytaten, but she laughs at the idea.

"No one could love Horemheb," she says. "One might as well try to get warmth out of a statue."

"Maybe that is what she likes," I say, "she's not very "warm" herself." But Merytaten wouldn't hear of it. Horemheb was unlovable. She pitied his wife. "They've probably never had children because they never make love," she said heartlessly. "Imagine making love to Horemheb!" I was surprised at the vehemence of her dislike.

But now that I am observing Nezem-mut so closely I begin to be convinced that it is Horemheb she loves. She is instantly aware of him when he comes into a room, and too assiduously, too deliberately, ignores him. Perhaps it is because I've made her self-conscious about him with my accusation—but I doubt it. He, for his part, is polite to her, but no more. It makes me wonder if he himself is aware of the plots of the priests of Amun.

MERYTATEN HAS VERY LITTLE MEMORY OF what happened to her. She claims she knows no more than that she fell asleep and that when she woke she found a long time had passed. I am glad she did not suffer, but I notice that she finds it difficult to get to sleep at night now. She hates to be alone and makes every excuse to put off going to bed without me. Even when I'm there she fights sleep till we are both almost desperate with weariness. I believe she fears she will lose time again. She fears that someone will take her over. No matter how I reassure her, my words cannot comfort her, for deep down, I too am frightened. I too dread sleep. I am having recurring nightmares. The monsters of my childhood are on the move again. Sometimes it seems I am being taken into my tomb with pomp and ceremony, the women wailing as for a king, the sistrums rattling, the priests chanting. I hear the heavy wooden rollers creaking and cracking on the uneven floor as sweating men guide the huge sarcophagus down the sloping corridor. And then—when the pit is reached—they suddenly let it go and it and I go crashing down into the dark—the void—the maw of Apep, the serpent of non-existence, ever on the watch and capable of swallowing the sun itself.

At other times I am walking in a huge city. It seems more like Men-nefer than Waset, for its streets are narrow and winding and the houses seem to be numberless. A turn here and a turn there and I know I am lost. I am trying to find the House of the Oracle for at least it is somewhere that is familiar to me. But I cannot. I walk and walk through identical and alien streets, getting nowhere. Darkness is coming and I want to be under cover before nightfall. There is something I fear that will be stalking the streets at night. I start running, but am still no nearer my destination. Every door is shut against me. It is dark and I hear something padding behind me, gaining on me. My lungs nearly burst with the effort to run faster. At this point I usually wake, shouting, and Merytaten is there to comfort me. "There is nothing there," she whispers, kissing me. "It is fear itself you fear." If I was not afraid I know I would find my way. But I do not know how to avoid being afraid.

Then I find out that Akhenaten dreams too and his dreams are always about Amun. Amun rising. Amun striding. Amun raising his sceptre to strike the golden disk of the sun.

TUTANKHATEN IS TOO YOUNG TO REALIZE the full implications of his displacement, or even that he has been displaced, but it will not be long before others make him aware of it.

Merytaten and I treat every moment we have together as though it might be our last. When we are alone we fall upon each other and make love until we are exhausted; then we rest and make love again.

Akhenaten avoids the question of our marriage adroitly. I am anxious and impatient but do nothing about it, waiting for the right moment. And then what I dread most comes about. Ankhesenpaaten's child by her father is born dead, and he announces that Merytaten will be taken as his wife.

Ankhesenpaaten retires with her younger sisters to the northern palace. Each time we see her she seems to have grown older and more worldly-wise.

Merytaten pleads in vain to be released from the obligation to bear the next king, but her father does not listen to her. Nor can I turn him from his resolution. She moves into the royal quarters and I am held back by guards when I try to visit her.

I believe Nefertiti genuinely cares for Akhenaten, though she is becoming increasingly impatient with him and when they are together it is clear the idyllic relationship they once had is not quite as it has been. She secretly studies day and night to master the ancient magic. She knows Akhenaten is in danger, and believes she will be able to protect him by countering spell with spell. She looks on me as an opportunist who had the intention of coming to the throne from the very first. I, in my turn, am not sure that I am not bitterly resentful that she has been chosen as co-regent, and not I. I remember the early days sadly. How promising and beautiful everything had seemed then. What dreams we had had of our great city of the sun being a centre of light for the whole world.

When I see Merytaten beside the throne in the position of honoured wife, I find it hard not to cry out and seize her in my arms. Why do we not flee the city and find a life for ourselves somewhere far from the centre of power? We do not need the double crown when the love between us is so satisfying. She is so young—torn between people she loves; surrounded by shadows, by whispers, by secret messengers coming and going, by old friends who talk smoothly, but whom she can no longer trust. We still meet secretly, illicitly, and sense, when we are not in the forgetful paradise of love-making, that a gigantic shadow is bearing down on us, but we, as though in a nightmare, cannot move our limbs out of its way.

Each day, I tell myself that the next day I will speak to Akhenaten, and we will plan together to turn about the process that is causing such disaffection in the country. He is behaving strangely. He spends most of his time in the temple praying to his God and when he comes out and everyone clamours for his attention, for his decision and his commands, he brushes them aside with a gentle smile and a wave of his thin and sensitive hand. Nefertiti makes more and more of the important decisions in the country.

"All is in the hands of the Aten," he says quietly. "Our enemies will not prevail."

I am torn between the naivety of this, and admiration at the strength of his faith. What if he is right?

I tell Merytaten that he is wrong to think he can overthrow the customs and beliefs of millennia in one lifetime, and that his changes will come about more quickly if, paradoxically, they start more gradually. She resents my criticism of her father.

"What do you know?" she says sharply. "You, too, may only be moving small pebbles about in the dust while the whole world is in danger!"

Her words shock me, and for a moment I lose faith that he or I, or indeed anyone, can ever effect changes of any significance in the world. Then, I remember that even moving one pebble effects a change in its immediate environment, and any change, however small, has a domino effect. Who knows but by moving one pebble today, one may eventually move a mountain.

ONE DAY I AM SENT TO Waset to sit in judgement on someone caught attempting the assassination of the king.

The accusers bring the accused forward.

I stare into the cold, dark eyes of Ma-nan.

As far as the laws of the land are concerned, the procedure is clear. The man must be sentenced to death and his name must be erased from all records, his body must be buried without ceremony, and without any mark upon it to distinguish it. He must be returned, in other words, to the great void.

Only the king has power over life and death, but I have the king's seal, and the king's permission and command to act on his behalf.

I stare at Ma-nan, remembering my childhood, and how I had feared to enter death without a name, how I had feared extinction... until despair had driven me to court it to escape his cruelty. The opportunity for revenge has been given me without my seeking it. Would I be so wrong to take it? Indeed, would it not be an act of treason against my brother-king to hesitate, or to set aside a single item in the expected punishment?

Time remains poised in the judgement hall. In that silence I know that Maat's scales are not in some faraway chamber under the earth where the sun goes at night. They are here, now, always at this moment, and the heart of the living *and* the dead is balanced at every moment against the feather of truth.

Ma-nan's heart is heavy with evil. He knows it, and I know it. He looks at me malevolently, smiling, knowing that I am as much on trial at this moment as he is, waiting for me to fail the test. It is important that I do not give way to fear. Flanked by armed soldiers, clad in shabby clothes very unlike his former robes, he seems a very different adversary now from when he used to terrorise me as a nameless boy. I knew that when he was arrested he would have been searched, and there could be no resin to give off hateful smoke, hidden about his body. Nor has he had time to work his word-spells on me. I am in the king's chair, knowing that I am descended from a line of kings, named and powerful.

"This man," I say, slowly and clearly, "shall not be put to death."

A gasp goes round the hall followed by an angry murmur.

I wait for silence, and struggle to suppress thoughts of revenge, knowing that to give way to them will mean that I will forfeit the help of the great eternal spirits when I need them most, and that Horus-Khurahtaten, will turn his golden eye from me. I want to cry out for help, but know that this decision has to be made on my own. When it has been made, then and then only help will come.

I speak at last.

"He and I will face each other in single combat," I say, my voice steadier than I expect. "The Judge will be Maat, the Spirit of Truth, Justice and Cosmic Order."

I leave the hall, the courtiers and soldiers moving back in stunned silence. I walk with confident dignity, as though I have no doubts about what I have just pronounced.

When I tell Merytaten, the royal queen, she holds her head high and looks straight forward. No one but I can feel how disturbed she is. She is seated on her gilded chair, her face painted as a queen's should be, the wings of the vulture crown folded around her ears. On her breast I can see the love-necklace I had given her, one large amethyst flanked by two water-clear quartz crystals and linked by golden ankhs. I can see it rising and falling on her breast more swiftly than it should. On her slender finger she twists our ring, lotus of lapis lazuli held by rods of gold and turquoise. She knows the power of Ma-nan, as I do, and fears him.

"Why do you let him go?" she demands.

"I do not. Have you so little faith in me that you think that he will win?"

"You know he won't hesitate to use sorcery."

"I have known him all my life. He will not take me by surprise." I cannot explain even to her how important it is for me to have this confrontation with Ma-nan and to win. If I take the easy way out and have him executed, I will never know if I have truly learned to live my own life or not.

And then, because I can see the depth of her fears for me I speak to her like an old man, wise in years, telling her that of course life is full of dangers, but none of them are random... A man can swim through a river full of crocodiles and come out unscathed. Another can stand in the safety of his own doorway and be killed by the falling of the lintel. Death will come only when we are ready for the next stage of life.

She listens to me, but I can see my words do not help her.

"Many people die suddenly, when they are not ready. Many people suffer when they don't deserve it..." she says.

"The readiness I speak of is not obvious to the ordinary eye," I say, "but only to the soul. Likewise, the suffering humans endure has reasons only the soul knows, sometimes punishments for deeds committed, sometimes lessons to be learned."

She shivers, although the summer heat of the sun is scorching the Two Lands and the air is visibly vibrating.

MA-NAN AND I TRAVEL IN SILENCE. We cross the river to the west bank, only the water speaking, and are escorted beyond the land of the living, beyond my father's mortuary temple with its colossal images in stone. There we are left to continue our journey alone, the soldiers staring after us in silence, puzzled no doubt by the orders they have been given.

We climb the mountain, pausing from time to time to draw breath and to look back over the landscape we have left behind, the green and fertile fields of barley and wheat, the pennants flying bravely from the temple pylons, the gleam of gold from the tall obelisks on the east bank: the teeming, fly-ridden, noisy life of the pharaoh's people.

And then we are in an empty world. Dry rock, dry sand and dry sky...

To the hawk soaring far above us we must be two moving specks. How could he suspect that in those minute dark spots on the vast, ochre-coloured earth, thoughts could take shape which are capable of making the entire universe as small as a mote in the eye.

The reality we had believed in, surrounded by the chattering minds of others, has long since fallen away, and, faced now by an immensity of silence, and left naked by the removal of the opinions, explanations and beliefs of others, we face a reality that has no compromises, no comforting padding of illusion. I have chosen the high desert deliberately, and the dawn is to see the beginning and the end of our duel.

We reach the plateau at sunset, and watch with awe as the huge red orb of the Aten disc sinks in the west. I don't know what prayer Ma-nan speaks in his silence, but my cry is to the one there is no word for, whose cipher, even, is too bright to gaze upon, who was and is and ever will be. . . After the disc has left us there is a great hush. Silently the huge vault of the sky is suffused with red light, slowly spreading, slowly deepening. We watch as the night shadow comes creeping over the desert to tug at the crimson mantle of the sky. We watch until the first stars appear. And then, when darkness has won, we settle on the bare earth to sleep, pulling our cloaks about us. I lie a long time on my back, looking up at the sky, feeling the earth wheel beneath me, the stars wheel above me. We give the stars names, we even identify them with our dead kings: we draw the pattern they make to us on papyrus or on stone, and give these patterns names of power: but who knows their real names, their real power: and who knows what part we play in those designs, and how we affect those who affect us?

The star of Isis, my star Sopdt, is not visible. It will rise just before dawn, heralding the sun and the inundation. It is appropriate that Ma-nan and I should face each other at this time. It is the anniversary of my birth and of my first rebellion. Such marking of the cycles of earth time might not be very significant in the huge splendour of the great design, but without them earth-children are afraid.

I watch the star's slow, slow movement across the heavens and prepare myself for the dawn. There are to be no physical weapons of any kind. This is a mind duel, a soul duel. I begin to be afraid, knowing Ma-nan's skill in mind-manipulation.

It is when my star rises, and only then, that I begin to feel confident. I have the living god and all the host of the beings of light to call upon, while his minions are lesser beings, failed souls and shadowy figments created by the dark side of himself.

He wakes, and I prepare the field.

I take the one object I have brought from Akhetaten, a doubled ended crystal of total purity, a shaft of frozen light. I draw, on the loose sand that covers the ancient bedrock, a perfect circle, symbol of Ra's disc, the Aten, in turn symbol of that One which alone Is and to which all Other eventually returns.

Ma-nan watches me as a cat watches a mouse.

When I am done, and have spoken prayers to my god, I invite my enemy into the circle. The sun is rising, waves of its energy are beginning to touch everything into life.

Ma-nan steps confidently into the circle and stoops down instantly, to draw with his finger a five-pointed star, a pentagram, around himself, two of its points defiantly facing the sacred centre of the circle, duality, a gesture of obscenity to the One. Opposite him I draw another, this time one single point leading the eye to the centre of the circle. The sacred pentagram—the One, becoming the Two, becoming the Three. . .

We stand within our two stars and look at each other. I know I should avoid his eyes: but if I do I cannot win, but only avoid the contest. I am no frightened child now, I tell myself, but an initiate and an adept as great as he, greater in many ways. It is not the time now to think of my failures and my weaknesses. I dare not doubt that I will win. After all he has no tricks of his trade with him, no resin that creates bad dreams, no amulets or charms, no figurines for sympathetic magic. But he has his mind—and he has his eyes.

I meet his gaze steadily, visualizing within my own mind as clearly as I can the brilliant disc of the sun, with the long rays of its energy reaching out, each ray terminating in a hand holding the ankh, the symbol of eternal life. I offer it to him without hate, but not yet with love.

He smiles, and the long rays become hissing snakes, the golden ankhs fall from the hands and become scorpions that race across the sand to me. At the centre of the Aten's disc I see a black spot, steadily growing larger as though the sun itself is diseased, like a rotten apple. For a moment I wonder if the dream we have of the pure light of the Aten giving understanding to all men's hearts is a false one, as corrupt as that which we strive to replace. For a moment I lose faith. For a moment I doubt.

Then I force myself not to run from the scorpions and the snakes; force myself to destroy the visualisation, and make my mind a blank.

I call to mind the gods of the Two Lands, carefully placing them where they belong, as aspects of the One, as named powers of the Great Spirit, limbs of the Great Body. Djehuti, the teacher of wisdom, the opener of eyes. Ptah, the fashioner of shape and form. Osiris the resurrection. Hapi, the eternal river of Life. Maat, Truth and Justice, the sustainer of Order and Harmony. Hat-Hor, the great Mother, the lady of intuition. Isis—ah, yes—Isis. . .

As I call each name, and the attributes associated with it, I deliberately avoid visualizing, trying to disassociate the traditional image from the meaning behind the image: but the images have become too powerful, too set after millennia of depiction; and under Ma-nan's skilled direction they take form and howl around me in the circle, jackal-headed, lion-headed, scorpion-headed—subject, as images always are, to the corruption of he who conjures with them.

I cower like a green boy against their onslaught, overwhelmed by the strength of my enemy's mind, mocked by the fact that it was I who had called their names and thus called them into presence.

But this is sorcery, I tell myself, and sorcery, though powerful, cannot prevail against the strength of spirit. It is of the earth, subject to time and space, as fragile and transient as the earth itself.

I take a deep breath.

Beyond the false images is the horizon, not of the desert, but of the burning ring of fire my crystal-drawn circle has become. Within the circle the two lions, yesterday and tomorrow, past and future, crouch back-to-back. Between them, the present moment is poised, and in great danger. I step over that threshold with courage and am instantly No-where, No-time, and Ma-nan is without his protective demons.

Now I have the advantage, because as pilgrim seeking truth I have come this way before; but it is unfamiliar to him. The power he has trained himself to have is over things, and over people. He has sought for knowledge only that he may use it to increase his power over others. I have sought it for its own sake, and because it brings me nearer to the One from whom I come, and to whom I yearn to return.

I choose my weapon carefully. It is a dangerous one, and one for which I have to seek permission. It is the right to question a man about himself.

Khurahtaten takes me before the three Assessors who examine my motives, my emotions and my conscience. I am given permission, with the proviso that I am not to ask anything I would not be prepared to answer myself.

I look at Ma-nan, and he is there.

He seems to have grown in stature. He towers above me, magnificent in the robes of an adept, the inevitable symbols of his trade, the staff, the sphere, the feather. Behind him, rising like a thunder cloud, his god Amun, with eyes of fire burning into mine.

I cannot help but tremble. Do I sense that beyond him there are others, waiting? Are they waiting to see what the outcome will be, or waiting to take part in shaping the outcome?

If I win I will defeat more than Ma-nan. If I lose, I will lose more than myself.

"Together," he says, "we will hold the Two Lands in our hands. It is ripe: we will pluck it and no one will have the strength to take it from us. Think of that, boy-with-no name."

The old jibe still hurts. I fall for the trick, and try to assert my little ego.

"I have a name. Djehuti-kheper-Ra, Beloved-of-the-Living-Aten. Beloved-of-Wa-en-re-Akhenaten—"

"Beloved-of-Amun, chosen by him to lead the world back to strength and health when the heretic is dead. The name he gives you will ring through eternity, and nations will tremble at the sound of it. If you stay with your dying prince you will be forgotten before the present generation of men has grown old, no trace of you will be found on earth, no memory of you will stir men's hearts. Your achievements will be accredited to others. The praises that should be yours will be sung to others. It will be as though you had never been."

"Nefertiti is co-regent. Akhenaten's son will be pharaoh—not his brother," I say.

How is it that I listen to what he says, knowing that the threats he uses are threats I should be using against him? But I have not used them. I am silent, thinking of the power he promises me, the glory, the fame that will last until the world's end. On Akhenaten's death I could marry Nefertiti, I think. She and I could have a son. Or, if she could not, I could father a son on Merytaten. Indeed, I might already have fathered a son!

"Amun is generous to his friends," Ma-nan continues smoothly. "Did he not make his priests richer than Pharaoh? A pharaoh who honours him will be cased in gold when he departs this earth."

"And while he lives. . .?" I ask hoarsely.

"There will be nothing that he requests that will not be granted."

"Except his freedom," I whisper, more to myself than to him.

"*Freedom!*" shouts Ma-nan angrily. "What is greater freedom than being the ultimate power in the land, controlling the lives and deaths of every creature in the kingdom?"

My heart is like lead. "With the weight of all lives and deaths on his breast, how can a man breathe?" I say.

"Ask your brother," he says sharply.

My brother? Myself? But we do not see ourselves as puppet-masters, as slayers of millions. We see ourselves as entrusted with a great task, we see ourselves as channels through which the waters of life flow from the source to the hidden grain. We are free in the sense that we have chosen this task, and we want to carry it through. In another sense we are not free, because the means we use to achieve it are dictated by the end we have in mind. We cannot choose to kill those who oppose us. I cannot choose to kill Ma-nan. For in doing so the means will corrupt the end, and nothing of what we want to achieve will be achieved. Freedom is a word more misunderstood than any other. But one thing I know is that there is no greater slavery than being a slave to one's own desires—whether it be for material possessions, for power, or, most insidious of all, for the good opinion and admiration of others.

"It is my turn to ask you a question, Ma-nan," I say now quietly, feeling my strength returning, knowing that I can resist the temptation of the throne.

"Ask," he says boldly, confident that he has won the first round.

"Who is there who loves you, Ma-nan? Who has ever loved you?"

"*Loves* me!" he exclaims, caught off-balance by the unexpectedness of the question. He says the word "love" as though it is an obscenity.

"Whom have you loved, Ma-nan? Whom have you ever loved?"

His face twists, and for a moment I could swear his whole body visibly shrinks. He has never loved. Never been loved. Behind him I see that even Amun does not love him; nor does he love Amun. They use each other, but they do not love each other.

"Why has no one ever loved you?" I ask.

Will he blame others as he always has done, or will he look to his own blame?

"Why have you never loved?"

Will he know that it is because he has been afraid to give? Afraid to share? Wanting everything, for himself?

How sad, how sad not to know even what love is. I do not want or expect him to give me answers. I want him only to examine his own heart. It seems that this is already happening, because he is squatting on the ground now, his cloak like a pool of shadow around him, a frown between his eyes, his lips a tight line. The questioning continues. I cannot stop myself now. It is as though the questions are being asked through me, rather than by me.

"Have you ever done anything for anyone that is for their sake alone, and not for your own?"

"Have you ever done anything for anyone that has made their lives better, happier, richer?"

"I have changed men's lives," he snarls. "I have changed many men's lives."

"For the better, or for the worse?"

"Why should I do anything for *them?*" he shouts. "What have they ever done for *me?*"

If you don't know the answer to this, I think, *there is no hope for you.*

"Whom have you hated? Who has hated you?"

Hate, he knows. I see his thoughts, and shudder at the shapes they take. Even Na-aghta, who might have been called "friend" distrusts, betrays: is distrusted, is betrayed. I see by his eyes that he is beginning to turn: beginning to regret: beginning to find the hate-feast sickening.

"Ask yourself why you hate," I whisper. "Why? Is it because in seeking self-respect you think it is easier to push everyone down below your own level, than to raise yourself up to theirs?"

"The knowledge you have gained as initiate and adept," I say. "How have you used it?"

Here, for a moment, the old spark flares up, as he remembers the triumphs he has had using his knowledge.

But then the question comes: "Do you remember the law that governs the use of such knowledge? The law that forbids the use of it for harm, for the exploitation of others?" The expression of triumph leaves his face. He knows what law he has broken, and what the punishment will be.

He turns his head away from me. He is rocking backwards and forwards on the balls of his feet and his heels, hugging his knees. Behind him I can no longer see the image of his god. We are alone, and it is very silent.

There is one more question I have to ask before I am through, and it is one I myself would not like to answer.

"Have you ever heard a cry for help, and it been in your power to help, yet not answered it?"

His hands are up, tearing at his face as though he would like to remove all the flesh of it and throw it away. The questioning has been no ordinary questioning. It has penetrated. It has hurt.

I sink down beside him and take his hands.

"Ma-nan," I say gently, "don't. . . There is no need. What is past, is past. Come, look at me."

Compassion has warmed my heart towards him and, at that moment, witnessing his despair, I begin to see how it is possible for him to change, for our relationship to change. I no longer fear him. I see in him what might have been: what could still be.

I have won the duel with myself. Whether I have won the duel with him, only time and events will tell.

The rising sun sees two men seated in the desert; the young one with the old one's head resting on his shoulders.

The dawn breeze stirs the sand and removes all traces of the two pentagrams.

The circle remains.

No time passes in eternity.

167

12

THE DEATH

I RETURN TO THE CITY OF the Aten, and am greeted at the quay as I step off the royal boat by one of my lector priests, white-faced and shaking. He tries to draw me aside, whispering incoherently that there is danger, and we must leave at once. But to do so is impossible. Already officials are crowding me, and I am caught up in the elaborate greeting ceremonial. But there is something wrong. I can see it in the eyes of the men who bow before me. I can see it in the faces of the crowds that the guards are holding back.

I LOOK AROUND FOR THE FRIEND who tried to warn me, but he is now nowhere in sight. Is it my imagination or am I being treated differently from usual?

As I climb into my golden chariot, and acknowledge the muted greeting of the young groom who holds the reins, I know that there is something that no one wants to tell me. I wind the reins around my hand, and steady my feet on the unstable wicker floor as the horse tramples the ground uneasily. Haughtily, from this height, I demand an explanation. I note the looks that pass between the men before one has the courage to step forward and speak. Impatiently I wait through the long preamble protocol demands, until I get to the nub of the answer—and then I go cold. It is as though all light has been extinguished.

The king is dead.

"An illness," they murmur. "Suddenly... without warning... only a few hours ago."

I can see by their faces that this is what they have been told—but not what they believe. It seems they had intended to keep the news from me until we reached the palace. There has been no official announcement and the people are not yet aware of what has happened, though rumours have already begun to fly around.

As I hurry through the streets towards the palace I see nothing of the city around me. My heart is pounding with the name of my brother, but the reality of his death has not yet fully penetrated.

I find the palace heavily guarded by Horemheb's men. The general had not been expected in the city when I left. Yet he is here now. There is no doubt in my mind that he is somehow responsible for my brother's death. I also have no doubt that he will be responsible for mine if I do not take care. My skin prickles when I think about him. A strong man, always watching, biding his time. He has always disapproved of everything we believe in, and I know that if he could he would reinstate the old ways. To him, religion is entirely an exoteric affair: a matter of words and rituals, performed to reinforce the ancient grid of order that has held the people quiet and docile for millennia. He supports Amun-Ra because the priests of Amun-Ra support the army and the army is the pharaoh's strong arm. Without fear of a pharaoh with a strong arm, he believes a land will fall into anarchy, and it is surely this fear that motivates him now. I respect him enough to believe that whatever he has done he believes it is for the good of the Two Lands. The trouble is—he sees only the body of the Two Lands, not the spirit.

WITHIN THE PALACE THE WAILING OF mourners is already mounting to a crescendo. Akhenaten's harem of secondary wives are beating their fists against the door of his chamber and against their own breasts, the cosmetics they have used on their faces streaking their cheeks with black and green. I am admitted at once to the presence of General Horemheb. Beside him is the Princess Nezem-mut with her two dwarfs. There is no sign of her sister Nefertiti. Horemheb is issuing orders to a group of officials gathered around him, and a few moments pass before he notices me. When he does, he breaks away from the people who surround him.

"My lord," he says. He bows. His action is followed by everyone in the room. Even Ay lowers his frame to the floor. In these uncertain times no one knows who will be in power next and, as king's brother, many must believe that I will take Akhenaten's place beside Nefertiti.

"Father of divinity," I say. "Bearer of the fan on the right hand of the king, acting scribe of the king and beloved by him, overseer of all the horses of his Majesty and head of his companions, rise." The others I keep down for some moments longer.

At last I release them and they scramble to their feet, Horemheb red in the face with annoyance, knowing that I have deliberately kept him down longer than necessary and also given him no precedence over the others.

All look to me now for instruction.

Time in that room seems to stand still as I gradually adjust to the realization that my friend, my brother is indeed dead. Pain begins to come to my hitherto numb heart, a lump to my throat. Huskily I ask to be escorted to my king, and that the physician who had been attending him be brought to me. I am told that his own physician is away from the city, and Horemheb's army physician had attended him. I demand the presence of the second court physician. It seems he, too, is away. I discover that all the men who had been closest to the king, his friends, his favourites, are mysteriously away from the city. I remember bitterly that I, too, was not there when he needed me.

Nefertiti and the princesses are in the northern palace, I am told, under guard for their own safety. "I have to inform you, my lord," Horemheb says quietly, "some believe the queen poisoned Pharaoh."

Is this possible? *Is it?* I look at Nezem-mut standing behind Horemheb. Her face is drawn and miserable. I meet her eyes and know that she is as afraid as I am. She recognises my question, and moves her head almost imperceptibly. I am assured that she, at least, does not think her sister is to blame. They have never been close as sisters, but I suspect Nezem-mut would know if Nefertiti were guilty of such a deed.

"I do not believe that, sir," I say coldly. "The queen loved her husband."

"The queen is ambitious."

"If to be ambitious puts one under suspicion of murder, General, then you yourself would be under suspicion."

I tremble as I say this, but am glad that I have the courage.

His expression does not change. He stares steadily into my eyes.

"And you, my lord."

I can feel the tension in those around me. I can almost hear the crack of the soldiers' knuckles as they tighten their grip on their weapons. I could point out that I was not in the palace when the king took ill, but that he was, but I know and he knows I will not say this. I, and all who loved Akhenaten, are in great danger.

I turn to the door of the king's bed-chamber, and with some semblance of authority indicate that the people crowding round it should he sent away. The mourners move, but I notice his soldiers stand their ground until Horemheb gives the sign.

I pass through the door panelled in ebony and ivory, and enter the chamber, almost overpowered as I do so by the smell of incense. My friend is on his bed, laid out on his back, his hands folded on his chest. I stand beside him looking down. The embalmers have not touched him yet, but he is already as stiff as a statue. I hate the thought of their cutting into him, of their pulling out his viscera, his brain, his heart.

"Will you not speak to me, my friend?" I whisper. But he does not reply—and a terrible loneliness fills my heart. *What will become of me?* I wonder. *Am I in a position to do anything? To make any decision?*

Horemheb is treating me with careful outward respect, but I know he does not fear me as I fear him. If I make one wrong move, I am a dead man.

My heart aches for my poor friend, lying so still. He was a great man; a dreamer, a believer, a reacher after the numinous essence of the world. . . and now he is an object lying helplessly at the mercy of the servants of Anubis, who are already gathering in the palace, bringing their jars of natron and their polished knives.

I turn from his side, and ask Nezem-mut in a low voice for Merytaten. "She is with her mother," she whispers. "Under guard," she adds.

"Release her!" I cry, suddenly rounding on Horemheb. "By what authority do you hold the royal family?"

"I do not hold them, my lord," he answers smoothly. "They stay under guard for their own safety."

"Send for Nefernefruaten Nefertiti and her daughters," I say coldly.

"With respect, my lord. . ." Horemheb begins.

"Send for them," I repeat firmly. I am thinking: If I go to them I may be trapped with them. This palace is larger, more open. It will not be so easy to guard and is not too far from the quay if we need to leave in a hurry.

Unwillingly the general gives the order.

I go to the throne-room to await their arrival, watched by soldiers, struggling to keep the violence of my emotions under control. I feel I am walking on an eggshell floor over a bottomless pit. Where is my brother? Where? I cannot feel him near me. It is as if he has never been. I command myself to keep control of myself. If they see that I am afraid I will lose everything. My strength, my calm must sustain others. There were many things my brother did I thought I could do better if I were pharaoh. Well, I might never be pharaoh, but I was my brother's partner in a great and potent dream. It must not die with his death. Will I have the strength? It is not only fear of Horemheb that makes my heart thud. It is fear of myself.

By the time the women arrive I am in control of myself. I have learned that many of Akhenaten's closest supporters have fled the city and gone into hiding, some talking of leaving the country altogether. Officially there is no talk of assassination, but there is no doubt in anyone's mind that that is exactly what it was. No one knows for sure who is responsible. I can sense that our friends are convinced it was done on Horemheb's orders, though nothing is said to that effect.

Nefertiti walks into the throne room as light as a feather, her head held high, her blue crown giving her a height she does not naturally have. Her beauty, even after the bearing of six children is astonishing. Behind her come her daughters, Ankhesenpaaten looking tired and sullen, the young ones terrified, clinging to their mother; Merytaten, my beloved, walking slightly apart from them, her face drawn and dark as though she has been weeping incessantly since I left her. When she sees me her soul flies to me, and although our bodies are separate, we are together. Horemheb is with them.

Nefertiti takes her place on Akhenaten's throne, leaving the throne of the co-regent empty. She looks from me to Horemheb and back again with a hint of mocking challenge in her eyes as though to ask which one of us will try to take Akhenaten's place beside her. I am aware of the fierce, penetrating eyes of the cobra on her forehead. She has the vision of past pharaohs, the mighty god-kings who built the pyramids

173

and are held in a continuing dialogue with the Two Lands as long as their mortuary rituals last, as long as their tombs contain the ancient holding spells. The golden band around her head burns. It seems to me she is not gazing at us with her own eyes, but with an eye of fire.

Horemheb begins to speak, his words picked and delivered with great care. He had come to Akhetaten, he tells us, to plead with his king once more for help on the eastern frontier. Vassal kings are rising against vassal kings and to keep the peace and protect the pharaoh's interests in the east, Horemheb needs more troops, more weapons, more supplies. He claims that Akhenaten agreed to give these things the night before he died. He suggests that someone, whom he does not name, has made the king weak, turning his heart away from the empire his forefathers had won for him, seducing him with music and art, and encouraging him in his policy, suicidal for the country, of destroying the stable network of belief in local gods under the central control of Amun-Ra. He claims it was when he or she realized Akhenaten had at last woken up to the fact that he had to defend his empire and had agreed to give Horemheb what he needed, that, fearing loss of control and power, this person decided to murder him.

I look at Nefertiti closely. Is he suggesting that she is the assassin? Could she be the one? Her skin is like alabaster, her eyes lapis lazuli. I cannot read her face. It is too beautiful, too composed. I know she supported and encouraged her husband in everything he did up to the death of their daughter, Maketaten. But at Maketaten's death a change had come over her; over them both. There is no denying that they had their differences, but I had not thought Nefertiti had veered so far from their original goal, that she would even contemplate such a deed.

Nefertiti looks steadily into the eyes of Horemheb. He meets hers as steadily at first, and then shifts uneasily, lowering his eyes. She turns to me. There is no murderous shadow in my eyes. I can see she is soon satisfied of that. Are we to be allies now against a greater evil, she and I who have had our differences, our jealousies? The man we both loved is dead.

Ankhesenpaaten, older than her years, speaks up suddenly.

"It seems to me," she says-coldly, "the only thing we know for sure is that my lord, the king, is dead. There was no mark of violence on him, no drop of poison lingering on his lips. He was not a healthy man. Anyone could see that. He died. Let that be an end of it."

Has she no love for her father-husband, this aged child, this pawn in the royal game? How different the two sisters are. How gentle Merytaten, how hard her sister. I pray that I will not drive my love to bitterness, and I fight the thought that slyly comes to me, that to marry Nefertiti now, and to become co-regent with her would give me great power. I cannot tell if it is because I want to further Akhenaten's dreams that I want to take his place, or whether it is because I am admitting to myself at last that I desire his queen.

Merytaten suddenly stands up, her face flushed with anger.

"What do you insinuate, general? My mother *loved* my father!"

"Your mother offered *me* the double crown," Horemheb says drily, looking hard at the widowed queen.

For a moment her composure falters and its seems my heart stops beating. Merytaten gasps and stands bewildered, not knowing whether to hit Horemheb in the face for insulting her mother or to spit in her mother's face for what she now feels is almost certain betrayal of her father. Being Merytaten she does neither, but in her eyes I see the dawning of a great pain. She has not realized before, this protected child of the City of the Sun, how complex and dangerous life can be even among one's own family. Her sister has, and is listening now to every word with close attention, apparently unperturbed and unsurprised by what she hears.

I feel as though I have suddenly fallen through that floor of eggshell on which I was so precariously balanced.

Suddenly I am tired and long to walk beside the lake at Per-hay talking with my friend. Let Nefertiti marry Horemheb and rule the Two Lands. . .

I do not realize how unquestioningly I have believed Horemheb until I hear Nefertiti reply to him.

"You lie, General," she says, with a deadly stillness in her voice, reminding me of the stillness of a snake before it strikes. "I offered you my body—not the crown."

The silence is almost tangible.

For me the courage of the queen in saying this has convinced me utterly that it is the truth. Had she made that offer to buy time for her husband—or simply to satisfy a passing need?

A dark stain of anger floods his face, his lips move, but no sound is

175

emitted. For the first time I feel almost sorry for him. I can see that it is possible that he genuinely believed that she had offered him the crown, and that all that he had done was in this expectation. But now, when he sees that he was mistaken, he tries to retrieve the situation by destroying her and turning his attention to me. I realize his disappointment in her is what has probably kept me alive. He and the priests of Amun need me as an alternative if she does not prove to be as helpful to their cause as they would like. If I too fail them—there is always Tutankhaten—a young and pliable child.

The tension is broken by Merytaten, who becomes hysterical and starts to cry and scream and beat her fists against her mother. Nezem-mut, who had been sitting silently all this while, thinking her own thoughts, moves forward swiftly and helps me drag her niece away. Nefertiti remains unmoved, straight and proud, challenging Horem-heb with her eyes. Ankhesenpaaten watches them both with a kind of unhealthy fascination.

WHEN MERYTATEN IS CALM AT LAST, and I can turn my attention back to the others, Horemheb has left. Nefertiti is sitting on the edge of her throne, her face buried in her hands, sobbing painfully. I leave Merytaten in the arms of Nezem-mut, and stand before Akhenaten's queen. My urge to take her in my arms, now that she is weeping, is very strong.

"Nefernefruaten Nefertiti," I say softly. "Horemheb must die. It is not right that a general should accuse a pharaoh and live." What would Khurahtaten say now?

Who am I to take the power of life and death into my hands?

Does she hear me through her sobs? She gives no sign. I stand silently in front of her, my hands hanging at my sides awkwardly, waiting. At length the sobs die down, and she raises her face to mine.

"If we could only go back Djehuti-kheper-Ra," she murmurs sadly, "back to before it all went wrong. There are things I would do that I did not do then, and things that I would not do now. . ."

My arms do not touch her, but my eyes hold her with great compassion and love.

"I used to hate you," she says, looking at me wonderingly, "because he seemed to want to spend more time with you than with me."

"I used to hate *you*," I say, "because there were things he shared with you he could not share with me."

At this moment I know for the first time that my love for Akhenaten was also desire, and that my desire for Nefertiti is also love.

Merytaten touches my arm. She has heard everything we have said—and not said. She can sense the beginning of the end.

EVENTS MOVE VERY SWIFTLY IN THE next few days.

Horemheb is nowhere to be found, though it is clear, wherever he is, he has real control over the country, and that nothing is done without his knowing it. He has been expanding the army over the past few years, using his own fortune when Akhenaten would not give him help, and now has what is virtually a private army. The displaced priests of Amun have aided him, and most of the considerable riches of their temples, which should have come directly to the king for use in his building programme, have found their way to Horemheb.

Nefertiti makes the decision not to challenge him at this stage.

"He is too powerful," she says. "We, too vulnerable."

I am inclined to agree, realizing that our only hope for personal survival, and for the survival of Akhenaten's family and ideal, is for us to appear to acquiesce in Horemheb's plans, while watching closely for an opportunity to subvert them. In the affairs of the world, when you do not have physical power you have to learn cunning.

Merytaten is shocked that I appear so docile. I do not accuse Horemheb openly of having brought about the death of Akhenaten, and he in his turn stops hinting that I or Akhenaten's widow might have been implicated. We both pretend to the nation that the king died of natural causes. As Ankhesenpaaten said, he was not a robust man, and for him to die suddenly of an illness would not be unexpected. That all his closest friends apart from Ay and myself have disappeared is known, but not commented on too loudly by those left at court.

Ay is a great help to us and it is he who finally persuades us that the waiting game is best. A man who was much respected by Akhenaten's father, he is also respected by Horemheb. He is the bridge that we must cross when we want to placate the powerful general.

The tomb Ay has been preparing for himself, in the valley east of Akhetaten, already has exquisite representations of Akhenaten and his family under the protective rays of the Aten. He now orders the artists discreetly to introduce the other gods.

WHENEVER I APPROACH THE CHAMBERS WHERE the embalmers are working on my brother, I am turned aside, politely but firmly, by one or other of the guards. I am drawn, by a need I cannot explain to myself, to ride out over the hot sands to his tomb.

At the entrance to the valley that breaks into the eastern range I rein in, and decide to walk the rest of the way to the royal tomb; the clatter of the horse's hooves and the rattle of the chariot wheels on the loose pebbles annoys me. I feel I need silence, I need to think.

Once out of range of my horse's gentle snorting as he crops the sparse, prickly vegetation, I have silence indeed. In some places I walk on rock and between high, hard cliffs, and have the uncanny experience of hearing the echo of my own footsteps, but for the most part I walk on soft sand and hear nothing. The funeral procession of Maketaten had come this way, and her father's will be following soon. Occasionally, I fancy I hear Hathor's silver sistrum being shaken and a brief burst of chanting; but faint and insubstantial, as though it is but the memory of the past haunting these still mountains, waiting to be used again. I must remember, I tell myself, to notice whether Akhenaten's music is all his own, or whether there is some ghost music closely mingled, with it.

Narrow valleys, roughly carved out by storm water, lead off the broad processional way, some overshadowed by pyramidal rocks, others having no distinguishing sign. I know which one to take, and stand before the entrance to my brother's tomb. Who would know from the outside that this crude hole in the rock hid so much.

I stoop and enter. It lies as it was at the moment of his death—unfinished—tools lying where workmen have dropped them, the rock silent and brooding.

I walk down the long corridor where I had floated once with Khurahtaten. There is a terrible emptiness, a feeling of desolation. I feel again what I felt the day of his death. It is as though he has never been.

I stand in the chamber where his sarcophagus is already waiting, and I begin to feel a strange and heady drowsiness. There is a faint lingering smell of incense, from the time he and Nefertiti tried to practise their magic rites, but this could not induce what I am feeling now.

I sit down beside the wall and lean my head back against the cold surface. I can feel myself drifting off to sleep and cannot stop myself. Gradually I notice that the darkness I had fallen into is lifting, and I am standing on a rock surveying a desert landscape. The sun is a burning hole in the sky, the land shimmering and insubstantial. Above my head vultures are circling. I stare into the glare, trying to see what is drawing their attention. There is a dark smudge on the sand. From this distance I cannot be sure what it is. There is an icy feeling in my heart as I walk over the scorching sands towards the shape. I know, somehow, what I will find.

Buckled and broken on the sand I find the body of a man, already stripped by the scavengers of the desert, yet still recognizable to my spirit-sight as my brother Akhenaten. A dark and malevolent shadow envelops him and I know that a spell has been cast to hold him to this place.

I tremble with rage. Is it not enough that they have murdered his body? There will be no elaborate burial for him, no prayers to take him safely to his god, no place on earth where his soul may be made welcome so that future generations might benefit from his guidance and protection. Even a ghost tied to his once-earthly habitation, ceaselessly remembering the moment of his death, has the chance of exorcism and release. But here—who will find my brother? Who will set him free from this desolate place? I know it will not be long before they will hack out his name from all his monuments, and then it will be as though he has never been. . .

I wake, shuddering, and find myself in his empty tomb.

I hurry away from the place, driving my light chariot swiftly back to the city. I see Merytaten and her sisters in the garden of the palace, but ignore them. I rush up the steps, along the corridors, through the halls, until I reach the chambers of the embalmers. There, I break through the restraining bands of the guards and fling open the door. On the slab where the body of my brother should be lying, is nothing. The embalmers are sitting around drinking beer and talking, and look up with astonishment at my precipitate intrusion. In one blinding second I know that my dream was a true vision. Akhenaten's body is not being prepared for burial. The elaborate series of coffins that will be carried in procession to his tomb and eventually lowered into his sarcophagus, will be empty. No ka is expected to inhabit the House of the Threshold through the long ages.

13

THE DOUBLE CROWN

HOREMHEB AND THE COUNTRY ACCEPT FOR the time being that Nefertiti is monarch, but watch her closely. Merytaten becomes my wife at last, but there is not a night in which she lies peacefully in my bed. We are surrounded by spies, and there is no such thing as privacy, even in the inmost chambers of the palace.

I try to challenge the mortuary priests about the disappearance of Akhenaten's body, but am lied to so plausibly that I am made to look a fool for doubting that the carefully-fashioned set of coffins contains his remains. I am even shown a bandaged figure with each costly royal amulet in place, but by this time, of course, the corpse is unrecognizable.

The funeral goes ahead with the usual elaborate ritual, the final feast taking place inside the tomb as is customary, so that Akhenaten can take his leave of us as he would if he were going on a long journey. Nefertiti and her daughters, Tutankhaten and I sit in the chairs of honour, garlanded with flowers, the effigy of Akhenaten propped up beside us. Food and drink is passed for him, and the pretence kept up that he is present. Even the ceremony of the Opening of the Mouth is performed before the coffins are lowered into the sarcophagus, that his soul may be empowered to communicate with those in the Otherworld, and with those left behind in this. I look at Horemheb's expressionless face, and wonder that he has so little faith in the gods he purports to champion that he may mock their rituals so.

Oh my love, my friend, where are you? If I could find your broken body perhaps I could at least avert some of the harm done to you, by giving you a proper burial. Nefertiti is highly skilled in magic—it may be that she can help with this.

The wine is heady, Merytaten's cheeks are flushed, her eyes too bright. I feel so dizzy I wonder if it is drugged, and whether it is intended that we never leave this tomb. The singing of the young girls with blue lotus flowers in their hair is very sweet, but seems very far away. . .

WHEN WE WAKE WE ARE BACK in the palace. So we are needed alive a little longer? I feel each moment I live is only by the grace of the stern general. Everyone around me seems to be waiting for something to happen. Everyone is afraid.

Merytaten begins to turn from my touch, and I read in her eyes that she despises me for not overthrowing Horemheb. She also knows her mother's beauty has seduced me, and watches bitterly as I flounder helplessly in my desire for Nefernefruaten and in my fear of Horemheb. When I can think clearly at all, which is not often, I am shocked that I have abandoned all I have learned from Khurahtaten. No wolf trap is a stronger snare than the body's fears and desires. My brother's eyes haunt me. I tell myself my pursuit of Nefertiti is for what she knows, not for her beauty, and I watch for an opportunity to be with her alone. It is not easy to escape the reproachful gaze of Merytaten, or the net of Horemheb's spies, but at last we manage it. By trick and subterfuge we slip away and push out a boat on to the lake at Meru-aten.

Nefertiti is marked by the strain of the past year. In her statues and her paintings she will always be beautiful, and her beauty will live forever, but in the flesh now her beauty is tinged with a hardness and gauntness that was not there in her youth. She looks at me in a way I do not like, seeing into my thoughts. She waits for me to speak first.

I hold myself back, careful not to touch her, careful to look straight ahead over the water to the small island in the centre of the lake, fringed with reeds, the home of Akhenaten's favourite rare breeds of waterfowl.

"Nefernefruaten," I say at last, "I have something to tell you that will hurt."

"Tell me," she says quietly.

I tell her for the first time about my scrying dream and then what

I know of the fake funeral. I dare not look at her face, knowing what she must be feeling.

After what seems a long silence she says that she had not felt his presence at the funeral, and so is not surprised to hear what I have just told her.

It is a relief to speak about my experience at last, to share the burden of it. I cannot see her face because her back is now turned to me, but she remains upright and there is no sign that she is weeping. I am strengthened by her strength.

"You are versed in magic," I say at last. "Do you know a way of finding him?"

She is silent a long time.

"He forbade my magic," she said at last, in a low and bitter voice. "It would be an irony to use it now to save him."

"I don't ask it lightly."

She looks at me with those marvellous eyes, turning her head suddenly, my hands beginning to tremble as though the look she gives me is a touch.

"I will try," she says at last, "but I would be surprised if whoever did that to him did not also put on a spell against his finding."

Na-aghta would have done that, I think, on Horemheb's command. Ma-nan probably knows about it. Perhaps that is where I should start. But if he doesn't—or if he is back under Na-aghta's influence in spite of my winning the duel. . .

That Na-aghta and Horemheb have left myself and Nefertiti alive, seems more and more sinister to me. They must be sure of their influence on us. They must be sure they have us trapped. For a few moments I despair, and then a duck lands on the surface of the lake throwing up a spray of silver water, which blazes suddenly in the sunlight. I am momentarily dazzled, and then my vision clears. Hiding-spell or no hiding-spell I will find Akhenaten's body, and ensure that its soul is free and safe to embark on its journey in the boat of millions of years. I only hope there will be someone to do the same for me if the need should arise.

NEFERTITI AND I SPEND A GREAT deal of time together, not only dealing with our official duties under the watchful eyes of Horemheb and his spies, but also in seeking secretly for a magic spell that will give us the whereabouts of Akhenaten's body. Merytaten is very much aware of the way things are drifting, and retires more and more to her own chambers, making excuses that she is not feeling well, even when I do manage to visit her. I can feel the sadness in her and I fight it, telling myself that she is being unreasonable—there is nothing between her mother and myself but concern for the good of the Two Lands, and for Akhenaten's Soul. I know I am lying to myself, but I continue nevertheless.

I try to win the friendship of Ay, for I suspect he has never really liked me, and still hankers to place his protégé Tutankhaten, on the throne beside his daughter. The boy is growing rapidly, and I can see that if I am not careful he could take my place beside Nefertiti. She has not declared me co-regent—but has given me hints that she is considering it. I know I have come to have quite an influence on her. I make public declaration of my relationship to Sitamun, in spite of my brother's wish to keep it hidden. I hope it will make my position stronger.

I invite Tutankhaten to live with me in the palace, thinking that in this way I will be able to keep track of everyone he sees and knows. I have learned the value of spies from Horemheb. But Ay prevents his coming, telling me blandly that the boy is not well and cannot travel. He is resting in his grandfather's palace at Per-hay.

Next I hear that Merytaten is ill. When I break down her chamber door at last I find her being delivered of a still-born child, her women around her, and her sister Ankhesenpaaten holding her head. The anger with which this latter looks at me almost freezes my blood. I push aside the restraining arms of the women and fall down on my knees beside by beautiful child-wife. The pain she has been through has aged her. By the development of the foetus I can see that the child is mine and not her father's.

If he had lived my son would have been pharaoh.

I put my head on her breast and sob. Her hands take my head and stroke it, her voice whispers words of comfort. Once again it is *she* who apologizes for *my* cruelty, it is she who needs comfort, who comforts me. Ankhesenpaaten's face is distorted with bitterness. She deliberately spits on me. I hear Merytaten chiding her, and ordering her to leave the room. She starts to leave angrily, and then stoops down and picks up the dead and bloody foetus from the basin in which it is resting.

Horrified, I look up to see her holding it high above me before she furiously dashes it to the ground.

"May the memory of you disappear from the earth and no child carry your blood!" she screams and runs from the room.

I turn to Merytaten.

She has fainted.

I INSIST THAT ANKHESENPAATEN LEAVES THE city. She does so willingly, taking her entourage of women with her, going, on Ay's suggestions, to Per-hay to join Tutankhaten. She does not even say goodbye to her mother, believing as her sister Merytaten does, that we are lovers.

I almost forget the dangerous position I am in, and the urgency of my mission to find Akhenaten's body, in my desperation to make it up to Merytaten for the way I have been neglecting her. She and I become inseparable again, and are seen even in public locked in embrace, as Nefertiti and her husband once had been. There is an ominous quiet in the affairs of the country for a while, and I almost begin to believe that we will win through to a kind of peace.

Nefertiti now keeps away from me as much as possible, and although this pains me it is obviously a relief as well. I do not want to see her face, so like her daughter's, yet so strong and subtle in comparison; her figure still tantalisingly seductive in almost transparent pleated robes. I am determined to love Merytaten as I used to love her. I *do* love Merytaten. But increasingly I know my love for her is not enough. I need Nefertiti. There are things I can share with the woman, that I cannot share with the girl.

Forgive me, I cry silently, as I kiss the young girl's hair and neck and lips, as I touch her nipples with my tongue and feel my way into her body. *Forgive me that with every touch I think of Nefernefruaten Nefertiti. . .*

If Merytaten knows what I am thinking, she gives no sign. Outwardly, everything between us looks well and she talks of another child. It is only at night when she cannot sleep she remembers her sister's curse—and trembles.

One night I receive a message that Nefertiti wishes to see me in her chamber. She has been absent from the great hall and the council chambers all day, and I hurry to her, wondering if she too has fallen ill.

She is on her couch when I enter, and her women silently slide away, leaving us alone. The lamplight flickers warmly on her bare shoulders. A wrap as insubstantial as a spider's web lies across the rest of her body. I stand beside her, looking down at her. I feel as though I am at a cliff edge, deciding whether to leap off or not. I am not sure if it is an illusion of the lamplight or a real smile that flutters briefly on her lips. I can hold myself back no longer, and stoop to take her in my arms.

I cannot believe I have never done this in all the years I have known her. It seems now so natural, so inevitable.

When it is finished we lie silently for a long time, watching the light and shadow play on the painted ceiling, the canopy of flowers and leaves and birds depicted there.

"Why?" I ask at last. "Why now?"

She shrugs and draws her wraps around her as though she is cold.

"I had a fearful dream. I was afraid," she says.

I hold her close; these are uncertain and dangerous times. My dreams are fearful too.

"And now?" I ask. "Are you less afraid?"

She kisses me long and deeply, but she does not answer.

If anything, I am thinking, I am more afraid than I was before. We can both feel it, the violence just under the surface, the darkness that will not be held back for long.

"Did Horemheb?" I want to ask her outright if she and Horemheb had ever been lovers. I am afraid of the answer, but I want to know. I tell myself I need to know, for, knowing, I will be able to deal with him more easily.

She puts her slender finger on my mouth and stops the question before it is spoken.

"You asked me to find Wa-en-ra," she says. "Have you forgotten?"

"No," I say quickly, but I know I had forgotten—this night at least.

I rest on my elbow, looking down into her face, my own shading it from the lamplight. Her eyes are dark pools, her thoughts unfathomable.

At last she draws away from me and rises from the bed. She pulls on a robe and crosses the room. She looks over her shoulder at me and indicates that I should join her at a little table in the centre of the room. It is ebony, finely carved, and panelled in silver and lapis lazuli. I sit opposite her.

She places what appears to be an ordinary box of palm wood between us. It is lightly carved and painted with marsh scenes. There are ducks swimming and flying. There is a boat pushing through the tall stems of the papyrus, with a young prince standing poised at the prow. At his feet a princess sits trailing her fingers in the water and playing with lotus flowers.

The queen touches the box with such reverence I know that it contains something of very great importance to her. She takes off the lid and lifts out another, smaller box contained within it. This is of a rarer wood, exquisitely carved and painted with the figures of the forbidden gods: Amun and Mut, Ptah and Sekhmet, Osiris and Isis, Set and Nepthys. I look up at her quickly, surprised that one who has been so active a priestess of the Aten, divine herself, should have such an object among her treasured possessions. She lifts the lid of this one too and brings out a third. By its scent I guess it is carved from the wood of the frankincense tree. The ghost of a memory stirs in my heart and for less than a moment I seem to be in another country among trees growing wild on high mountains, a hot breeze sighing softly through their leaves. The mountains run range after range into the blue distance. . .

On the lid of this box is carved the ibis-headed god Djehuti, the ancient god of wisdom, and on its four sides there are inscriptions from the traditional wisdom texts.

She shuts her eyes and places her fine and slender hands on the lid of the box, resting on the image of Djehuti. I notice her nails are reddened with henna.

Then she lifts the lid and takes out what lies inside on a little cushion of finely woven linen. It is a green stone, rounded and polished. It is not as clear as emerald, nor as opaque as malachite—but somewhere between. She holds it with the tips of her fingers over the open box and gazes intently into it. I see that her lips are moving in some invocation or prayer, but I cannot hear what she is saying. I sit very still, knowing that this may be the moment my brother is located.

After staring at the stone for some time, fascinated—waiting for something to happen—I glance up at Nefertiti and am startled to see the expression on her face. Her eyes are very wide open, unblinking, the dark pupils expanded so that the iris has almost disappeared. On the black surfaces of her pupils the green stone is reflected. It is as though the green stone, now twinned, is looking out of her eyes at me. I am so shocked by this I cannot look away but continue to stare into them, into the images of the green fire in her eyes. My heart is beating fast and I pray for Akhenaten's forgiveness that we are using the ancient magic when he has expressly forbidden it. I ask for Khurahtaten's blessing and protection but do not feel that I will receive it. Would my brother have done this for me? Would he have understood why I am doing it?

Nefertiti begins to speak in a deep, man's voice. Her face is distorted and ugly. I am horrified, but I feel I have gone too far to turn back now.

I ask the being who has taken over her body where my brother, the king, lies—where I may find him and how I may save him from the void.

The voice booms out, speaking in archaic phrases, using what to me are meaningless jumbles of words. The voice rolls and thunders but makes no sense. My fear and awe turn to rage. I want to take Nefertiti by the shoulders and shake the creature out of her. It is so frustrating to be given what is apparently an answer, but be unable to understand it. We are being mocked.

I lean across the table reaching out my hands. In doing so I cut across the line that joins Nefertiti to the sight of the stone, and she screams and raises her hands to her eyes. I can see that she is herself again, but is sobbing with the pain in her eyes.

"Why do you use these methods?" I shout angrily. "They are danger-ous. They tell you nothing!" I am furious with her and furious with myself. I have subjected her to what Ma-nan used to subject me to and which I so hated. Khurahtaten's voice rings in my ears: "All that you need to know is already within you. Trust yourself."

I put my hand on her shoulder, gently.

"Can you see?" I ask solicitously. What if she is blind?

She lifts her hands tentatively from her eyes and opens them frac-tion by fraction, squinting at the light. She can see, but the whites are very bloodshot. I lead her to her bed and lay her down, a cloth soaked in cool water over her eyes.

"What is that stone?" I ask. "Where did you get it?"

"A foreign magician brought it to me."

"Did Akhenaten know that you had it?"

"Yes. But he told me to destroy it, or give it back to the one who gave it to me. But I couldn't destroy it and the one who gave it to me couldn't be found."

"Why did Akhenaten tell you to get rid of it. It is beautiful. Might it not have made a ring?"

"He said he could feel it had a power that was too strong for us. He said we should never take a step without a good look as to where it would lead. We knew nothing about the stone."

"You should have thrown it into the ocean or the river. "

"I enclosed it in these three sacred boxes. I thought it would be safe until we could find out more about it."

"But why did you keep it when he told you. . ."

"Why did you ask me to try magic to find the body of Akhenaten?"

I was silent. I bit my lip.

"What did the magician tell you it would do?"

"It would answer any question."

"Have you used it before?"

She hesitated to answer and then said, "Yes."

"Did it answer your question satisfactorily?"

"Yes."

"And the next time?" I guessed that she had not been able to resist using it more than once. It is so much easier being given answers to questions than seeking them out oneself.

She was frowning.

"What happened?" I persisted.

She took a long time to reply. She was thinking.

"I see now that what I was told was wrong," she said at last, "but at the time I believed it and acted upon it."

"Because the first answer was correct?"

She nodded. Ma-nan had played these tricks too. He would give one or two correct "predictions" in order to trap his victim into obeying him unquestioningly thereafter.

"You should never give up control of yourself," I said, remembering my youth. "Seek advice by all means, but test it against your own experience and wisdom. Never blindly obey anyone, alive or dead, natural or supernatural."

She took the cloth off her eyes and sat up impatiently. I could see they were clearer, healthier looking. I wondered what would have happened had I left her longer under the spell of the green stone.

"You came to me and asked for my help," she said irritably. "I have done what I can and we have gained nothing. I can do no more. It is possible the Lord of the Green Stone does not know the answer to the question you ask. It is possible he does, but he is being prevented by a stronger magic from telling us. It is even possible that he would have given us the answer if you had not interrupted."

"I had to interrupt," I said. "I felt I was losing control of myself again—and I couldn't bear the feeling. I'll try other means to locate Akhenaten." I was thinking of Ma-nan. He might well know where they had taken the body and, after our duel, he might not be so loyal to Na-aghta and the others as he had been before.

14

THE SECOND DUEL

THE NEXT DAY I LEAVE FOR Waset to make enquiries about Ma-nan. It is not easy to locate him. As far as I can establish he has not been seen since the duel. The people who might know—the dispossessed priests of Amun scattered about the town, living very different lives from the ones they lived before—are resentful and suspicious and will tell me nothing. I wonder if he has returned north to Men-nefer where I presume his family once lived. I hope not, for the journey will waste precious time.

My persistent enquiries produce at last a hopeful lead. One of the kitchen servants in my father's old palace is brought to me. He is a thin, ungainly man, standing first on one foot and then the other, his eyes darting here and there, as though watching out for enemies at his back and sides, when they should be steadily on my feet. I have allowed him to rise in my presence because I want to flatter him into loyal co-operation. I have come up against too many blind alleys to risk another one. Of what is he afraid? Did Na-aghta still have the power to control and terrorise? Even here—in the king's house?

"I am told you know where the ex-priest Ma-nan may be found," I say coolly.

This seems to bring about an even greater fit of eye-darting and body cringing. He does not answer at once but his hands almost involuntarily come together, palms cupped, as though mutely demanding a reward before he will tell me anything. I despise the man and want to dismiss him in disgust. But I have been the victim of a conspiracy of silence and he knows, and I know, I am desperate. I could have him beaten, but he knows, and I know, this is not my way.

"You will be rewarded," I say coldly, "if your information leads me to the man."

He grovels gratefully, but still does not speak.

I take a golden bracelet from my arm and hold it lightly between my fingers, looking pointedly at him. His face lights up and at last his eyes are still, fixed on the bracelet.

"My lord," he mutters in a low, cracked voice—then clears his throat.

I wait.

"He is in the village of tomb workers. He lives now with his sister."

The village is at the foot of the western cliffs. For centuries it was a flourishing community, but since Akhenaten's move to Akhetaten it has become something of a quiet backwater. Most of the skilled crafts-men have moved to the new city and are working on the royal tombs in the eastern cliffs there. Some have stayed behind—those who could not bring themselves to leave the old gods, and those whose work is not up to the standard my brother demanded. Many houses stand empty. Some had been taken up by drifters and wanderers, others by families who for one reason or another dislike living in the city.

"You will take me there and show me the house," I say.

He trembles. "Please, my lord. . . p-please. . ."

"You will take me there."

I throw the bracelet into the air, his eyes following it. I catch it and replace it on my own arm. His face darkens.

"You will have it," I say, "when you bring me face to face with Ma-nan."

It is clear the man is terrified. I can see the conflict between fear and greed in his face. I have become hard, I think. I have become ruthless. I believe I can play any game to win. He could melt away as others have done, but he wants the bracelet which will make him a rich man. One bracelet on my arm, I think, so light I hardly notice it, and it can change the course of this man's life.

I do not want Ma-nan to know that we are coming so I take no entou-rage and disguise myself as best I can. I could send for him, but I want to face him privately, man to man, once more. Shadows are closing in around me and who knows but he and those like him hold the power now? I need to know that I can rely on myself alone.

We find him in his sister's house, squatting on the dried mud floor like a peasant, watching an old woman spinning. It is difficult for me to believe that this is the same man I once feared so much. I hear a sound behind me and it is my guide wanting to withdraw, but not without his reward. I toss the bracelet at him. His fingers reach out and catch it, and, as though it is magic and has made him invisible, he is gone.

I turn to Ma-nan and look into his eyes. He has aged beyond belief since I have last seen him, even his skin looks grey and he shakes continually. It seems his evil genius was his only strength, and without it he is nothing. Momentarily I pity him, and then dismiss the thought. He owes me something.

His sister does not realize who I am and continues spinning. Ma-nan, remains squatting, looking at me, not even curiosity in his gaze. It is as though he knew I would come.

I nod in the direction of the old lady and he tells her to leave. She starts to argue but then looks again at me and hesitates. Does she recognize me? Or is it just that I have the bearing of a noble and the expression of a man who has important business with her brother? She heaves her heavy bulk off the little wooden stool and, grumbling, goes into the yard. I hear her calling to a neighbour that a visitor has come unexpectedly and she has nothing in the house to offer him. I wonder if she will borrow eggs and bread. I wonder if Ma-nan has beer. My throat is parched.

He offers me nothing, but waits to hear why I have come.

"You know why I have come," I say sternly.

He does not reply.

"What Na-aghta has done has not passed unnoticed," I say darkly.

Again he says nothing.

"Ma-nan, you and I have fought a long duel. All this life we have been linked, and who knows how many lives we still may be. Do you long so much for the void that you will keep silent when you should speak?"

"What is it you want to know?" he asks at last in a dull voice.

"Where is Akhenaten? Where is my brother?"

"You know where he is. In his tomb."

"Do not play games with me."

He shrugs and stares at the ground beneath my feet. There is no fear in his face; only indifference.

"Have you forgotten so soon the vision that you have seen?"

"I have not forgotten," he says reluctantly, almost sadly.

"Why do you betray it?"

"It seems unreal now. How can I be sure. . ." His voice fades, his gaze withdraws from the outside world, seeking the inner world with something like despair. . .

"It *is* real," I insist. "You will be sure it is once you stop hiding in this nowhere-place, this shadowy hole, this refuse pit of regrets and aborted good intentions. It will come back if you take up life again. It will come back if you come with me and show me where Akhenaten is."

He shakes his head. He is a man who had seen the splendours of the universe, but not his place in it.

I remind him that we are both on a great journey and if we take a wrong turn we could easily end up on the way to the void rather than on the way to the realms of light. I talk and talk, surprised at my own eloquence.

"It is not Akhenaten only who has been condemned by the actions of the priests of Amun: it is all who connived at his destruction, all who stayed silent when they could have saved him, in fact, could still save him."

Worn out by my persistence he at last agrees to show me where Akhenaten's body is.

We leave late at night for Waset, not wanting anyone to see and report our movements to Na-aghta. My old enemy comes with me on the royal boat to Akhetaten, but no one recognizes the ragged old man who sits in the stern staring at the passing landscape. He speaks to no one, and no one speaks to him. I remember how I had come to Waset, sitting as he is now, silently watching the cliffs slide by, a prisoner with no visible bars.

EARLY IN THE MORNING AFTER A night of fitful sleep in Akhenaten's beautiful city, we set off.

Together we make for the ridge of pale gold cliffs lining the eastern horizon of Akhetaten. We walk on a dry river-bed, and pass the silent tombs of the royal family and the nobles of Akhetaten—empty shells waiting to be infused with life by the death of those whose names are carved on their walls.

We work our way through the mountains and pass out into the wilderness beyond.

Heat and thirst make me exhausted and dizzy, but Ma-nan leads on and I follow. The landscape is yellow, vibrating with the heat; the sky a blank and pitiless blue. The Aten disc has no helpful hands to give us cups of water, only rays like swords that cut into our flesh. We wear the long desert cloaks of cotton and our heads are swathed, but still I feel the heat will kill us if one of the desert cobras does not. Ma-nan has insisted that I leave everything behind that could distinguish me as prince or priest, and when we occasionally meet a camp of desert nomads we are given hospitality like ordinary travellers, and like ordinary travellers searched thoroughly when we are asleep. Nothing is found but dusty cotton wraps, leather sandals and waterskins; and in the morning we are sent on our way with supplies of meat and drink.

Soon even the nomads cease to appear and we are alone, held to the hot, flat land by the huge suffocating hand of the sky. I have long since ceased to trust Ma-nan or not to trust him. We hardly speak, but make our way as best we can, thinking only of how we can get through the day without collapsing. Only at night my thoughts expand beyond this, and we lie side by side on the sand looking up at the stars. I think of all I have learned, and know that I have not begun to ask all the questions I want to ask—nor ever will. I may know the name of everything in our world and beyond; I may learn to weigh the stars and understand the nature of disease, so that no one will die of it; but I will still not know *why. . . why. . .*

I wonder if Ma-nan ponders these thoughts, or whether he lies plotting my death, I no longer care. The questions of who shall rule and not rule, who shall worship and not worship, who shall love and not love no longer torment me. Life is stripped down to survival or not survival: the outcome a matter of chance.

I sit up suddenly in a huge darkness and wonder about this thought. *Is it so?* Is the answer to all the questions no more than this? Ma-nan has wandered off, and I could be alone on the earth waiting for the dice to fall.

There was the void. Why did it become non-void? Why?

195

I strain my eyes to see into the darkness, hoping that something, someone, will answer me.

I feel totally alone. Lonely beyond belief.

I am conscious: but conscious of nothing.

I am thinking: but have no thoughts.

I am alive: but have no extension in time and place.

It is as though I am the god who was alone in the great dark and was lonely: who said: "Let there be OTHER", and there was OTHER: who then enjoyed this otherness, and was no longer lonely.

Ra utters a syllable of light, and the sand and the hills and the rocks gradually become visible. Lying below me in a little valley I see the bones of a man picked clean by the vultures. Behind them Ma-nan is squatting, himself like a vulture in his black cotton cloak. I run down to him through the cool sand, and know that I have found my brother, his legs buckled and broken beneath him, his arms flung out beside him, the skull grinning. He is as clean and dry as crystal.

Ma-nan watches me from the shadow of his hood.

I am suddenly at a loss to know what to do. When a pharaoh dies there is always a structure of accepted procedure and ritual to rely on, a hierarchy of officials each with his own duties to perform, an elaborate pattern of movement and sound, of spell and prayer, each tiny part of which is believed to be vital to the survival of the man in the after-life. Akhenaten has been denied all this—how can I alone hope to take its place?

I look at Ma-nan. "Help me," I say. He has been a priest most of his life, though he has long abused the privilege.

He shifts from one haunch to the other but says nothing.

I am suddenly angry. I need his knowledge. I have never presided at a funeral before. He has. I approach him and seize his shoulder roughly, pulling him upright. As I do so his cloak falls away from his face. I am looking into the eyes, not of Ma-nan, but of Khurahtaten. I start back, shocked.

"Where is Ma-nan?" I demand.

"Here."

"No!" I cry. It can't be.

"This is the second duel," he says. "It is my turn now to question you."

My mouth is hanging open and I am staring like an idiot.

He draws a circle in the sand, as I had done before, this time to contain the two of us and the bones of Akhenaten.

"Look at him," he says quietly. I turn my head and look into the eye sockets of my brother, friend and king. I see Khurahtaten there too.

I am questioned step by step about my life, my love for my brother, for my brother's wife, for my brother's daughter. I am questioned about wanting to be king; my motives for planning the reforms I intend to make.

Gradually, as the sun climbs higher I feel myself becoming dry and empty. Every pretence I have put up, has been knocked down; every lie I have told myself, has been uncovered. I stand at last in the full blaze of the sun at noon, naked of everything I have believed about myself, knowing that I am no better than the least among men, knowing that I have failed miserably, through fear, through desire, through laziness and procrastination, to achieve the task I had accepted.

I can think of nothing but of lying down beside my brother and being wiped off the face of the earth with him. I have had an opportunity not given lightly, and have wasted it.

Khurahtaten looms over me like a giant, his head blocking out the sun so that I cannot see his features. . . but around him the rays blaze out.

"*Now!*" he says, and the voice that had been so cold and relentless before, softens. "Now, my friend, you are ready to help your brother."

Help him? How can I help him, when I myself deserve oblivion?

Khurahtaten steps out of the circle and vanishes. I am alone in a vast wilderness with the broken bones of my friend, my partner. . . I kneel beside him weeping.

When I cease at last, exhausted, and sit back on my haunches, I know what prayer I must say, and to whom, to free my brother from the imprisoning spell of the false priests—it is written on no papyrus, chiselled on no walls. I know also that life and death have their own logic and are unaffected by long and elaborate rituals. I wish my friend and I could talk together as we did all those years ago beside the lake at Per-hay—now older, wiser, knowing what we know about ourselves.

It seems to me I feel his presence beside me. It seems to me I hear his voice in my own thoughts. There is no sense of defeat. No sense of loss. I am confident that the body of Akhenaten may have been broken by enemies and picked clean by vultures—but his spirit lives on.

I wrap my brother tight in my cotton cloak. He has no amulets or jewels, no rich and beautiful grave goods to lie with him through the centuries. I search the desert around me and find some fragments of crystalline rock. Carefully I choose the pieces, holding them in my hands, letting their silent voices speak to me of the first creation before the separation of sky from earth, before the exile of air from water. They speak to me of the first thought in the Creator's heart, the first utterance of light, the first joy of being. Ah, these crystals are fitting companions for my brother, my king. I lay them one by one in the folds of his makeshift winding sheet. I set them at the crown of his head, at his eyes, his mouth, his throat, his chest, his genitals and his feet.

Ma-nan, himself again, helps me to dig a deep pit. Is the old priest sorry for his part in this? Does he have any idea what he has done? He and his companions have not only killed a pharaoh, a man who was also a divine king, and spitefully denied him the benefit of burial, but have destroyed an ideal, set back a process that might have changed the course of the world. If Akhenaten had succeeded in what he originally intended, he might have freed future generations from the manipulations of false priests, led them to seek the unity behind the diversity, the one, true and abiding principle of divinity that holds us together against dark and violent forces of chaos.

As I throw the handfuls of shimmering sand on to what is left of his bodily form, burying it deeper and deeper in the earth, I know that he had a noble ideal, but that he had not yet been pure enough, powerful enough, divine enough, to achieve it.

"There will be another time," I whisper. "Another time!" And then I pray as he taught me to pray:

"I have come with praise to the Aten, the living and sole God, Lord of rays for giving light. I have come with love in my heart for thy child, issued from thy rays, Son of the Sun, living in truth, Akhenaten. Thou hast given eternity to him, thou art indeed the living Ra, who produced Maat, truth, justice. Mayest he travel freely to the gates of the Otherworld. Mayest he see Ra at dawn when he rises in the eastern horizon, and mayest he see Atum when he sets on the western horizon of heaven... Mayest he take changing forms as a living soul. Mayest he go out and in at the bidding of his heart."

Ma-nan watches and does nothing to avert the power of the words as they flow over the grave of the dead pharaoh...

198

Is it my imagination or does the sunlight suddenly flare up around us? I look up, startled, and see the outline of a huge bird winging its way towards the sun.

WE TURN FOR HOME, AS SILENT as we were on the journey out, but now for different reasons. I ponder that Khurahtaten had taken the form of Ma-nan and then of Akhenaten himself. And then I put the thought aside. In the night the howling of a dog to the full moon may make a man question his soul; in the day, the silver spray from the landing of a duck on water. Who knows what form the Questioner may take? Who knows when he will come?

15

THE RETURN

My MIND IS FULL OF PLANS for the future; how I will stand up to Horem-heb; how I will follow through the task my brother and I had been set; how I will make sure the religion of the people is a true religion, and not a beautiful mask over an ugly and cruel face. I feel strong, confident, capable of great deeds. I know I will not see Khurahtaten again. He has done for me what he can, and now I must stand alone. I no longer desire to be king. As high priest I can do what I have to do.

My heart is singing and my feet tread lightly on the burning sand. How wonderful the sky, how light and high and full of joy! What scope we humans have, I think, what infinite potential!

But just before we enter the cleft in the mountains, through which we must pass before we can see the plains of Akhetaten, I experience a strong sense of foreboding. The forces of darkness have not finished their work.

I look at Ma-nan, wondering if he has suddenly reverted to his old ways and is working his spells on me, but he is plodding behind me, wearily, not thinking of anything but how he can take the next step. I had forgotten how old he is. I tell him that I intend to hurry on ahead, and that he should take his time. He nods. I begin to stride and soon leave him far behind.

As the heat of the day builds up my pace slackens, and I am forced to rest for a few moments. I doze in the shadow of a thorn bush, and fall into a kind of half-sleep. I find I cannot relax and am haunted by formless anxieties. I force myself to travel on in spite of the heat.

At last the plain of Akhetaten lies before me in a haze of white light. From the limestone ridge that holds the tombs of the nobles I can see the gleam of the distant river, the city shimmering in the heat, unreal, insubstantial, mirage-like—as though one blink and the whole rich and marvellous creation could disappear for ever. I look across the farmer's fields, squared off neatly by the canals, to the city streets, the low houses, and beyond them to the palace complex and the temples. This city rose so suddenly; will it as suddenly cease to be?

I hurry down, the rough, loose stones hurting my feet, grazing my shins, yellow dust following me like a plume of smoke.

The guards at the palace do not recognize me, covered as I am with dust, my cotton kilt plain and shabby. Without adornment how can one tell a prince from a commoner?

I am challenged and I answer, but the captain of the guards has to be called before I am allowed to enter my own home. As I wait for him there is a chill on my heart. I am looked at with suspicion and hostility. I feel I no longer belong here. These are new men since Akhenaten's time.

The captain recognizes me at once and bows and gives the order for me to pass. He dares to meet my eyes though no subordinate should be so bold to a prince of my rank, to a high priest of the Aten. I see no respect or loyalty there—only a careful and cautious sense of duty. I get the impression that he is under instructions to be, for the time being, no more than polite. I wonder where these people were when Akhenaten was alive. When I stood beside my brother as he rode through these gates every face was lit with adoration, every head touched the ground.

I FIND NEFERTITI IN HER FAVOURITE room. As I enter I seem to step into the tall papyrus swamp in which Isis hid from the wrath of Set with her infant son Horus. There is no depiction of the myth here, for this is the city of the Aten where such myths are not encouraged, but I cannot help thinking about it as I see the woman seated on a low stool, her elbows on her knees, her head in her hands. Everything about her indicates despair and loneliness; indicates that she is hiding from a world that has become almost too difficult and hostile for her. On every wall the scenes of a rich and fecund marshland are depicted.

Tall papyrus stems create a forest around her; marsh birds nest peacefully beside her; lotus flowers bloom; fishes swim. The scene is one of the natural world going about its business unmolested. There are no pictures of hunting and fowling here as there are on so many walls. Even the ceiling has paintings of ducks flying overhead, and the still pool at the centre has water-weed painted on its sloping sides. Nefertiti in this room is contained and hidden in the marshlands away from city life; away from court intrigue and political manipulations.

I hesitate to disturb her, but I bring her good news of a sort, and decide to intrude. I clear my throat.

As soon as she hears the sound she looks up, the slender, long neck straightens, lifting that beautiful but now lined and pale face like a lily on a stem. Her back and shoulders stiffen and she rises to her feet with one flowing, graceful movement. She gazes at the intruder as a royal pharaoh would, all traces of a woman's fear and despair gone.

When she sees who it is she relaxes and her shoulders sag a little. I stride to her and reach out my arms. Her eyes show me that she would like to come to me, but I am subtly told by an almost imperceptible movement of her body that she is not ready for this intimacy now. She wants to hold herself to herself. She wants to face whatever she has to face alone.

My arms drop and I stand close, but not too close. I tell her I have found Akhenaten's body and how I have given him something of the dignity of burial. She has turned from me and listens with her back to me, as though she does not want me to read the emotions in her face. As I finish she faces me and I see in her eyes all the pain she has been suffering at his loss. We are lovers. She is Pharaoh—a busy and competent woman who has achieved her highest ambition, but none of this compares to those early years she had with Akhenaten; nothing takes the place of the joy they had in dreaming together, of the excitement of implementing those dreams, of the intimacy of body and soul and heart, of shadow and double and name, of ba and ka and akh, that they shared. I know I am her lover because she is a lonely and a sensual woman, but I will never be to her what Akhenaten was. My pride is momentarily hurt, but not for long. There is no place for personal pique and selfish possessiveness in the great drama we are engaged upon.

I bow and leave her.

At the door I turn. She is standing close to the wall, her forehead resting against the painted papyrus stalks, her hands above her head, flat against the flowers. I can see by her shoulders that she is sobbing.

As I TAKE A REFRESHING SHOWER, and as I lie on the alabaster slab afterwards for the massage and sweet oils, I remember with extraordinary vividness the splendours and the triumphs of former times.

In year twelve of my brother's reign a huge festival was held to which every foreign king was invited. Most came and those who did not sent crown princes as their representatives. It was called partly because Akhenaten wanted to show his beautiful city to the world, and partly because he wanted to establish in the minds of his people, amongst whom there had been some murmuring against his changes and reforms, that the world acknowledged him and honoured him for what he had done.

Not even his father had staged such a pageant. In his day the foreign princes, though lavishly entertained, tended to approach the throne of Egypt as separate entities, at most in twos or threes. Perhaps the wily Neb-maat-Ra did not want to give them an opportunity to meet and form alliances against him. But Akhenaten wanted them all, the whole world, to see the splendours of the Aten and to believe, with him, that all and everything was under its control and care.

I remember I stood with the princesses, slightly to the left of the king and queen, watching from the bridge that joined the informal royal residence that was home to the royal family, to the great state palace on the other side of the road. I was glad the logistics of organizing the arrival of the boats and the marshalling of the processions was not my concern. I was there as priest of the Aten and close companion of the king and his family. My concern would be only that the rituals to be performed at the Aten temples were perfect, as Akhenaten or his queen brought one after the other of the foreign rulers to do obeisance to our god.

For now I could enjoy the spectacle as procession after procession filed past the Window of Appearances. I could still almost hear the chattering of the princesses as they excitedly commented on the differences in clothes and style of each country, from the Syrian's dark, oiled and curled beards and long embroidered robes, to the Nubian's almost naked and barbaric magnificence. I particularly liked the light and slender representatives of the Keftiu, from the island in the Great Green I have always longed to visit. The steps of the king and his entourage were relaxed and free swinging and they did not appear to be at all overawed by the might of Egypt. Behind the king his servants walked bearing the delicate and flowered pottery of the island that was always Nefertiti's favourite ware.

After the processions there was the offering of tribute in the great hall specially erected for this purpose. Akhenaten and Nefertiti sat high up on a stepped throne under a canopy of gold with their daughters beside them and I not far behind. Below us the stewards were sweating profusely as they tried to keep orderly lines of tribute bearers flowing. White doves fluttered overhead by the thousand, cattle lowed, lions roared, the princesses chattered in delight, laughing hilariously at any and every hitch. Nubians brought ingots of gold so heavy the bearers staggered under them; tusks of ivory so long and curving their points caused havoc among the closely packed throng; logs of ebony; live leopards on chains; squealing and chattering monkeys that leapt from shoulder to shoulder and on more than one occasion displaced a wig; huge trays of myrrh; shields of stiff hide, and bows and arrows later, no doubt, to be used to kill their own countrymen. The Syrians brought fine, light chariots and horses; antelope and oryx. Even the animals filed into the hall and out again the other side. Never was such a scene! Never such a noise! We could hear the drum beats of the musicians stationed behind us only as an emphasis of our own heart beats.

Half way through I could bear it no longer and retreated to the quiet, empty courtyard of my temple to prepare for the visit of the foreign kings. I knew Akhenaten was accepting the tribute because it was the custom, but the religious aspect of this great international event was of much greater significance to him.

It was during the offering to the Aten in the blazing white heat of noon before the altar in the courtyard, that the purpose of this great gathering became clear. One after the other the foreign kings bowed to the ground before the golden sign of the Aten, its life-giving rays touching each upon the forehead, hopefully marking their thinking forever.

Time would tell how deep the impression of that golden touch penetrated, but now it seemed all had forgotten the Beloved of the Aten, Son of the Sun, Wa-en-Ra. That magnificent and bustling time seemed very long ago and far away.

The servants put a thin linen robe over my shoulders and I leave the room. Do I detect a glance between them indicating that in their hearts they also know the great days are over, and no matter how skilfully Nefertiti rules, the impetus has gone out of the dream, and the dawning of a new, and maybe not such a pleasant day, is near.

THE NEXT DAWN SEES ME BACK in the temple preparing for the first ceremony of the day. As though nothing has changed junior priests carry in the food offerings from the peasant farmers and pile them on the altars. Others replenish the flowers in the tall vases and sweep footprints away when all is ready. The torches that burn around the four sides of the great court are extinguished as the light that precedes the rising of the sun grows stronger.

Nefertiti enters and we stand ready. The stars go out one by one and the square of sky we can see above us becomes a pale grey-blue. We wait, and it seems as though the whole world waits for the Aten to enter in pageant. I miss my brother at my side. He had always particularly loved this ceremony.

From the shadowy colonnade around the otherwise unroofed court I can hear the chanting as the priests begin the great hymn to the Aten Akhenaten had composed. It starts low and rises and falls throughout in rich and moving cadences. It is already sounding in my heart.

As the sky begins to stain with red Nefertiti lifts her arms so that her fingertips may touch the descending rays of the god—so that she may be transformed in light.

I have watched this ritual more times than I can count and each time it is for me the most potent moment of the day. Everything is potential—nothing is set and certain—yet the impression of a comfortable permanence, an eternal and immutable pattern, is very strong. But this day, for some reason, the magic is not working. I remain detached from the ceremony, and then, as the light floods the temple court, there is a momentary break in the rhythm of the hymn and the voices that had sung in such harmony a moment before, take up the song again hesitantly. I sense a difference in Nefertiti too. She is still standing as she had been, but there is a stiffness, a rigidity in her stance that is new.

Something has gone. Something is not as it has been. I lower my eyes from the sky and look at the altar before me, puzzled.

And then I see what others have already seen.

At first glance the altar looks exactly the same as it has always looked. No one had noticed anything wrong when they brought the offerings in the dim light before the dawn.

Now we can see that damage has been done to the sacred carvings on the altar sides. Where Akhenaten and Nefertiti, divine pharaohs, lift their arms to the Aten, someone has chiselled a great gash across the rays of the sun, so that the beneficial power and energy of the great god can no longer reach the royal lips, nostrils and eyes: can no longer reach the hearts of the people, transmuted and transformed through the golden body of their king. There is a fatal break in the transmission from heaven to earth. What before had been a ritual of power and beauty, now feels empty and ineffectual. Nefertiti lowers her arms. The hymn falters to a stop. We all stare, disbelieving, at the sacrilege that has been committed here at the very most sacred and protected heart of the Aten worship. Not least among our questions is how someone with such an intent could have penetrated to this holy of holies. The question of why it was done is easier to answer.

Nefertiti turns to the priests staring helplessly from the colonnade. She orders them to disperse and search the temple for any other signs of vandalism. I bow myself out of her presence and join the search. We find three other such desecrations, each one at a place that will be most likely to hurt the energy and effectiveness of the temple. Whoever has done this knows exactly what he is doing.

Meanwhile, unperturbed, the great sun rides higher and higher in the sky.

MORE THAN EVER AKHETATEN BECOMES A city of suspicion and shadow. We no longer know whom to trust, even among the ranks of the Aten priesthood. Before it had been clear to us that anyone loyal to Horemheb or who had ever been connected closely with the cult of Amun must be watched, but now it seems those whom Akhenaten and I had personally chosen to serve the Aten in the heart of the temple might be traitors. I remember my brother's speech about how Akhetaten could never fall unless someone from inside opened the gates to the enemy.

One by one the priests, from fellow prophets of the highest standing, to the lowliest and newest of novices, are called into my private chambers and questioned. Before each one enters I try to achieve a state of silence and readiness in which I will be capable of hearing what is not spoken, seeing what is not revealed. It is not the answers that are given to my questions that interest me, for I regard words as smoke blown hither and thither by the winds of expediency, while the fire in the heart starts small but can destroy a city.

I almost abandon sleep I am so intent on my task, but for all my persistence I find no one I can accuse unequivocally. It seems to me that the clarity and innocence Akhenaten and I had been striving for has been abandoned and we are all reverting to the bad old days before his reign when prayers were spoken without feeling, when lies and greed and jealousy were rife, and no one felt the presence of the divine.

Akhenaten had destroyed faith in the traditional gods, and now his own god is being challenged. If this faith goes too, what will be left? I shudder to think of a world with no means of guidance and no sense of value and purpose: a world where we are all at the mercy of the vagaries and whims of selfish and foolish people, where there is no order, no truth, no justice. In such a world, on one dark night, Apep, the serpent of non-existence, might well win against Ra, and there will be no dawn.

FOR MORE THAN A YEAR THE country limps on under Nefertiti's rule. The defaced reliefs in the Temple of the Aten are restored.

We are aware that temples to other gods in the Two Lands are gradually being restored. The restoration is not done on Nefertiti's command, but she turns a blind eye to what is going on.

What is happening now reminds me of the start of the inundation when the first mud walls around the fields are breached and the first trickle of water reaches the parched land. I warn her that if we are not careful there will be nothing left of Akhenaten's golden dream. I advise a policy of controlled restoration with royal approval, a gradual reinstatement of the old gods, with the Aten still pre-eminent. I suggest it is better to compromise from strength than be forced to surrender everything from weakness.

One morning, lying in bed in that strange state of not knowing whether one is awake or asleep, it seems to me I can hear a whispering, a murmuring, a muttering, as though all the people in the country are turning against us. It seems to me a crowd had gathered round my bed and I can see their hostile faces. Their words are indistinct, but the sound they make is like the swelling whine of wind through palm groves at the approach of a storm.

I sit up, preparing to defend myself, but when I am fully awake I see that I am alone with Merytaten at my side. There is no voice sound or wind sound, only the silence of a deep, dark night.

I lie awake for a long time wondering about the experience. I fear it is a premonition, a warning, that some storm is gathering, some menace growing. I turn on my side and gather Merytaten into my arms. She sighs from a deep sleep. I rest my cheek on her hair. I stroke her, losing the uneasy memory in the comfort of her limbs.

Day after day passes and the sun blazes down as usual. The rituals of the temple follow one after the other in careful sequence. Nothing seems changed, yet I know it has. In Akhenaten's time there was the sense of energy on the move, of things being done, of changes being made, of flux and flow. But it seems to me now the country is in suspended animation—waiting.

Nefertiti who had been such a dynamic power during her husband's lifetime, the two of them sparking off each other to keep things on the move, seems now to have lost impetus. Since that day I had seen her weeping in the marshland chamber, she has avoided me. In public she is cold and distant, and in private, when I do manage to be with her alone, though her eyes are troubled and sad and I long to take her in my arms, she shakes her head and turns away—not in hostility or revulsion—but rather as though she has made some secret resolution not to be touched by any man.

It becomes clear that even in matters of state the great lady has lost her touch. She hesitates over decisions and gives the impression of being as unpredictable as Akhenaten was in his last days. I sense she wants to do one thing, but is being influenced against her better judgement to do another.

I wonder if it is the work of the priests of Amun. Are they chanting spells and sending their dark energy through the clear, dry air to confuse a mind already weakened by sorrow and fear.

I advise her, whatever the cost, to destroy Na-aghta and his closest associates.

"There are other priests less dangerous who could be groomed to take their place," I say. "Even Horemheb must see the power of these men is unhealthy for the Two Lands."

It is a wonder to me that after all they have done, they still walk free.

"After all they have done. . ." I ponder this thought. Nothing they have done can be traced without doubt to their door, and I know nothing of which they are suspected that could have occurred without a weakness on our part.

I determine to take matters into my own hands. I am no longer enfeebled by my desire for the double crown. I am clear in my mind that I have nothing to lose but everything to gain if I act as I intend.

A boat is prepared for me and I take leave of both Merytaten and Nefertiti without ceremony and without telling either where I am going or what I am about to do. I try to make it as casual as I can, but both women sense something dangerous in the air. Nefertiti still does not let me touch her with my body, but her eyes speak to me and I see that she does not want to let me go. Merytaten tries to persuade me to stay and then when I refuse, bursts into tears and leaves the room. Just as I am about to walk the plank bridge from bank to boat, I hear a commotion behind me and look around to see the royal chariot drawing up in a cloud of dust and my wife stumbling off it in undignified haste.

I shout to the boatman and, before she can reach the quay, the boat pulls away and I am out of reach.

I watch her standing on the quayside for a long time, my heart aching to see the forlornness of her figure.

"Ah, my dear," I think. "It is for you I do this. It is for all of us. It should have been done a long time ago. Na-aghta cannot change. He has to be destroyed."

"Everyone can change," a voice in my mind whispers. "Even you. Yes, even you, Djehuti-kheper-Ra."

My heart is full of vengeful hate; full of schemes for killing a man. Tears fill my eyes and I can no longer see the young woman on the river bank, staring so sadly after me.

I sit for a long time in the prow of the boat staring at the water and then I call the boatman and his son to me. I give them a golden ring if they will agree to help me. I see that they need no further persuasion. There is no hostility in their eyes. This is not a royal boat, but one of the many that ply between the east and west bank at Akhetaten. The man is old and is loyal to the royal family though I notice a small figure of Hapi, the river god, hanging from his belt, half hidden by the folds of his garment.

We did not leave Akhetaten without being noticed, but here in the wide reaches of the river, there are many boats similar to ours, and the people we pass have not witnessed our departure from the royal city. Once again I divest myself of all the trappings of my priesthood and my royal lineage and become a commoner. I keep only a gold handled dagger in my kilt.

I ask that I be put ashore on the outskirts of Waset, far from the quay where I would certainly be recognized, cover myself with dust as though I have been working in the fields, and set off along a path that leads into the town. Donkeys laden with huge bundles of dry reeds waddle past; women carrying water pots on their heads and urchins chasing dogs and pigeons pass by. Country scenes give way to narrow streets of mud-brick houses, tired women sweeping doorsteps, men arguing. Through open doorways I glimpse sandal-makers sewing leather, basket-makers stripping reeds, vintners stacking earthenware jars, no doubt each stamped with the throne name "Smenhkhare: year one." Or is it already year two?

In the town centre there is an atmosphere of nervous excitement. Rumours are rife. The murmuring I thought I heard in my dream is a reality here.

I wander about feeling like a ghost—no longer part of the society I observe.

I catch sight of the young prince Tutankhaten being carried in a golden litter. His face is so covered with paint, and his body enveloped in such rich garments, I can hardly believe it is the same young lad I saw not so long ago, swimming joyfully naked like a brown fish, in the lake at Meru-aten. He was laughing then. Now his face is pinched and tired.

I glimpse a dark figure hurrying through the streets, and recognize Ma-nan. I follow him, hoping he will lead me to Na-aghta. He slips down crowded alleys and I almost lose him. At last he taps on the huge wooden door of a mansion. When the door is opened I am just behind him and I slip in with him, touching him on the shoulder, calling his name. We have shared so much. Do I believe he will now be my friend?

But he does not turn and greet me. He hurries across the courtyard. At the other side he stops as a tall figure emerges from the house. Now he turns. Beside him is Na-aghta. Na-aghta has him by the arm, and I can see that he holds him tightly, as though he is not sure whether he has complete control or not. Ma-nan looks at me, silently pleading for forgiveness. I see in his eyes that he now has shame for what he does, where before he had pride. But the mood of the country has changed, and he now has the chance to be a power in the land again. He yearns for power as much as he ever did—but I know, and he knows, he will never have the pleasure in it again that he once had. I feel a kind of pity for him, and detachment from my own fear.

I walk calmly towards them. Am I under spell or do I believe even now that there is something I can do to change things. My hand tightens on the hilt of my dagger. I know what I intend to do is wrong and I will have to pay for it—if not in this lifetime then in another—but I cannot bear to see all that we have tried to do undone.

"This is not the way," the voice I don't want to hear insists. "It is not too late. Go back. Go back!"

I hesitate. I turn.

Too late. The huge bolts of the door are drawn behind me, and Na-aghta signals with his eyes to someone behind and to the right of me. Ma-nan suddenly moves and pulls away from him, running towards me, shouting a warning.

I stand irresolute only for a moment, but it is too long.

A spear is thrown and I stare with amazement at the point of it protruding from my chest. I am puzzled that there is no pain.

Will it be so hard to die? I think. I had wanted to die so passionately once. Perhaps I do again.

Ah, but to die with a task unfinished!

IT IS ONLY WHEN I NOTICE the triumphant face of Na-aghta, and Ma-nan kneeling over me weeping, that I know that I am dead.

Let your wings be my wings
O Horus, the sun's companion.
Teach me the currents of the air. . .
the high spiral
of the sky's heart. . .
the breathless pause
as the earth holds still
for the god to speak.

Fear has held my feet to the ground.
Fear has weighed me down.
My eyes and ears are blind and deaf with dust.

Immortal Bird
shake me free,
turn me loose
in your splendour. . .
Under your protection
Let me soar.
Let me see the sun before its rising.
Let me see the world
at the point of transformation.

16

AFTERMATH

NA-AGHTA LOST NO TIME AFTER THIS in trying to destroy anyone and anything that threatened his security.

He and his supporters infiltrated the crowds in Akhetaten and within days had so roused their fear and their passion that mob violence did all his work for him.

Though Horemheb must surely share the blame with the priests of Amun for what happened in Akhetaten that terrible day, he was, at the time, not in the city. He was on his way from Men-nefer, a few hours rowing from Akhetaten, when he heard the news, and those who were with him could testify to his shock and anger. It was true that he had encouraged the Priests of Amun in their bid to place upon the throne a king who would return the Two Lands to the way it had been before. It was true he hated Akhenaten for his obsession with the Aten and his disregard for the traditional and orderly network of gods and their priests and temples that had kept the Two Lands peaceful and undisturbed for so many centuries. He was a stern and righteous man and liked everything in its place and everyone attending to well-defined duties. The dissolution of the temples under Akhenaten had released many disaffected people upon the country. As the sacred places of the old gods were no longer revered, the thieves and vandals moved in and what Akhenaten's iconoclasts did not destroy systematically and ritually, fell victim to gangs of youths aiming rocks.

It was not Horemheb's idea to assassinate Akhenaten—he was too much of a traditionalist for that—but one day after a tour of inspection that left him enraged, he had finally and reluctantly agreed that something had to be done, however drastic, to return the country to what he considered to be order. He agreed to execution by poison. For the pharaoh to be seen to be assassinated would defeat the purpose of the exercise and bring about a further breakdown in respect for the old values. The god-king was supreme and should remain so. It was only after much heart-searching that he convinced himself that what he was doing was truly in accordance with the laws he considered the gods to represent, truly the best for the country he loved.

Horemheb administered the poison himself. It was he and he alone who would have to justify the act before the forty-two assessors in the court of Osiris.

Akhenaten was not a robust man and the people were soon persuaded that he had died of natural causes. They joined his funeral procession with grief and respect as it made its way to the tomb prepared for him in the eastern mountains. It was Na-aghta and the priests of Amun who, without Horemheb's knowledge, added a macabre touch by stealing the body before the embalmers had time to work on it, and casting it into the desert to be devoured by vultures and jackals. It had been they who had tried to prevent his return to earth in revenge for what he had done to their privilege and power.

As the stern general stood on deck watching the oarsmen pull against the current as though their lives depended on it, the story of the massacre at Akhetaten pleased him less and less. The very disorderly forces he was trying to control seemed to have struck and this time, in his name. He was aware that if he did not act quickly and ruthlessly to punish those who had done the deed, he would be giving licence to any band of bloodthirsty rebels who felt like overturning the system and, next time, the system might be his own.

His careful and secret execution of Akhenaten, his judicious planning to give the appearance of a natural death, or, at worst, a family murder, had apparently failed to fool anyone. Who had led the mobs in and set them to burn and kill and loot? Was it spontaneous, or were those arrogant priests behind it? Horemheb pursed his lips grimly, his feet wide apart to steady himself against the motion of the boat, his arms folded over his chest. If they had started to manipulate mob violence for their own ends, they must be curbed at once before their power, the power he was helping to reinstate, got out of hand.

He would not have harmed Nefertiti and Merytaten for the world. Yet the crowds who had smashed their way into the palace and murdered the two women had chanted his name and the name of the army's god, Amun.

Once at Akhetaten Horemheb surveyed the wreckage of the royal palace with a stern, cold face. He stood over the bodies of Nefertiti and Merytaten, their arms around each other as though in that last terrible moment they had forgotten all the hurt of the past year. Nefertiti's crown had been ripped from her head, and it was only congealed blood that ringed her forehead now. Horemheb pondered how easy it is to manipulate the emotions of crowds. Irrational and excessive love is easily turned to irrational and excessive hate. The very crowd that used to sing her praises and run to glimpse her as she drove past in her chariot, reaching up their hands to catch something of her beauty and her life-force, had rounded on her and destroyed her on nothing more substantial than an ugly rumour.

Horemheb commanded that they be given royal burial.

He ordered a search, a rounding up of suspects, clearing up of the debris.

Akhetaten suffered a second purge of blood. Horemheb was a harsh man and could not afford to let anarchy go unpunished.

In Waset too his men were ruthless and thorough. Horemheb doubted that the prince Djehuti-kheper-Ra would have been strong enough to restore order—he was too close to Akhenaten's dream world—and he was not sorry to hear that he had been found dead in the streets of Waset with a spear through his back—but justice must be seen to be done by those in authority. Na-aghta was accused and arrested, and it was the boy Tutankhaten's first duty as pharaoh to pronounce judgement on him. His piping voice delivered the fearful and merciless words he had been instructed to say, hardly knowing what he was doing or why he was doing it—a child seated uneasily on a huge throne with Ay, the vizier, on one side, and Horemheb, the general, on the other.

* * * *

HOREMHEB AND AY ARRANGED FOR THE first ceremony of Tutankhaten's coronation to be at Akhetaten. They planned other important ceremonies for other centres as soon as the temples and palaces there had been sufficiently restored. A new selection of priests and prophets would be made by Horemheb and Ay, but would be officially sanctioned and instated by the child pharaoh.

ANKHESENPAATEN WAS CHOSEN FOR THE NEW pharaoh's Great Royal Wife though she was several years older than he was.

Since she had learned of the massacre at Akhetaten she had stayed close to her chamber in her grandfather's palace at Per-hay, where luckily she had been with her three younger sisters when the mob went berserk in Akhetaten. She listened intently to the news and rumours brought to her by her spies. There was nothing she missed, nothing she did not understand. She had no illusions about what was happening, and knew that when the priests of Amun were sentenced to death it would not be the end of the opposition to her father and his ideas. Carefully she weighed up what she was told and worked out who her enemies would be and who her friends. She knew that she and her younger sisters would either be used or thrown away in the current shake-up of power. Whatever was to be her fate she felt she could handle it, but she wanted a better life for her sisters.

One night she came to their chamber in the Women's House and stood looking down on them. Setepenre, the youngest, was sleeping on her back, her mouth open, and her arms flung out on either side, her breasts, not yet rounded, rising and falling regularly as though the child were sleeping without a care in the world—yet vulnerable to every kind of evil. Neferneferure, the second youngest, was curled up in the foetal position, the filmy sheet drawn up over her head as though she were trying to hide from the world. The third, Nefernefruaten Tasherit, was muttering in her sleep and tossing from side to side as though the victim of nightmares.

Ankhesenpaaten quietly woke them one by one, and explained that, for their own safety, they were being sent away, far away. In answer to their anxious questions she would tell them no more than that when everything was peaceful and settled again they would be sent for. Meanwhile they were going to live like ordinary girls, not princesses, with a family remote from the court, in the delta lands, and they must be very careful not to tell anyone who they really were.

Before dawn they were all gone from the palace in the care of trusted servants.

Wide awake, Ankhesenpaaten waited for sunrise in her chamber.

At first light she crept out into the garden, and, after making sure that no one was watching, she raised her arms to the emerging Aten and whispered her father's favourite prayer, unaccustomed tears running down the cheeks of the princess everyone thought so cold and hard-hearted.

It was later that day that she was told she was to reign as queen beside her young half-brother. She showed no emotion—neither pleasure, nor sorrow, nor dismay.

AFTERWORD

Most of what we know about the lives of the pharaohs and the nobles who were close to them comes from their tombs and mortuary temples. It is lucky for us who are curious about and fascinated by this magnificent and ancient civilization that they buried their possessions with them and wrote their autobiographies in enduring stone.

Tutankhamun's tomb, found in AD 1922 by Howard Carter under the patronage of Lord Carnarvon, caused a great amount of excitement because it was one of the very few tombs from ancient Egypt discovered almost intact, with the royal body still present in its nest of priceless golden coffins. Nearly every other tomb had been picked clean by robbers long before we could get to it. The marvellous monuments of ancient Egypt have been quarried for building stone, burnt for lime to spread on the fields, smashed up and re-used in every possible way, goats have been tethered to columns delicately carved and painted, and mud-brick Arab villages have been built inside courtyards and on the roofs. Christian hermits have lived in some of the temples and tombs defacing the images of the gods, believing them to be the images of demons.

In ancient times some of the royal bodies were taken from their tombs by the superintendents of the necropolis when they found they could no longer protect them from the vandalism of robbers, and two separate caches of them were found in the late nineteenth century of our era. One was in a cave in the cliffs north of Hatshepsut's temple at Deir el Bahri. In this were found the bodies of Ahmose, who founded the magnificent eighteenth dynasty and freed Egypt from the hated rule of the foreign Hyksos kings; Thutmosis III (Men-kheper-Ra, Hatshepsut's stepson-nephew); Amenhotep I, his son; Sety I, who built the great temple to Osiris at Abydos that we still visit with such pleasure, and Rameses II, his son, one of the mightiest and best known of the Egyptian pharaohs who ruled for seventy years or so and fathered more than a hundred children. The body of a woman was also found—believed at first to be that of Hatshepsut herself, the female Pharaoh who was so instrumental in raising the priests of Amun to unprecedented power. But whether it is or not is now uncertain.

The second cache was discovered when the tomb of Amenhotep II (son of Thutmosis III) was opened. In it were found several later kings of the nineteenth dynasty, but also, of most interest to the readers of this book, the body of Queen Tiye, the mother of Akhenaten, with long auburn hair.

These royal mummies are now mostly in the Cairo Museum, but since 1982 they have been kept in a sealed room, not open to the gaze of idle passers-by.

In the early years of this century a magnificent tomb with everything still in place was found in the Valley of the Kings. This time it was not of a king but of Yuya, Master of the King's Chariots, and his blonde wife, Thuya. They were buried with such honour among the royal tombs because, while not royal themselves, they were the parents of Tiye, the Great Royal Wife and favourite of Amenhotep III, and grandparents of Akhenaten.

In 1907 a small tomb, badly damaged by flood water, was discovered. It is known as Tomb 55 and the controversy as to who was found buried there still goes on. The names of Tiye, Akhenaten and Tutankhamun have been found among the goods scattered in it, but it has proved to be the tomb of none of these. The body found there is of a young man between the ages of twenty and thirty. Medical examination establishes that he is of the same family as Tutankhamun. He seems to have been hastily buried in a coffin designed for a woman, and in a tomb that was not meant for him. Names have been scratched out. I like to think this is the body of the prince Djehuti-kheper-Ra who tells the story in this novel.

As the first archaeologists who entered the tomb touched the body, the flesh disintegrated into fine grey dust. Only some of the bones remain. And from the foot of the beautiful but damaged gold coffin the following poem has been pieced together:

"I breathe the breath which comes forth from Thy mouth.
I behold Thy beauty daily.
It is my desire that I hear Thy voice, even as the north wind, that
my limbs may be rejuvenated with life through love of Thee.
Give me Thy hands, holding Thy spirit,
that I may receive it, and may live by it.
Call thou upon my name unto eternity,
and it shall never fall from Thy lips in vain."

Akhenaten's body has never been found—not even in his carefully prepared, but unfinished, tomb in the cliffs behind his city of Akhetaten, now known as Tel el Amarna. From the pictures on the walls of his empty tomb and the tombs of his nobles, we can glean a considerable amount of information about the religious revolution he instituted, but very little of what happened at the end of his life.

Now we have the archaeologists sifting through every grain and scrap left over from the 3500 years of robbing and vandalism, taking what they find to the soulless security of museums. A friend whose grandfather was an early archaeologist in Egypt told me he had recalled how when the coffins and mummies of the ancient kings were loaded on the boats and taken away down the Nile, villagers all along its length gathered on the banks and keened for the passing dead. One traveller early this century described seeing bodies being taken from the royal tombs at Amarna (ancient Akhetaten) and burned with full funeral honours presumably to keep them from the archaeologists. He could not tell whose bodies they were, and we will now never know.

Akhetaten as a city was short lived. Founded by Akhenaten on virgin ground, much of it reverted to wasteland in only a few years after his death. Small areas continued to be inhabited for some centuries, and there are scattered villages on the site even today making the exploration of the remains of it difficult, but it ceased to be a city of any note when Tutankhaten changed his name to Tutankhamun and moved his capital north to Men-nefer (Memphis), the ancient capital of the Two Lands. Eventually the exclusive worship of the Aten became anathema and Akhenaten himself was declared a criminal and a heretic. His name and the names of the kings who briefly succeeded him, Smenkhkare, Tutankhamun and Ay (known to us as the Amarnan kings) were left off all king lists as though they had never existed. It is only in the last century that archaeologists have pieced together something of their stories.

For a long time Smenhkhare was thought to be a male king who succeeded Akhenaten and reigned for less than two years. But recently there has been a growing body of opinion among Egyptologists (led by J. R. Harris and Julia Samson), that Smenhkhare was the name taken by Nefertiti herself when she reigned briefly after her husband's death. Tutankhaten succeeded after this, dying aged between sixteen and eighteen years, circa 1323 BC.

He was succeeded briefly by the elderly Ay, Master of the King's Chariots under Amenhotep III, probably father of Nefertiti, and vizier under Akhenaten. He in turn was succeeded by Horemheb who ruled Egypt for something like twenty-seven years. He was not of royal blood but married Nefertiti's sister Nezem-mut (Mutnodjeme). He died childless, handing on the double crown to one of his elderly generals, a member of a powerful delta family. He became Rameses I—who then fathered the nineteenth dynasty. It is probable that Horemheb saw the qualities in the son of Rameses and chose him knowing that there would be a strong and reliable dynasty to follow. The son of Rameses I was Sety I, and his grandson, Rameses II.

The power of the priests of Amun steadily grew.

Notes

Notes and comments on the themes and ideas in this book can be found at www.bladudbooks.com/extra/son-of-the-sun-notes.html

Lightning Source UK Ltd.
Milton Keynes UK
UKHW011850170822
407466UK00009B/453/J